Mr. Darcy's Daughter

A Pride & Prejudice Variation

By Melissa Halcomb

Contents

~~~*✳*~~~

Prologue
Pemberley, Derbyshire
August, 1808
✳*✳

Rain lashed at the windows with relentless force, trees whipped and bent in the ferocious winds, lightning flashed across the sky, illuminating the faces lined with worry, fear, and agony of those waiting within the house. The storm cast a shadow of eerie foreboding, and all within the walls of Pemberley felt it. Someone had angered the gods and Fitzwilliam Darcy was convinced it was he at whom their fury was directed. Yet, like many a

Greek tragedy, he would not be the one to pay the ultimate price.

Pacing the floor before the library fire, Darcy had never felt so helpless, and helplessness was a feeling he detested. As the master of two grand estates, several smaller holdings, hundreds of servants, and the stewardship over dozens of tenant farms, Darcy was a man of action and decision. If there was a dispute, he settled it; a problem, he fixed it. But this? There was nothing in the world even he could do. There was no amount of money he could pay to undo what had been done. His wife would die, and he could not stamp down the feeling that the blame rested squarely on his shoulders.

"Mr. Darcy," a voice broke through his tortuous thoughts. "I must have a word with you." A blank gaze met the surgeon's request and so the man simply spoke in the straight forward manner he had learnt was the kindest way to handle difficult situations; he would not give even a hint of hope where there was none. "Mrs. Darcy's body is not strong enough to push the babe from her womb. Your wife is exhausted and weak. But if we cannot deliver the child soon, both mother and babe will die."

"What can be done?" Darcy heard himself ask.

Mr. Graham sighed as he wiped his hands on the blood-stained cloth in his hands. "I fear the only way to save the child is to make an incision in Mrs. Darcy's abdomen and remove the babe that way."

"You want to cut my wife? She will surely die!"

"I am sorry, Mr. Darcy," Mr. Graham replied with a slight shake of his head," but there is likely nothing that will save your wife at this juncture. She simply is not strong enough. We must focus on saving her child, though I am not certain how much hope I can grant you there, either."

Placing shaking hands on his hips as he stared into the fire, Darcy took a ragged breath and nodded once, sealing his wife's fate. He continued to pace the study long after the surgeon had left him. How long he waited, he knew not. His thoughts festered and twisted inside him, the conversation with the doctor increasing his already abundant supply of guilt. With the absurdly simple action of one single nod, he had signed his wife's death warrant. It did not matter that he did not love her as he ought; he had meant to save her, not stand as her executioner.

"Mr. Darcy, sir," his housekeeper's trembling voice sounded softly from the door what felt like moments later but must have been at least an hour. When he looked up, Mrs. Reynolds said nothing more; only frowned and indicated that he should follow. Knowing there was no alternative, he picked up his glass of brandy from the mantelpiece, drained it in one swallow to fortify his courage, and left to face the consequences of his actions.

The air within the room hung heavy with the oppressive feeling and stench of death; it was a sensation with which he was all too familiar. Darcy looked about, waiting for his eyes to adjust to the dim room. All candles had been extinguished and the only light came from the fireplace across the room and the occasional flash of lightning through the partially curtained windows. A few maids stood off to the side, looking frightened and unsure of what they were meant to do; as if there was anything that could be done. On the bed, he could just make out the dark outline of where his wife lay against the pillows, heaped with bed clothes. Before he could take a step towards her, however, the surgeon approached and requested a private word. With a curt nod, Darcy stepped back into the hallway, despising himself for the rush of relief that washed over him at being given a reason to stall the moment when he must face his wife.

"You know what I have to say, Mr. Darcy," said Mr. Graham with grim frankness.

Darcy swallowed hard and nodded, his fists clenched at his sides. "I do. How long?"

The man shrugged and shook his head. "I cannot say. Not long. It is as I feared. She has lost too much blood. I have closed the incision but there is still bleeding within her. I am powerless to stop it. I am sorry, sir."

Darcy nodded to indicate that he understood. "And the child?"

"The babe came sooner than I would have liked, but I cannot say I am surprised. To be honest, as ill as Mrs. Darcy has been, I am amazed the child survived this long."

"Sir?"

"She is small, but has already taken nourishment from the nurse. I believe she will survive."

"She?"

"Aye," Mr. Graham confirmed with a small but warm smile. "You have a daughter, sir."

Another nod and Darcy excused himself to sit with his wife for as long as she would last. When he re-entered the room, no one remained but Mrs. Reynolds and his wife's maid who both stood and quickly exited to give the couple some privacy.

Slowly, he closed the space between himself and the bed, his guilt building with every step. When he was close enough to make out the ghostly pallor of his wife's face, he nearly turned and bolted from the room. How could he face her when he was responsible for having inflicting this terror upon her?

"Stop that, Darcy," said Anne, her voice little more than a shaky whisper.

"What am I to stop, my dear?" he asked, attempting to school his features into something that would appear more confident than he felt as he sat on the edge of the bed, desperately trying to ignore the crimson-stained sheets, and took up her cold, clammy hand. It felt limp and weak in his own.

"Blaming yourself. I know you, cousin" Anne teased with a weak smile. She drew a ragged breath and said slowly, "You think that because you are Fitzwilliam Darcy, master of Pemberley, you must control everything. But you cannot save me and so you will take the blame upon yourself."

"Did not I do this to you? I never should have...Forgive me. I do not mean..." He turned his face away, knowing he ought to offer some comfort; profess his love, even if he did not mean it. Yet the words caught in his throat. It mattered not—Anne already knew.

"You do not love me, Darcy," she stated baldly, as if she had read his thoughts on his face.

"I do love you, Anne…"

"Not as a man loves his wife. And that is well. We both knew that was not what this marriage was about."

"I do not regret our marriage, Anne. I have been happy these last three years. I only wish I had not…I ought to have been stronger."

"Look at me, Darcy." Slowly, he turned his head to meet her gaze. Her words were slow and quiet, but filled with conviction. "I am dying now, but you *have* saved me. I was not destined for a long life, that was never any great secret. But you have made my last years on this earth truly the happiest I have ever known. Had you not married me, I may have lived a few more years yet, but I would have died, lonely and miserable, at Rosings, a prisoner of my mother's cruelty. I love you for the gift you have given me and for being so dear a cousin and friend to me. I am only sorry that these years have been wasted for you when you might have married a proper lady to whom you might have given your heart."

"You have nothing for which to be sorry, Anne. As I said, I do not regret my decision. I never have."

They sat in silence for several minutes until Anne softly requested to see her daughter. Darcy rang the bell on the table beside the bed and requested their child be brought. A few moments later, Mrs. Reynolds returned with a small bundle in her arms. Pillows were carefully propped under the mother's arm as she had no strength to hold the tiny child. When the baby was placed gently in the crook of her elbow, Anne boasted a weak but joyful, watery smile.

"Look at her, Darcy," she breathed. "Is she not the most beautiful thing you have ever seen?"

"She is, indeed," he whispered gruffly, his gaze transfixed on the face of his daughter.

"If not for you, I would never have known what a mother ought to feel for her child. Oh, I love her so dearly! I did not know it was possible to love so much." Slowly, she reached up to gently stroke the sleeping baby's satin cheek. "You must promise me, Darcy, that you will care for our daughter."

"I promise you, Anne, I will do all within my power to ensure her happiness. She will want for nothing."

"Protect her," Anne demanded with a fierceness one might not have believed possible in her weakened state. "Protect her from Lady Catherine. She will try to take our daughter. You must not let her. My mother does not know how to love. You must not allow my mother to do to my child what she did to me."

"I promise, Anne. I will protect her with my life. Lady Catherine will never harm our daughter."

"And promise me, William, that you will love." She fixed him with a tender, imploring gaze. "You married me out of duty and kindness, and I am forever grateful. But now you must find a woman worthy of your heart. A woman who will appreciate the man that you are beneath the wealthy, nobly connected gentleman. A woman who will love our sweet girl. Someone who can be a true companion to you."

"Anne..."

"Promise me. You have a good heart and such a capacity for love. Do not waste it. Promise me that you will love." Darcy nodded curtly but said nothing. "Say it, Darcy."

"I promise, I—I will try."

Seeming to know that was the best she would get from him, Anne lowered her gaze once again to the precious bundle in her arms and smiled at the tiny face. She gave her husband instructions for the naming of their daughter and her choices for godparents then encouraged him to hold his child.

Darcy moved to the other side of the bed and propped himself up against the pillows beside his wife. He had not held so small a child in more than thirteen years, when his sister Georgiana had been born. Awed and more than a little emotional, he laid the sweet baby girl in the crook of his arm. She made the sweetest sounds which brought a smile unbidden to his lips and when she yawned and stuck out her tiny tongue, he had to suppress a laugh for fear of waking her.

Anne leaned her head against his shoulder and watched with misty eyes, grateful to have lived long enough to experience this moment and to have been able to have given him this precious gift.

The family lay together, Darcy holding his daughter against his chest with one hand and Anne's in his other. After some time, he drifted off and the next thing he knew, he was opening his eyes as the brilliant morning sun was beginning to shine through the windows, the storm exhausted and gods apparently appeased. His daughter was no longer on his arm and the hand he held was cold and stiff.

~~~*✳*~~~

<u>*Chapter One*</u>
Meryton, Hertfordshire
October 1811

✳*✳

Anticipation buzzed about the assembly rooms as the locals excitedly awaited the arrival of Netherfield Park's newest occupants to the ball. In the small market town, the coming of a man of fortune to reside in the neighbourhood had caused such a stir that everyone seemed to know everything of import about him before he had even taken up residency at the grand estate. It was soon common knowledge that Mr. Bingley, as it had been learnt was the gentleman's name, was a young, single man in possession of a large fortune—no less than five thousand pounds a year—he rode a large, white stallion, and was exceedingly handsome in his fine blue coat.

It was also circulated that he was coming with a large party of wealthy friends, though the number varied wildly depending on whom one spoke to. The latest rumour that there would be an additional twelve ladies with which to compete for dance partners in a community already lacking in the commodity gave no one any great joy. Seven extra gentlemen was certainly not enough to satisfy all the hopeful mamas wishing to marry off their single daughters.

Drifting blithely through the crowd, Elizabeth Bennet hid her amusement behind a gloved hand. A curious creature by nature, she was just as eager as anyone to catch a glimpse of her new neighbour, but simply could not understand what all the fuss was about. She could not believe that Mr. Bingley was anything more than a man; a wealthy man to be sure, but a man nonetheless. So, it was no hardship to her when the music was struck up and her hand solicited for the first dance and the newcomers had yet to materialise.

In fact, the Netherfield party did not arrive until the third set had commenced and some, her mother most of all, had begun to despair that they would come at all. With a scarcity of gentlemen, Elizabeth had been obliged to stand the set out and was happily chatting with her dearest sister, Jane, and good friend, Charlotte Lucas, when a hush fell over the room and the musicians slowly ceased their playing. She turned her gaze to the front of the room, along with every other attendee, in time to see naught but five people enter. Sir William Lucas rushed forward to welcome them to their little assembly.

"Only three gentlemen, after all. Charlotte," Elizabeth addressed her friend as the music resumed and the newcomers ventured further into the room, "what can you tell us about them? Which is the highly anticipated Mr. Bingley?"

"Mr. Bingley is the gentleman on the left, in the blue coat."

"Ah, yes. The much talked of blue coat. It certainly is very fine," Elizabeth said with a sagacious nod, though her eyes danced with amusement. "And mercifully only two ladies. Can you tell us anything of them?"

"They are Mr. Bingley's sisters, I understand. One is married to that gentleman there." Charlotte nodded in the direction of the two gentlemen who stood just behind the three siblings.

"The taller?" asked Jane.

"No, the other. A Mr. Hurst, I believe."

"Even better," Elizabeth teased with a wink. Though she could not see him clearly, being a rather diminutive woman standing in the back of the room, the other gentleman at least appeared to have a full head of hair and to be younger and taller than the stout Mr. Hurst.

As the music commenced, she watched the group advance into the room, Sir William offering introductions to the more prominent families, particularly those with single daughters. A long-time studier of character, Elizabeth observed her new neighbours with great delight, forming her first impressions.

Mr. Bingley, she liked immediately. Handsome with tawny blond curls and bright cobalt blue eyes, he bowed and smiled and shook hands, greeting everyone with enthusiasm and friendliness. With each new acquaintance made, the gentleman bounced on the balls of his feet and seemed to verily tremble with delight. He had a great likeness to an energetic puppy, seeking any new friends that were to be had and eager to play with anyone who might have a treat or a tempting stick to throw.

He seemed, however, to be the only member of his party who took any pleasure in their surroundings. The sisters, two very fashionably dressed ladies with the same tawny blonde tresses as their brother—though Mrs. Hurst's was a slightly darker shade—kept close to one another, looking down their noses at everyone and endlessly whispering behind their fans. It was obvious to Elizabeth that they were far better pleased with themselves than what lay before them. The younger sister, Miss Bingley, seemed particularly disgusted with what she saw.

Of Mr. Hurst she struggled to form any opinion at all. He did very little besides follow his wife about until he found a chair near the refreshment table and settled in with a large glass of wine. He spoke to no one and the ruddiness of his cheeks and glazing of his eyes spoke of a man who imbibed too often and perhaps was not entirely sober now, rendering him incapable of any meaningful interaction. It was a shame, she thought, that he did not even appear to be a very entertaining drunk.

The final member of the party, a Mr. Darcy Charlotte informed them, took the greatest share of her attention for he was quite possibly the handsomest man upon whom she had ever laid eyes. A clear head taller than any other man in the room with broad shoulders and long, strong looking arms, she might have swooned had he looked her way and she been more her mother's daughter. Thick, nearly black hair fell across his brow in a most becoming fashion and if not for the fact that he seemed as displeased with his surroundings as the ladies of the party—wearing a deep scowl that never wavered and frequently pulling out his watch to check the time as if counting the minutes until he could make his escape—she might have considered him the very definition of masculine perfection.

As the group neared where their mother stood, Mrs. Bennet frantically beckoned Jane and Elizabeth to join her. With a shared long-suffering sigh, the girls left their friend to weave around the dancers to where their mother stood.

"Do you see that man there, girls?" she demanded of her eldest daughters in a loud whisper. "Lady Lucas has just informed me that he is Mr. Bingley's oldest friend. He has a vast fortune and a great estate in Derbyshire! Bingley's wealth is nothing to his! A clear ten thousand a year! At least! Is he not the handsomest man you have ever seen?"

While Elizabeth agreed that, yes, she had never seen a man so well favoured, she would never admit such to her mother. Mrs. Bennet needed no such encouragement to throw her daughters into the path of a wealthy man. But, as Mr. Darcy would soon prove, there were some slights which even Mrs. Bennet could not ignore, not even for all the wealth in Derbyshire.

In no time at all, Sir William stood before the Bennet matriarch with Mr. Bingley as Mr. Darcy stood a few feet back looking as if he desperately wished to simply disappear. Introductions were made, many blushes and smiles exchanged between Jane and Mr. Bingley, and her mother's exuberant raptures barely contained when that gentleman solicited the next two dances from her most beautiful daughter. Seeing an opportunity to put her second daughter forward, Mrs. Bennet addressed Mr. Bingley's friend.

"And you, sir? I hope you have come to Hertfordshire just as eager to dance."

Like a stag sensing danger, Mr. Darcy froze, eyes wide. Looking as though it pained him to condescend to address the woman before him, he managed a stiff nod. "I thank you madam. I rarely dance."

Undeterred, Mrs. Bennet cheerily pressed on. "Well, let this be one of the occasions. For I am sure you will not easily find such lively music, nor such pretty partners." She eyed Elizabeth pointedly before nudging her forcefully forward.

"Mama!" Elizabeth admonished in a hoarse whisper before stepping back. But it mattered not. By the time she had gotten over her mortification at her mother's blatant improper behaviour and looked to see his reaction, he had bowed and was walking away. An embarrassed Mr. Bingley quickly excused himself and bounded off after his friend.

Insults to any of her children was one thing which Mrs. Bennet could not stand in the least, even towards her least favoured daughter. Despite his ten thousand a year, Mrs. Bennet declared him to be the most disagreeable man she had ever met and not nearly so handsome as she had first allowed. She pitied Mr. Bingley his odious friend's company and wasted no time informing anyone who would listen of what a horrid man had darkened their neighbourhood.

Though disappointed that such a handsome man could not be more amiable, Elizabeth was not a creature made for unhappiness and determined not to allow one ridiculous incident dampen her enjoyment of the evening. She had come with no expectations beyond dancing and perhaps making a new acquaintance or two and so, rejoicing in Jane's conquest of Mr. Bingley, put the matter behind her.

But no amount of determination could conjure up more men with whom to dance and so Elizabeth, and, indeed, nearly every other lady, was

22

obliged to sit out at least another dance or two. It was during one such occasion that her dislike of Mr. Darcy was very nearly decided. That gentleman had danced only once each with Mr. Bingley's sisters and spent the rest of the evening stalking the perimeter of the room, glaring at anyone and everyone he passed. An entire half hour had passed where he had been seated beside Mrs. Long but had not so much as looked upon her, let alone uttered a single word. After the musicians had taken a short rest and were beginning to take their places again, he had come to brood a few feet from where Elizabeth sat when he was accosted by his jovial friend.

"Come, Darcy," said he, "I will not have you standing about in this stupid manner. You had much better dance."

Moved not at all, Mr. Darcy proceeded to insult nearly everyone in the room by declaring it would be nothing short of a punishment were he to be obliged to stand up with any young lady in attendance. Elizabeth's only consolation was his concession of Jane being the only handsome girl in the room and Mr. Bingley's enthusiastic praise of her dearest sister. She was all astonishment when she heard Mr. Bingley point out a very pretty young lady just behind his friend and realised he was speaking of herself.

"Which do you mean," Mr. Darcy drawled, turning slowly around. Never one to be easily intimidated, Elizabeth looked him in the eye, offering a slight smile and a nod before determinedly breaking her gaze. "She is tolerable," she heard him say, "but not handsome enough to tempt me. Bingley, I am in no humour at present to give consequence to young ladies who are slighted by other men."

A quick glance told her that this comment had been overheard by more than just herself. She was acutely aware that, as Mrs. Goulding had quite obviously heard his unflattering evaluation—if the hungry glint in her wide eyes was anything to go by—the entire assembly would be well informed of this rich man's slight of herself long before the night was over. Before she could make her escape to lick her wounds, however, Mr. Darcy spoke again and she felt she might have her revenge.

"Bingley, go back to your partner," he growled. "You know very well I came only at your insistence and wish for nothing more than to return to Amelia."

Elizabeth stood, arms folded across her chest with wounded pride, and took aim. "I pity the lady, that she might be made to endure such a disagreeable man. But perhaps she is as uncivil and ill-mannered as the company she keeps." With a triumphantly raised brow as he turned slowly at her words, she waited for the sputtering of his awkward response and the acknowledgement of his ungentlemanly behaviour which never came.

With a slight smirk, which she begrudgingly noted made him all the more handsome, he raised his own answering brow and calmly replied, "Yes, her manners occasionally leave something to be desired. As she is but three-years-old and currently suffers from a slight cold, however, I hope she might be forgiven her faults and I my worry over my daughter. Excuse me." He bowed stiffly and, informing his friend that he would return to Netherfield and send the carriage back for the rest of the party, strode away, leaving a highly mortified Elizabeth to no greater satisfaction than to see a rather sheepish looking Mr. Bingley return to her sister.

It was too much. She had behaved abominably and she knew it. Fleeing to a darkened corner of the room where she could reflect on her shame in peace, Elizabeth cursed her damnable vanity which had caused her to speak so uncivilly. She knew full well that she had only reacted to her disappointed hopes of being looked upon favourably by such a handsome man but such was a paltry excuse. There was no call to insult a lady unknown to her. To then learn that the lady in question was an ill child; her dishonour was complete, indeed.

She stirred not from her self-imposed exile, but sat in silence, considering the man to whom she had spoken so rudely. With her newly gained knowledge, her perception was entirely altered. What she had previously interpreted as pride and disdain, she now saw clearly as worry and distraction, perhaps even a fair amount of reserve around strangers. She recalled having scoffed each time he checked his pocket watch throughout the night and cringed inwardly as she imagined what he must be feeling, having been pulled away from his ill daughter for such frivolous pursuits and counting the minutes until he could return to her side. Oh, she was a wretched creature!

"Lizzy?" her sister's sweet voice pierced through her self-castigating thoughts as she sat with her face buried in her hands. When she looked up, she saw that Jane was not alone; Mr. Bingley stood at her side, looking down on her with sympathetic eyes.

"Oh, Mr. Bingley. I must apologise for offending your friend. It was unpardonable for me to speak so, especially as regards a poor, ill child!"

She returned her gaze to her twisting hands in her lap and her shoulders slumped.

"Be easy, Miss Elizabeth," Mr. Bingley said with a kind smile. "Darcy insulted you first, and with no such provocation as he provided you."

Elizabeth shook her head. "'Tis no excuse. I ought to have risen above his words. I cannot even imagine why I should care for his good opinion," she lied, and not only to her companions.

They were not fooled and, if Elizabeth had looked up, she might have seen the look of understanding which passed between them.

"Pray, allow me to apologise for my friend. He has always been a rather quiet, reserved fellow but he is truly the best man I know. He has not had an easy time of it the past few years, ever since his marriage. No, even before then. In truth, Darcy seems to have had more than his fair share of misfortune."

"What happened?" The words tumbled out of Elizabeth's mouth without thought. "Oh! Forgive me. 'Tis none of my concern."

"No, I shall tell you. Well, I shall tell you what I know. Perhaps you might help me make some sense of it." Bingley paused and seemed to gather his thoughts. He turned a chair to face the two sisters and began his tale.

"Anne de Bourgh was Darcy's cousin, the daughter of his mother's only sister. His aunt had long claimed it was the greatest wish of his mother and hers that the two be united in marriage, that they had planned the union whilst Anne was in her cradle. His aunt beleaguered him about it constantly, wrote him almost weekly, demanding to know when he would come to Kent to do his duty and marry his cousin. Darcy ever denied it, insisting he had never heard such a wish from his mother and would never marry his cousin. That it was neither of their inclination.

"Then, one day whilst I was still at Cambridge, I received word from Kent informing me that they were to be wed and would most likely be so by the time I received his letter. There was no explanation, and nor has he ever given one but to say that it was his duty.

"I did not see my friend much during those years. He married his cousin and they retired to Pemberley and, excepting for occasional business which brought him to Town, remained there. Anne never left as far as I know. There was much talk as to why he suddenly changed his mind about marrying Anne and why the rushed wedding. 'Twas all balderdash. Darcy is not the type to dally with any lady, in fact, he is famous for it. He never dances the first set, he never takes to the floor with any young lady more than once to avoid raising expectations, and he is exceedingly careful to pay any lady no more attention than is strictly polite.

"Personally, I believe it had something to do with Anne's health. I only met the lady once, shortly after their marriage when Darcy invited me to break my journey at Pemberley as I was making my way north. She was of a poor, sickly constitution and seemed so frail one might worry a light breeze would carry her off. Perhaps he took pity on her, knowing she would likely never marry otherwise. Darcy had no great interest in a society marriage, so I suppose it suited them both well enough.

"Once, when he was in Town and paid me a rare visit, I teased him about soon becoming a family man, but he emphatically declared that there would be no children, that Pemberley would be left to his sister's second son. And yet, just as with his marriage, I received another letter naught two years after they wed announcing that Anne was with child. His letter was...not enthusiastic. In fact, he seemed rather displeased by the notion. I think he knew it would be the death of his wife. And, indeed, it was. Anne died, I understand, a very few hours after the babe was born.

"And that is to say nothing of the rest of his family," Bingley said with a heavy exhale. "Darcy's mother died not long after his sister's birth, when he was naught more than twelve-years-old. His father died five years ago, shortly after Darcy was wed. My friend was left, only just two and twenty, a newlywed with a sickly wife, the master of not one but two vast estates, and the guardianship of his then eleven-year-old sister. He is exceedingly fond of Georgiana and has long struggled to do right by her. I know none of the details, only that something occurred this past summer that has rendered him desperately worried for his sister. I know he feels completely unequal to the task of raising two young girls, but he is determined to do his best by both."

Jane and Elizabeth listened to this tale in silence, clutching one another's hands and blinking back tears. That one man's history could contain so much pain and tragedy seemed wholly unfair. For Elizabeth's part, she found she could not hold his harsh words against him. She pondered Mr. Bingley's story and imagined what it must be like to be to be Mr. Darcy. He was exceedingly handsome, incredibly wealthy, and the master of two grand, profitable estates. Certainly, he was highly coveted amongst the ton as a very desirable marriage partner; not for the man he was, but for the social and material boon he could be for anyone seeking to aggrandise themselves. Even here, she had heard whispers in every corner of the assembly room as to his estimated worth. Suddenly, she was grateful to be naught but a poor country gentleman's daughter! Any man who wished to marry her could never do so for her fortune, for she had none.

"And, his daughter?" she asked, trying to control the tremble in her voice. "It must be difficult for him, the ever-present reminder of his late wife."

Bingley surprised the sisters with a small smile and a light chuckle. "Not at all. Darcy adores Amelia. I believe she is the one bright spot in his life. I have never known so devoted a father. 'Tis not fashionable for fathers to dote on their children," he said, wrinkling his nose with distaste, "but Darcy cares naught for that. His daughter travels with him nearly everywhere and anything which can be done for her happiness is accomplished in a trice. I hope to be half the father he is someday." Bingley shot a quick glance at Jane and Elizabeth could not help but smile, despite the ache in her heart for the gentleman they had been discussing.

Chapter Two

The quiet and stillness of the darkened room eased much of the tension in Darcy's shoulders. He could not stomach the petty, disparaging remarks Bingley's sisters had fallen into when they returned to Netherfield and so excused himself to retire for the night, but found himself in the nursery.

For the past several nights Amelia had slept ill, fits of coughing and wheezing shaking her small body. What little sleep she had gotten was only as he rocked her gently in his arms or nestled tightly beside him in his bed. This had only added to his irritability and disinclination to attend the assembly, as he had not slept much and feared for her ability to rest in his absence. Upon his return, Amelia's nurse, Mrs. Lawson, had assured him that his girl was on the mend and, on seeing her still, sleeping form, he gave himself permission to set his worries for his daughter slightly to the side. Lowering himself quietly into the oak rocking chair next to her bed, he reflected on the events of the evening.

Though he did not wish to admit it, he had not behaved well. He also knew that it reflected poorly on his friend and he was sorry for it. Bingley had asked Darcy, an experienced land owner, to aid him in learning the art of estate management before he took the step of purchasing his own estate. Darcy had willingly accepted, wishing to put many of his own troubles out of his mind and earnestly desiring to assist his friend. But his behaviour this evening, and that of Bingley's pernicious sisters, had done the man no favours.

He had not acted the gentleman and insulted an innocent lady who had committed no greater crime than to be the one unfortunate enough to be singled out by Bingley and brought to his notice. He had hardly even looked at her when he said those vile words. When he did look properly, when she had stood and boldly challenged him as no woman had ever done before, there was a fire in her eyes that strangely intrigued him. She was quite lovely with her colour raised and her accusing brow arched, and he now greatly regretted his ungentlemanly words.

What truly picked at his conscience and would not allow him to be easy, however, was the expression of true remorse and chagrin he had observed in her magnificent eyes in the wake of learning of her mistake. It was clear she had a good heart. The young lady had been visibly appalled with herself to learn that she had spoken ill of a child and he was ashamed of the vindication he had felt when he had walked away from her.

He wished he could put aside his cares as easily as he knew other men did, but his worries for his precious little girl and his heart broken sister in London weighed heavily upon him and he was not a man who easily shirked his responsibilities. This was no excuse for his actions this night, however, and he was well aware of it. He would certainly never have excused any man for speaking of Georgiana as he had spoken against Miss Elizabeth.

A sound at the door drew his notice and he turned to see Bingley standing in the doorway, beckoning him towards the hall. Ensuring Amelia was covered and sleeping soundly, he placed a gentle kiss on her soft cheek and followed his friend. But Bingley did not stop in the hallway; he led the way down the stairs to the master's study. Darcy was very nearly amused when his friend took his seat behind the desk, looking every bit the master of the house, and turned a harsh gaze upon himself. He was nothing short of astonished when it became clear that the amiable, jovial Bingley meant to chastise him.

"Darcy," said he, sounding far more serious than Darcy had ever know him to. "How could you do that me? You are meant to be helping me!"

He knew full well to what his friend referred; had he not just been castigating himself for the same? But this was wholly new to him. The master of Pemberley and Rosings had not been made to answer for his actions since he was a boy in short pants and so he dissembled. "I beg your pardon?"

"You insulted all my new neighbours tonight! What with your haughty attitude and Caroline and Louisa sneering down their noses at everyone, I shan't be surprised if the whole of Meryton should appear at my door with torches and pitchforks demanding my immediate removal from the neighbourhood!"

Darcy hoped he did not look as flushed as he felt. It rankled to have his behaviour compared to that of Bingley's sisters—no matter how warranted. "Surely, you are overreacting," was all he could say aloud, though it did not convince even himself.

"Am I? You did not speak one friendly word the whole evening, doing nothing more than stalking about, glaring daggers at anyone who dared look in your direction. You slighted Miss Elizabeth most cruelly *and* publicly, and a more delightful young lady, excepting her sister, I am hard pressed to imagine. She did not dance again the rest of the evening."

Despite having already acquitted the young lady, he used his only defense; the words coming out as nothing short of a deplorable, petulant whine. "She insulted my daughter."

In a show of uncharacteristic severity and authority, Bingley stood, leaning over the desk with his hands placed atop as he fixed Darcy with a stern gaze and spoke in a voice as hard as stone. "Only *after* you insulted her for no other reason than that I pointed her out as a possible dance partner. Oh, yes, let us have her drawn and quartered at dawn for her crimes! She did not know who Amelia was, and you had just deemed her not handsome enough even for one dance within her hearing!

"I did my best to explain your affection and concern for your daughter, but I really think you owe her an apology. In fact, I demand it! The lady did nothing to deserve your censure and, I assure you, she is exceedingly repentant for having spoken ill of Amelia."

To continue to deny his friend's accusations was beyond foolhardy and churlish. Were they not the very same that he had been contemplating not ten minutes ago as he sat in the nursery? Had he not come to the same conclusions? Why was he now attempting to justify his inexcusable actions? He knew why; his friend was right and he was thoroughly ashamed of himself. It was not a feeling to which he was accustomed nor one he liked overmuch.

He released a loud sigh and rubbed his forehead. "Bingley, you are right and I am sorry. You know I am not fond of society at the best of times. I have not been sleeping well since Amelia has been ill and I am worried for Georgiana." He stopped and shook his head. "No, there is no excuse. As you say, I am meant to be helping you establish yourself, had even hoped to distract myself from my own concerns for a time. I failed to do so and allowed my worries to overcome my better judgement. I do see how my actions tonight have reflected poorly on you and I humbly beg your pardon, my friend. I will apologise to the young lady at my earliest opportunity and endeavour to comport myself with greater civility and propriety from now on. I would be most grieved if your reputation here were to be tarnished by my bad behaviour."

"Thank you, Darcy" said Bingley, looking quite relieved. "I must say, I think you would like Miss Elizabeth a good deal if you got to know her."

"Did she truly not dance again?" he asked, guilt twisting at his insides. It was not his favourite activity—in fact it was among his least—but he was sorry if she had been denied the pleasure as a result of his ungentlemanly words.

"The example of the very rich can lead even those she has known all her life to shun and look down upon her. After you left, she took herself out of the way for a time—she was quite cut up over her own behaviour. But when she did reenter the ballroom, her hand was not solicited again."

"Then I am sorry. I shall do all I can to remedy the damage I have caused," Darcy assured his friend. "Are we finished?"

"Yes, thank God!" Bingley exclaimed dropping heavily back into his seat. "I have never been so nervous in my life."

"*You* were nervous to tell *me* off?" Darcy laughed.

"Yes! You can be a rather intimidating figure and God knows I have always relied heavily on your advice. To feel that I had need to chastise you was terrifying in the extreme!"

"You did exceedingly well, Bingley. And I hope you will always feel equal to calling me out when I have behaved badly."

"I shall. Not that I expect the need to arise often. I cannot remember another time I have believed you to be in the wrong."

"I am sure I have, though it has ever been my study to avoid such behaviour as invites censure. I am ashamed of my conduct this evening. But, may I, in turn, offer you a bit of advice now?"

"Please do! We must put the universe to rights again," Bingley joked, falling back into his usual light-hearted manner.

Darcy then proceeded to gently advise his friend to take his role as head of his family to heart and exert some control over his sisters. Caroline, at least. Louisa was her husband's problem, but a strong word to Hurst and perhaps a hint that Darcy was displeased might be enough to rouse him to check his wife. In any case, Louisa was not so terrible; she had only an unfortunate habit of following her younger sister's lead. Caroline would be far more difficult to rein in. She was headstrong, conceited, and volatile; she would not take criticism well, if she listened at all.

The night ended with several glasses of brandy consumed and Darcy listening with great amusement as Bingley enthused heartily on the virtues of Miss Jane Bennet. She was declared a veritable angel and the most beautiful creature he had ever beheld. If he were a little more reflective and seemingly sincere, Darcy brushed it off. Bingley was forever falling in love with every pretty face he encountered. His admiration always wore off within a week or two. Surely, this infatuation would be no different.

The following morning, Elizabeth woke much earlier than was her wont after a ball. In fact, she arose very near her accustom hour. She had slept ill with dreams haunted by coughing children, her neighbours whispering behind their hands as they stared and pointed at her, and a tall, handsome man with dark hair and penetrating eyes declaring her naught but tolerable and condemning her in a disgusted tone, "She is but a child!"

Knowing there would be no use in attempting to gain any more sleep, she slipped from Jane's bed where she had spent the night after listening to her dearest sister wax long on the qualities of a certain handsome, young gentleman with tawny curls and kind, blue eyes who was everything a gentleman ought to be. Quietly, Elizabeth padded across the hall to her own chambers to don a walking gown before pinning her long, dark curls up into a simple knot and wrapping her dark blue cloak about her shoulders. She stopped back in Jane's room to tuck the bedclothes snuggly around her sister.

"What time is it?" Jane asked sleepily.

"Far too early, dearest," Elizabeth whispered. "Go back to sleep. I am sorry I woke you. I am only going for a walk. I shall be back for breakfast."

"Shall I come with you?" Jane mumbled through a yawn as she rolled over to her side.

"Not at all. It truly is too early. I could not sleep and only thought to—" Jane's soft snores stopped her speech and Elizabeth had to stifle a giggle. Even on mornings that did not follow a night of dancing and charming new neighbours, Jane was no lover of the dawn. This thought sparked another that Jane would do well with a gentleman from

Town who was accustom to keeping later hours; a man very much like Mr. Bingley, perhaps...

Elizabeth crept silently from the room and down the hall, descending the stairs with her walking boots in her hands. No one would thank her for disturbing their rest after a long evening of dancing and making merry so she waited until she reached the kitchens to don her footwear.

This was Elizabeth's favourite time of day. In a house with so many people, it was nearly impossible to find time to one's self without taking drastic measures. She loved her family, but her mother's constant, erratic nerves and younger sister's boisterous spirits often became wearing and she had long ago learnt that taking time in the morning to fortify her own constitution went a long way in helping her survive life at Longbourn.

The sun was only just beginning to crest the horizon and she smiled at the marvelous show of pinks, oranges, and yellows that painted the morning sky, the songs of the birds as they called out to their mates and danced among the treetops, the chittering squirrels as they argued over nesting trees and carefully hidden winter caches.

She knew her reflections were too many for a quick ramble down the lane and so turned her feet to her favourite haunt, the path which would lead her to Oakham Mount. The views from the top were nothing short of inspiring and the walk itself was invigorating. It was where she most loved to go when she had a difficult query to ponder or a problem to solve—or was feeling particularly vexed with her mother or one of her younger sisters.

Her path chosen, Elizabeth gave her mind free rein to wander and, predictably, her thoughts turned to the mysterious Mr. Darcy. She liked puzzles and that was what he was to her; a riddle she desperately wanted to solve. Why had he married a lady he had sworn he would not, and then given her a child when he had been adamantly against the idea?

She thought of the two females in his care; one in ill health and the other suffering from some unknown grievance, according to Mr. Bingley. It could be an illness as well, but she thought not. That was likely something her new neighbour would have known and she did not believe Mr. Darcy would have ventured so far from his beloved sister if she were also ailing. Surely, he would wish to be at hand to offer whatever comfort or cure was in his power. Mr. Bingley had said that their father had died five years ago, leaving Mr. Darcy with the care of his eleven-year-old sister, which meant that she was now sixteen years of age, or near to it.

She knew not what afflicted the young lady but could sympathise with Mr. Darcy. If Jane were suffering in any way, Elizabeth knew that she would grieve with her dearest sister. She could see how fear or concern for one's most beloved family members could render something so trivial as a ball a great annoyance. No, she could not blame the man, not even for his uncharitable words against her. She did not consider herself to be a stunning beauty, being far too used to Jane's unattainable pulchritude and her mother's oft repeated reminders that Elizabeth was nothing to her sister. It was why she had worked so hard to develop her mind, devouring the books in her father's library.

It was little wonder Mr. Darcy had been unmoved by her meagre physical attractions. Now, by the light of day and with time to reflect, she felt how silly it had been to take such offense at his words. A man such as he was, with all his wealth, connections, and own breathtaking good looks would not seek a merely tolerable, poor country maiden to whisk away to his grand estate. Men such as Mr. Darcy married the daughters of earls or dukes; ladies of his own sphere. It was ludicrous to have entertained even the slightest hope he might have spared her even such slight notice as a passing glance.

She paused at the base of Oakham Mount; her gloomy thoughts having robbed her of her enthusiasm for the lovely views to be found at the top. It would pass; she was not one to wallow in melancholy and would soon be at rights again. Plucking a sweet little daisy that grew against the rock upon which she had settled, she lifted it to her nose as she attempted to clear her thoughts of all maudlin reflections. After gathering a few more blooms, nearly enough to life her mood, she heard the huffing of a horse from around the bend. Assuming it would be naught but a farmer or servant on an early morning errand, Elizabeth paid no mind and began absentmindedly plucking the petals from one of the blossoms.

"And, does he love you?" a deep voice asked as the horse came to a stop some yards away, causing her to startle and drop her flowers.

When she looked up, her surprise was great on perceiving Mr. Darcy astride a large, black stallion, looking every bit as handsome in his morning riding clothes as he had in his evening finery.

"Forgive me, I did not mean to alarm you," he atoned. "I thought you must have heard my approach."

Hastily, she stood, brushing away the plucked petals from her gown. "Oh, I did, sir. Only, I had expected perhaps only a tenant farmer or a servant at this early hour. I do not often meet with many others on my morning constitutional." Her words trailed away and she chewed her bottom lip, wondering at the words he had said when he came upon her. "Excuse me, does who love me?"

One corner of his lips quirked up in a very becoming and roguish half-grin as he slipped off his mount then pointed at the wasted blooms at her feet. "Do not young maidens pluck the petals of a flower to ascertain the devotion of their suitors?"

"Perhaps, I suppose. As I have never had a suitor I really could not say," she answered without even stopping to consider her words. When she realised what she had inadvertently implied of herself she hurried to cover her mortification. "I was merely resting before I began my ascent." She waved vaguely towards the path that led to the top of the rise.

He looked to the path and then to her and she thought he looked rather anxious and she wondered at it. In fact, she wondered at his stopping to speak to her at all after her shameful behaviour of the previous night. She was nothing short of astonished when he requested to join her on her hike and acquiesced before she knew what she was saying.

The gentleman tied off his horse to a sturdy branch and together they began to climb. It was not a difficult trek, being not particularly steep, but each put a good deal more concentration into their steps than was strictly necessary. Elizabeth knew not what he was about but felt that she had been given an opportunity to make amends for her offences and was determined not to waste it.

Taking a deep, fortifying breath, she spoke before her courage could fail her. "Mr. Darcy, I fear I am a selfish creature and must relieve my feelings, even if it should wound yours. I must apologise for the horrible things I said to you last evening. I have no excuse to offer but that of injured vanity. I heard the words you said of me," she admitted sheepishly, "and, while I hold no great estimation of my own beauty, I was offended and childishly wished to assuage my own mortification by wounding you. Such behaviour, however, is beneath me and I do, from my heart, beg your pardon, not least of all for the insult to your poor daughter."

Mr. Darcy stilled his steps and, for a moment, it seemed as if he knew not what to say. He did not look upon her, but rather surveyed their surroundings as if he might find the words he ought to say hidden in the trees or written upon a boulder. When he did, at last, turn his gaze upon her, she held her breath in fearful anticipation of his words.

"Please, be easy, Miss Elizabeth. You would not have spoken so if I had not provoked you. I am pleased to have met with you this morning as I also wish to apologise. I should never have said what I did. Such ungentlemanly words are unpardonable. More so, for they were decidedly untrue. I was in a foul mood, determined to be displeased, and desired only for my friend to leave me be."

"Then, perhaps we might forget the whole terrible evening and agree to begin again as friends?" she suggested with an outstretched hand, which he took.

"With pleasure, Miss Elizabeth. May I introduce myself? I am Mr. Fitzwilliam Darcy of Pemberley in Derbyshire," he said with a gallant bow over her hand.

"It is a pleasure to make your acquaintance, Mr. Darcy. I am Miss Elizabeth Bennet of Longbourn." She offered a bright smile and a curtsey as she endeavoured to check her laugh. Quickly, however, she sobered. "May I...may I ask after your daughter? How does she fare?" Elizabeth asked hesitantly as they resumed their walk. Despite what she said about forgetting the evening previous, she felt she had no right to speak of the little girl after the way she had spoken of her, yet Elizabeth had always loved children and truly felt concern for the girl.

But Mr. Darcy seemed intent to hold no grudge and when he answered she heard nothing but relief in his voice. "I thank you. She is on the mend. Which is the only reason I was persuaded to leave her at all last evening. My dear girl slept soundly all the night in her own bed, which meant that I was able to sleep all the night in mine. That also means that I am well rested and able to be far more civil today and promise not to insult anymore beautiful ladies."

Elizabeth bit her lip to temper her smile at such words and lowered her face in a vain attempt to hide her blush. Deciding it would be safer to tease than to entertain any kind of foolish hope, she raised an arch brow. "I assure you, sir, Jane was not the least bit offended. You did acknowledge her to be the only handsome lady in the room, did you not?"

A deep chuckle rumbled from his throat and a warming sensation coursed through her insides. "A ridiculous assertion." After gazing quietly on her a moment he spoke again. "You truly think so little of your own beauty?"

"With a sister such as Jane and a mother who feels it her duty to remind me regularly of my inferiority, it is only natural that I would be aware of my lacking." Elizabeth answered with a shrug. "It matters little to me. I am quite content giving greater heed to improving my mind than improving my looks."

"Do you truly mean that?" he asked with a look she could not quite decipher.

"I do. Beauty is subjective and will one day fade. I can expend my energy trying to hold on to it, doing what I can with a pretty gown or a bit of ribbon. But, while I enjoy a lovely dress as much as the next lady, 'tis a futile exercise. Knowledge, on the other hand, that is mine to keep."

This statement led to a rousing discussion on books, philosophy, and, strangely, the latest farming techniques that carried them the remaining distance to the summit of Oakham Mount. For nearly the first time, Elizabeth gave scant attention to the vistas before her as she was so thoroughly entertained by her companion.

When asked upon his return to Netherfield, Darcy was hard pressed to remember anything of what he had seen but for the image of a bright-eyed maiden with the morning sun shining on her hair who intrigued him far more than he was ready to admit.

Chapter Three

* * *

In the week he had spent at Netherfield, Darcy had not given much attention to the house within which he resided except to ensure any room he entered was not solely occupied by Caroline Bingley. That lady had no dearth of opinions about the house her brother had taken, and each of them seemed to compare it most unfavourably with Pemberley, which the lady had never seen. She was not, strictly speaking, wrong. Netherfield could not even begin to compare with Darcy's estate; but there were few houses in England which could.

Tonight, however, in the absence of his hosts, he began to see its charms and thought that his friend had done very well in choosing this estate. The house was large, but not overwhelmingly so, well furnished, and in good repair. There were two sitting rooms; one formal, one for family use, a parlour, a breakfast room, a formal dining room—which Miss Bingley insisted be used every evening despite it's being far too large for their intimate party of five—and an elegant ballroom. There was a nursery in the family wing but he had requested that the adjoining chamber be used as Amelia's nursery; it would not do to have his daughter so far from him. The master's study was large and well situated without being overly intimidating. The library was pitiful; that, however, was not the fault of the house, but rather Bingley's disinterest in the written word.

If there was a fault, it was that the family and guest rooms were situated on opposite sides of the house. At Pemberley, these chambers were, indeed, separate but remained in the same wing. Guests were kept near enough to be comfortable, yet not so close as to interfere with the family. Here, Darcy sometimes felt as though he were the sole inhabitant of the house. Though, after only just a week living with Caroline Bingley, Darcy could not but be grateful that his chambers were so isolated. With a quiet chuckle, he recalled how he had been contemplating inviting Bingley and his family to stay at Pemberley next summer to thank them for their hospitality. He wondered if he would not prefer the guest chambers to be further from his own with Bingley's sister in residence.

For a man of Bingley's status, Netherfield was exactly what Darcy might have expected. It was a testament to the progress his friend had made in becoming his own man and establishing himself amongst the gentry. Darcy chuckled lightly as he remembered back to when Bingley had first entered Cambridge and positively floundered, seeking his advice on everything from which tailor he ought to use to what colour horse he should ride.

During Darcy's marriage and the difficult years that followed, however, Bingley seemed to have come into his own, Darcy thought with a mixture of guilt and pride in his friend. He was happy for the man, and it was certainly for the best, but he could not but feel that he had not been a good friend to Bingley. He had done his duty and focused on that which was most important, and he knew Bingley held no ill will against him and was better off for it, but Darcy was a man who desired to be in total control of his own affairs and it galled him that there had been an aspect of his life which he had neglected.

That had been the impetus which had decided him to come to Netherfield. He felt that he had owed it to his friend to be here and offer whatever guidance was asked for. He missed his sister and wished he could be with her now, but there was nothing an eight and twenty-year-old older brother could do for a heartbroken and humiliated sixteen-year-old girl. This rankled him greatly, as well, but he was astute enough to know that Georgiana was in good hands under the care of their kind Aunt Elaine and he was only a four-hour ride away—three if he rode hard—should he be needed.

Now he was grateful he had come. He had not seen Miss Elizabeth since their walk up the side of Oakham Mount, as she had called it; though he had teased her that it was smaller than many of the foothills that surrounded Pemberley. He had not seen her but he was surprised at how often her sparkling eyes, rich, chestnut curls that shimmered in the early morning sunlight, and her exceedingly pleasing figure were called unbidden to his mind. That encounter had left him feeling more relaxed and lighter than he had in...he honestly could not remember ever feeling so at peace, especially not with a woman. She had a way that put him at ease effortlessly; when she laughed, it lifted his soul to another plane where sorrow, fear, and guilt could not reach him. He had no idea what he wished from his acquaintance with this enchanting lady, but he knew he desired to know her better.

As he sat in the pitiful library with a glass of brandy, wondering when he might see her again, it occurred to him that she was likely at the party at Lucas Lodge he had declined to attend. Between business with Bingley, riding over the estate, and attending to his own correspondence and estate business, he had not seen a great deal of his daughter but when she slept since they arrived in Hertfordshire. Darcy had begged his friend's indulgence to offer his apologies and allow him to remain behind to spend the evening with his little girl. Bingley had been exceedingly understanding, especially considering his behaviour at the assembly. Darcy knew it was possible the locals would see his absence as further proof of his disdain and he was sorry for it, but it could not be helped. He would muster as much charm as he was able at his next opportunity to be in company.

Miss Bingley had been most reluctant to leave Darcy behind, offering to remain herself to keep him company as she struggled with the effort to look pleased with the idea of spending the evening with a child. The truth of the matter was, she had long nursed hopes of securing the role of mistress of Pemberley; ever since she had learnt that her brother had befriended the very wealthy and highly connected gentleman. Yet, they had met only once before he had married Anne, and Bingley had confided that his sister had been most put out when she learnt soon after that Darcy was no longer a single man. Though there had been countless insincere offers of condolence by young ladies when news of Anne's death had reached London, Miss Bingley had been among those most eager to offer her gleeful sympathies.

Tonight, Darcy had been adamant that he desired only his daughter's company and together, he and Amelia had spent a lovely evening dining in her nursery, having a proper tea, snuggling together as Darcy read *Gulliver's Travels* aloud and sang his daughter songs he remembered his mother singing to him until she fell asleep in his arms. This girl was the light of his life and, even if Bingley were shunned from Meryton society forever, he could not find it in him to regret having stayed.

Now, however, Amelia was tucked in bed, sound asleep and he was faced with several hours alone. Normally, this would have been a welcome respite, far preferred over a night out amongst strangers. When he thought that he might have the opportunity to be in Miss Elizabeth's company, however, he purposefully did not delve deeper into why he suddenly had the desire to be amongst society. He only gave word to Mrs. Lawson, ordered his carriage prepared and hurried to change, unsuccessfully attempting to convince himself all the while that he went only for Bingley's sake.

"Sir William, Lady Lucas," he addressed his hosts when he arrived, digging deep for every ounce of civility he possessed in the face of two people he barely knew. "I beg you would excuse my late arrival. Perhaps Mr. Bingley explained, I could not pass up an evening spent in the company of my daughter this evening. She has gone to bed now and I find myself desirous of good company. I hope I am not intruding?"

The stunned looks they gave him at this speech filled him with remorse; he truly ought to have made a greater effort at making a better first impression when first he entered Meryton society.

"No, no. Not at all, Mr. Darcy," Sir William gushed. "You are most welcome! I am exceedingly honoured to welcome you to my home."

Entering the party, he seemed to float upon a sea of uncertainty as he looked about the room of unfamiliar personages. Certainly, he had been introduced to some of these people at the assembly but he found he could not recognise more than a very few faces and no names. His guilt doubled. When had he become such a snob? His parents, his father especially, had certainly taught him better manners and to treat all, even those beneath him in station, with respect and kindness. This lesson had somehow become lost and replaced by self-importance and conceit. Had Anne not teased him more than once for his arrogance? He could not remember but he would not dwell on such thoughts now. This was the time to prove he was a true gentleman, good and honourable.

"Darcy!" Bingley's voice pulled him from his thoughts and he spun around to find his friend approaching from a corner of the room where Miss Jane Bennet stood, a serene smile on her lovely face. "You came!"

"I did. After Amelia was put to bed, I found myself in want of company."

Bingley snickered at this answer. "You? In want of company? Are you well, Darce? Have you perhaps caught Amelia's cold?"

"What?" Miss Bingley's shrill and most unwelcome voice broke into their conversation. "Is Mr. Darcy ill? We must return to Netherfield at once!" In a low voice which only Darcy heard, she added, "And, then to London, for God's sake."

"I assure you, Miss Bingley, I am perfectly well," he rejoindered. "Your brother was only teasing me."

"What could Charles possibly tease you for, Mr. Darcy? Surely you are perfection itself," she cooed and simpered while ferociously batting her eyelids.

Fighting the urge to laugh in her face, which would go decidedly against his efforts of acting gentlemanly, he only replied, "You give me far too much credit, Miss Bingley."

"Come, Darcy," Bingley rescued him. "You remember Miss Bennet?"

Bingley pulled him to where Miss Bennet stood and for several minutes, he joined them in conversation. Yet, soon enough, he found his company was rather superfluous amongst their agreement on every subject and exchanged smiles so excused himself to see if he might manoeuvre himself into the company of another Bennet lady. The moment he thought it, he mentally kicked himself. *No! Remember Bingley. You are here for him. If you are granted the privilege of speaking with Miss Elizabeth, all the better...*

After nearly a half hour of standing on the edge of random conversations, not *all* of which were Miss Elizabeth's, he was beginning to question the wisdom in coming at all. He had never possessed the talent of feigning interest in topics which simply did not interest him, had never learnt to catch another's tone or inflection, and was entirely inept in the art of small talk. He much preferred to listen, speaking only when he felt he had something of value to add to the conversation. Fighting the impulse to fall back on his custom of finding a window to gaze out of, pretending his mind was deep in contemplation, he felt absurdly pleased when a melodic voice addressed him, throwing him a lifeline as he struggled against the tempest of social etiquette.

"Do you call this being sociable, Mr. Darcy?" Elizabeth asked, her bright smile and arched eyebrow lifting his spirits and warming his heart at once. "Listening to other's conversations but never offering your own opinion? Tell me, did I not express myself uncommonly well just now when I was teasing Colonel Forster to give a ball?"

"With great energy, madam," he answered, pouring all his focus into listening to her words and not the delightful sparkle in her eye and the intoxicating scent which hung about her, not to mention the tasteful, yet very alluring, view he was afforded by her décolletage and the great difference in their heights. "But it is a subject which often renders a lady energetic."

"You are rather severe on us, Mr. Darcy!" Elizabeth laughed and his stomach performed a rather delightful feat of acrobatics.

"Fear not, Mr. Darcy," said another voice and he turned to see a lady whom he had not even noticed with mousy brown hair and plain features standing beside Elizabeth; Miss Lucas if he was not mistaken. "I shall soon open the instrument, then it shall be Lizzy's turn to be teased."

"You are a very strange thing," Elizabeth laughed, "by way of a friend. Always wishing me to display before anyone and everyone! Had my vanity taken a musical bent, you would be most invaluable. As it is, certainly there are those present who are accustom to hearing the very best of performances. I would not wish to injure myself in their estimation." Her friend would not allow the matter to drop and soon Elizabeth relented. She turned with a sigh towards Darcy and shrugged. "There is an old saying with which we are all familiar. 'Keep your breath to cool your porridge.' I shall keep mine to swell my song!"

She was, by no means, a capital performer. Elizabeth missed the occasional note and slurred her way through the more difficult passages. Yet, even so, Darcy could not but feel that he had heard few performances which gave him greater pleasure, and he had heard some of the best talent in the world. Elizabeth's was a true gift. She not only played the notes, but seemed to feel the music to the depths of her soul which, in turn, enhanced the experience for the listener. Her voice, a clear and flawless mezzo-soprano, touched his very soul and left him desperate for more. He was only to be partially obliged for, after her second song, she was proceeded at the instrument by one of her sisters, though he could not remember which, and her playing was not near so pleasing though more technically correct.

He was absurdly gratified when Elizabeth returned to his side after her performance. "You play beautifully, Miss Elizabeth. I am coming to see that you are reluctant to give yourself any credit."

"I assure you, sir," she laughed, "I am well aware of my meagre abilities. Come, let us find someone with whom it shall not be so arduous for you to converse," she teased with a wink and Darcy allowed himself to be led away.

The entire evening passed most delightfully. Elizabeth introduced him to those with whom he might share some commonalities. He met several of the local gentleman farmers and was surprised to find that, indeed, they were not so very different from himself. They dealt with tenant disputes, drainage issues, drought, flood, and predators the same as he, though on a much smaller scale.

He discovered a nearly kindred soul in Elizabeth's father, whom he had not thought he would like. Darcy had heard reports that Mr. Bennet was a lazy, indolent man who neglected his estate and gave scant attention to his daughters, excepting his second, and rarely stirred from his bookroom. He was therefore surprised at the elder man's knowledge of new planting techniques and various harvesting methods, sheep breeds and livestock diseases. The two stood in conversation for over half an hour discussing books, philosophy, estate management, anything which struck their fancy, and did so with an ease and flow Darcy rarely managed in conversation with even some of those with whom he held years long acquaintances.

Throughout their conversation, Mr. Bennet smirked often and Darcy recognised the same sparkle in the gentleman's eye that his daughter possessed. He was left with the distinct impression that Mr. Bennet was not all he portrayed, and that he took a great deal of delight in pulling the wool over everyone's eyes.

Never had he so enjoyed an evening amongst company with which he had only just become acquainted. Perhaps the most enjoyable moment of the evening had also been the most surprising: a dance, of all things. After Elizabeth's sister had completed a long and rigid concerto, her youngest sisters entreated her to play something to which they might dance. Standing beside Sir William at that moment, Darcy forced himself to suppress a groan; dancing had never been a favourite pastime. His host expressed his pleasure in the young people's delight in the dance and Darcy endeavoured to make a civil reply, though he was uncertain as to his success. By some force of serendipity, however, Elizabeth happened to chance by at that moment and Sir William called out to her.

"Miss Eliza! Why are you not dancing?"

"Why, because I have not yet been asked," was her cheeky reply. "Are you looking for a partner, sir?"

"Oh, ho!" laughed the jovial gentleman. "If I were but twenty years younger, I should happily do the job, my dear! But I have a better idea." Taking up Elizabeth's hand, Sir Lucas turned to present it to Darcy. "Mr. Darcy, you must allow me to promote this young lady to you as a most desirable dance partner. I defy you to refuse in the face of so much beauty!"

Much to Darcy's disappointment, the lady withdrew. He wondered at the blush on her lovely cheeks, hoping it did not indicate displeasure, for he found, much to his surprise, he genuinely desired to lead her to the dance floor.

"Forgive me," said she. "I hope you do not suppose that I moved this way in order to beg for a partner. I would not wish to force Mr. Darcy's hand in engaging in an activity I know he does not enjoy."

This was singular indeed. Darcy had never known a lady who did not positively leap at the chance to dance with him given the slightest opening. It was clear Elizabeth took pleasure in a dance as she had already taken to the impromptu floor with Bingley and some of the officers present with obvious enjoyment. Perhaps it was only the idea of standing up with him to which she objected, but he thought not. She smiled sweetly when she looked upon him and there was a look of apology in her eyes as she shot a glance at Sir William. It seemed her reasoning was genuine; she demurred purely for Darcy's sake. The sensation within his chest he had been striving to disregard all evening amplified. The words Anne had spoken to him as she lay dying drifted across his mind. *You must find a woman worthy of your heart. A woman who will appreciate the man that you are beneath the wealthy, nobly connected gentleman.* Was it possible, when he had not even been looking, that he had found just such a woman?

"You are everything gracious, Miss Elizabeth. But I would be exceedingly pleased if you would honour me with a dance." He held out his hand, trembling in anticipation of her touch, and waited. When she placed her own hand in his with a shy smile, he felt his own lips stretch across his face and hoped he did not look too ridiculous.

"If you are certain, sir, I should be happy to dance with you."

"I am very certain, Miss Elizabeth." With that, he led her away, feeling greater anticipation to dance a reel than he could ever remember feeling before.

The only blight on the evening was, rather expectedly, Miss Bingley. During a moment when he had been standing alone, only having just been left by Elizabeth after their dance and lost in watching the delightful way her graceful hips swayed as she walked away, the former lady accosted him and sought to gain his indulgence in disparaging the present company.

"I believe I can guess your thoughts at the moment, Mr. Darcy," she cooed into his ear far too closely, forcing him to take a step away and temper his facial expression.

"I should image not," was his unenthusiastic response.

She was not to be deterred, having never been talented in reading his disinterest in her company or simply being unwilling to see what was so plain to others. "You are thinking how insupportable it would be to spend many an evening in such tedious company! And, I must say, I cannot but agree. Never was I so annoyed. The insipidity, and yet the noise! The nothingness, and yet the self-importance of these people." At this perfect depiction of her own character, he was forced to turn an incredulous laugh into a cough.

"You are entirely wrong, Miss Bingley, I assure you," he managed when he could trust his voice. "My mind was much more agreeably engaged. I have been meditating on the very great pleasure which a pair of fine eyes in the face of a pretty woman can bestow."

Miss Bingley, who ever saw only that which she wished, manoeuvred herself directly before him and looked intently up into his face, furiously batting her eyelashes. "Might one dare asks whose are the eyes which inspire such pleasant reflections?"

"Miss Elizabeth Bennet," he answered with not the slightest hesitation and not even bothering to remove his gaze from that lady. Darcy had ever sought to politely discourage Miss Bingley's vain hopes, doing everything he could think of short of stating baldly that he would never offer for her. Perhaps an expression of admiration for another woman, no matter how new and unexplored it may be, would be enough to encourage her to turn her attentions elsewhere. He held no ill-will against his friend's sister, and truly wished the best for her. As she continued to turn down eligible offers, however, in her doomed aspirations to become his wife, her manners and machinations were wearing on more than just himself as her brother and sister were burdened with her care.

"Miss Elizabeth Bennet?" The lady swallowed hard before positively spitting with bitterness. "I am all astonishment. How long has *she* been a great favourite? And when am I to wish you joy?" This must have been rhetorical, for she did not remain to hear his answer, stalking away looking very much as though she might scream.

Chapter Four

***

The walk to Netherfield was wet and muddy, just as Mrs. Bennet had predicted, but Elizabeth could not find it within herself to care overmuch. Her purpose was to see to Jane's health and comfort; if those at that fine house were offended by her appearance, that was their concern. Of course, she had no wish to offend Mr. Bingley or Mr. Darcy, but she did not think they would hold the state of her hems against her.

The morning previous, Jane had received a letter from Miss Bingley begging her company for dinner while the gentlemen were out dining with the officers. Of course, the invitation was to be accepted, Mrs. Bennet would allow nothing else; though she was deeply annoyed to learn that Mr. Bingley would be absent. Proving herself as scheming a matchmaking mama as ever there was, Mrs. Bennet vehemently denied Jane's request for the carriage and insisted her daughter arrive at Netherfield on horseback, citing the dark clouds on the horizon. If it rained, her hosts could not, in good conscience, send Jane home again and would be obliged to invite her to stay the night, ensuring she would have a chance to see Mr. Bingley.

"This would be an excellent plan, Mama," Elizabeth had pointed out with a heavy dose of exasperation, "if you could be certain they would not send Jane home in their own carriage."

But her mother waved her ever present handkerchief to dismiss such a notion. "No, indeed. Why would they not wish for sweet Jane to remain? Besides, the gentlemen will have the carriage."

"The gentlemen will likely take Mr. Darcy's carriage, Mama, leaving Miss Bingley and Mrs. Hurst with Mr. Bingley's."

Rather than winning Elizabeth her point, this only diverted Mrs. Bennet's attention. "Mr. Darcy...yes. Lizzy, go and change. You must accompany Jane to Netherfield!"

"Accompany Jane?" she asked, incredulous. "Whatever for?"

"Mr. Darcy!" Mrs. Bennet exclaimed as if that answered all. When Elizabeth met this answer with naught but a blank stare, her mother elaborated as though she were speaking to a simpleton who could not comprehend that two and two equals four. "Though he was slow to see your charms, the gentleman was most attentive to you at Lucas Lodge last evening. I am certain he regrets his slight at the ball and I believe he has taken a fancy to you. You ought to go to Netherfield and do what you can to secure him. He is far richer than Mr. Bingley!"

While Elizabeth was far from objecting to spending more time in the company of Mr. Bingley's handsome friend, she refused to throw herself in his path like some desperate fortune-seeker, and she certainly would not confess to her mother his recent apology for the alluded to slight. She was still working out her own feelings towards the gentleman. Mr. Darcy was handsome and interesting, but their acquaintance was still so new.

Her mama would care little for such reasoning, however.

"Mama, the invitation does not include me. It was sent specifically to Jane. I cannot simply appear where I have not been invited."

Even Mrs. Bennet could not refute this and the matter was dropped, at least that of Elizabeth's attendance. Her mother won her point when Mr. Bennet reluctantly admitted that the horses were, in fact, needed on the farm and he would need his stallion, Hephaestus, for some business with one of his tenants, therefore only old Nelly could be spared. So, Jane left, alone and on horseback. She had mounted as soon as she could be readied, desirous of making Netherfield before the rain let loose. No more than a quarter hour had passed after her leave-taking when the heavens opened up and released their fury.

Mrs. Bennet did her best to assuage her own guilt—she did have a care for her children, Jane in particular—by assuring all that Jane was an able horsewoman and certainly made the journey in good time; and a damp cloak would be well worth it when she was Mrs. Bingley.

Elizabeth made up her mind to go to Jane at Netherfield the moment she had read her sister's note, received that morning, detailing how she had been soaked through upon arrival at Netherfield and had taken ill at dinner, prompting her hosts to offer her a room for the night. She wrote that she had awoken this morning with a sore throat and a headache but insisted there was nothing much the matter with her. Elizabeth, who knew her sister well, easily read what had not been written. Jane's sweet disposition and obliging manner was loath to give trouble to anyone and she would never ask another soul to go out of their way on her account; she would, of a surety, downplay her discomfort so as not to give her dear family much alarm. But the shaky handwriting, normally so elegant and fine, the very admission of feeling unwell, and having addressed her letter to Elizabeth told plainly that Jane wanted her.

Mrs. Bennet was all in support of this idea, eager as she was to throw her second daughter in Mr. Darcy's path, until Elizabeth declared her intentions of walking the three miles to Netherfield.

"Walk three miles," she protested, "after a rainstorm, in all that filth and mud? You will not be fit to be seen!"

"I shall be fit to see Jane, Mama, which is all I want." There was no use arguing with her most stubborn daughter. Mrs. Bennet knew this well and so pushed the matter no further, praying Elizabeth would at least be mindful enough to avoid the deepest and muddiest puddles.

Her father's offer to call the horses from the farm was declined, Elizabeth having no desire to avoid the walk. She did, however, accept her youngest sister's company as far as Meryton where they were headed in hopes of meeting with an officer or two who were quartered there for the winter.

Crossing field after field, jumping stiles and springing puddles, Elizabeth pulled off her bonnet to enjoy the warmth of the sun's rays on her face as her thoughts wandered the entire way and quickly drifted to a certain gentleman residing at her destination. They had certainly had a wretched beginning, one that reflected well on neither of them. But, in the two meetings they had had since then, she had found Mr. Darcy to be rather charming, in his own way; and it was a way she rather liked. He did not pile on heaps of false flattery nor flirt incessantly. In fact, she could not say that he flirted at all, yet she felt a certainty within that he...well, it was clear that he enjoyed her company. Often throughout the evening at Lucas Lodge, her eyes would seek him out and, more often than not, his own soulful, dark brown eyes would be fixed upon herself.

He made an excellent effort to make himself agreeable to her neighbours but, inevitably, the gentleman always found his way back to her side. She had repeatedly told herself that it was only due to the familiarity they had already established, all the while fighting the hope that it might mean more.

But could it? Mr. Darcy was an exceedingly wealthy man who was the master of two vast estate in Derbyshire and Kent, with smaller holdings throughout the kingdom, connections to the nobility, and occupied the highest echelons of society. Such men did not take notice of poor, pitifully dowered country gentlemen's daughters.

As she thought it, she was surprised at the surge of disappointment that swelled with in her. From whence had that come? She had previously held no aspirations towards the gentleman. He was handsome and kind and she thoroughly enjoyed conversing with him, but that had been all; until the party that was. The way he had gazed at her across the Lucas' drawing room had made her feel things she had never felt before. Her insides quivered, her heart raced, and, each time she caught him looking her way, she felt her face flush and she was forced to tamp down the ridiculous urge to giggle. She felt discomposingly like Lydia and more than once she

had lost track of her thoughts mid-sentenc
earning her strange looks from her compa

Stop it, Lizzy, she scolded herself.
*only intrigued because he is a very handsome man
who is intelligent, kind, and compassionate. And his
love and care for his daughter is endearing in the
extreme. But what the gentleman needs right now is
a friend, and that is what you shall be.*

No sooner had she made her resolve than it
crumbled to the ground. Having thus decided, she
shook her head, squared her shoulders, and looked
about her only to find that she had entered the park
at Netherfield and the object of her reflections was
not twenty feet away in his shirtsleeves, a beautiful
little girl in his embrace, wrapping her tiny little
arms around his neck.

Elizabeth's steps halted, so mesmerised by
the sweet scene was she. The girl pressed a noisy
kiss to her father's cheek then cried "'Pin me,
Papa!" Elizabeth watched as Mr. Darcy lifted the girl
by the waist high above his head and spun in place,
the girl's giggles and squeals of delight echoing over
the lawn. He continued to turn as he brought her
back down into his arms and peppered her cherubic
cheeks with kisses, bending over double as he held
her tight in his embrace.

When he straightened, it was to face Elizabeth and Mr. Darcy started only slightly.

"Miss Elizabeth!" he cried happily, seeming not at all chagrinned to be found informally attired in such an undignified activity, which only endeared him to her all the more. He took a few steps closer and bowed as best as he was able with his precious burden in his arms. Elizabeth smothered her smile at the sight of a tiny flower tucked behind his ear, obviously a gift from his daughter. "Good morning!"

Roused from her enchantment, Elizabeth smiled brightly and closed the distance between them. Reaching the pair, she returned his greeting with a curtsey and, catching sight of her muddy hems, suddenly wished she had taken greater care on her walk. But then, if Mr. Darcy was not ashamed of being caught at play with a child, she would not be ashamed of what it had cost to come to her sister's aid. "Good morning, Mr. Darcy."

"I hope you are well today?"

"I am, sir. And you?"

"I am quite well, thank you." Then, as if he were acquainting a pair of duchesses, Mr. Darcy introduced the two young ladies. "Miss Elizabeth, may I introduce my daughter, Miss Amelia Darcy. Amelia, my love, this is Miss Elizabeth Bennet." Dark blonde curls were half tied up in a blue ribbon that matched the sash around the waist of her white gown. Large, dark eyes were identical to her father's, right down to the intensity with which she appraised this woman who had interfered with their play.

"It is a pleasure to meet you, Miss Darcy," Elizabeth smiled. "My, but are you not just a lovely little lady! Mr. Darcy, she is beautiful."

"Yes, beautiful," he said softly, gazing upon Elizabeth with a half-smile gracing his lips. It was a moment before he shook his head slightly. "Ah, that is, thank you." With heightened colour, he turned his attention to the little girl in his arms. "Amelia, dear, how do young ladies greet new friends?"

The child's sweet little mouth formed a perfect 'O' before she wriggled to be let down. Once steady upon the ground, she turned to Elizabeth and, grabbing fistfuls of her skirts, bent her knees to squat most adorably in what was obviously her attempt at a curtsey. "Nice to mee'choo, Miss, um..." Scrunching up her nose, she looked to her father for guidance.

"Miss Elizabeth," he bent down and whispered as Elizabeth bit her lips together to contain the giggle which threatened at the adorable display.

"Miss Lebitaf…Lelibeff." Her little brows contracted in frustration and her lips pursed to one side of her mouth. Mr. Darcy very patiently knelt down on one knee beside her.

"Nearly, darling. E-liz-a-beth." Hearing her Christian name drawn out in his deep, rumbling voice made Elizabeth's breath hitch.

"E-lib-i-teff."

"Miss Darcy," Elizabeth crouched down to the girl's level. "Can you say Miss Lizzy?"

The girl thought for a moment then dropped another darling curtsey. "Nice to mee'choo, Miss Lizzy." Her 'z' bordered on a hard 'th,' but that only made it all the sweeter.

"How very ladylike, Miss Darcy!" Elizabeth smiled and stood to return Amelia's salutation.

The girl's eyes lit up excitedly. "Weally? I a lady?"

"Oh, indeed," Elizabeth said earnestly. "A very proper lady. Your papa must be exceedingly proud." She smiled down at the man still kneeling beside the girl.

"I confess, I am," Mr. Darcy replied with dazzling smile and fond look at his daughter.

Finding it easier at that moment to continue conversing with sweet little Miss Darcy, Elizabeth spared one last glance for the father before turning her attention. "And are you having a lovely time with your papa, Miss Darcy?"

"Papa 'pin me!"

"Yes, I saw. It looked like great fun. And did you give your papa that lovely flower he is wearing?"

"I did! Pwetty Papa!" Amelia giggled.

Mr. Darcy furled his brows in confusion. "Excuse me?" Elizabeth bit her lips together and silently tapped her right ear prompting him to reach up and investigate his own, pulling out a tiny purple and yellow pansy as he stood to his full, impressive height. "Ah, yes. I had forgotten. Amelia is quite fond of gathering flowers." As if taking this for a directive, Amelia scampered off to a nearby patch of pansies growing in the lawn.

"That is very kind of her. And, I must say, it suited you very well."

"Well, in that case..." He tucked the wilting flower back into place and turned his head slightly and raised a brow, seeking approval.

"Very handsome," she said before she could stop herself, hoping her cheeks did not appear as flushed as they felt.

Luckily, Mr. Darcy's attention was at that moment diverted when Amelia toddled to his side and tugged at his trouser leg. She held out a fistful of plucked pansies for him to bend down and sniff. While he was still doubled over, she leaned in close and loudly whispered, "Give dis to Miss Lizzy, Papa."

"Wonderful idea, my love." Mr. Darcy placed a kiss to her cheek then stood and held out the flimsy bouquet as if they were prize roses. "Miss Elizabeth, these are for you."

Beginning to curse her traitorous cheeks, Elizabeth accepted the flowers with a shy smile. "Thank you, Mr. Darcy." She crouched to address Amelia. "And thank you, Miss Darcy. They are lovely."

For a moment, a silence fell over the threesome, to which Amelia, at least, seemed oblivious as she examined the blossoms she held. At last, as if just realising that Elizabeth did not belong to Netherfield and the strangeness of finding her there, Mr. Darcy cleared his throat. "Can I assume, Miss Elizabeth, that you have come on purpose to see your sister?"

"Oh!" she started and jumped back up. "Oh dear! Some sister am I. I had nearly forgotten with the lovely scene I stumbled upon. Yes, I received a note from Jane this morning explaining that she had taken ill and have come to see what comfort I might be to her."

"I am sure she will be nearly as pleased to see you here as I am. May I take you to her?"

Elizabeth gratefully accepted his offer and Darcy gathered his folded coat from the lawn then beckoned Amelia. "Darling, 'tis near time for your nap. Shall we escort Miss Elizabeth to the house?"

"Yes, Papa." Amelia tossed away the flowers that remained in her tiny fist then brushed her hands on her gown before reaching up for Elizabeth's. "Come wiff me, Miss Lizzy."

Elizabeth looked uncertainly towards Mr. Darcy, but he only smiled and gestured towards the house. Elizabeth took hold of the sweet little hand with her thanks and together, they crossed the lawn to the manor house, Amelia jabbering adorably the whole way.

Chapter Five

***

This was turning out to be an absolute nightmare. First, her brother had taken this horrid house in this unfashionable, backwater county. Netherfield was by far too small and insignificant to show Mr. Darcy that Caroline knew how to be the perfect mistress of a grand estate such as Pemberley. The society was nothing short of savage; there was no one worth exerting herself to throw a party for to highlight her hostess skills and she would not dream of calling upon any of her

London associates to witness her in such a miserable situation.

Why had Charles not listened to her and taken an estate in Derbyshire? She was wild to visit Pemberley and see with her own eyes what she felt sure was to be her future home. Had he done so, they might visit often and, in time, Mr. Darcy would certainly see that she was eminently suited to be his wife.

Secondly, Mr. Darcy had brought his daughter along. Why he insisted on carting the brat around everywhere with him was beyond Caroline's ability to comprehend. Was that not what nurses and governesses were for? She did not like children, noisy, smelly little things, and it was exhausting trying to pretend every little thing the girl did was so pleasing and adorable. Then the girl had fallen ill and Mr. Darcy had all but disappeared. The child had monopolized all of his time for several days and Caroline had been greatly put out. Her relief at hearing of the child's recovery had been genuine. She could not care less for the child, but now, perhaps, Mr. Darcy would spend more time with herself.

Except now, and worst of all, that dirty hoyden, Eliza Bennet had fenagled an invitation to remain at Netherfield under the pretense of nursing her sister. Caroline saw through that in an instant. It was clear that Miss Eliza wanted only to get her claws in Mr. Darcy. Well, she would not stand for it. It was time to turn up the charm and elegance and show the gentleman just how perfect she was for the role of Mrs. Darcy. Miss Eliza being here might actually work in her favour, now that she stopped to think on it. Next to that country bumpkin, Mr. Darcy could not fail to see Caroline's superiority.

"Oh, Mr. Darcy! We were all just agreeing how ill Eliza Bennet looked this morning," she enthused gaily when he had returned from checking upon that bothersome child after dinner. If Mr. Darcy noticed the fine new gown she had run off to change into, he did not say and she swallowed down her disappointment.

"We agreed on no such thing," Charles chided her. "You and Louisa were sniping the poor lady. Neither Hurst nor I said a word."

"Come now, Charles. You must have seen the state of her petticoats!" Caroline sneered.

"Her hems *were* rather muddy," Louisa agreed nervously. In truth, she had said very little but neither had she done anything to discourage Caroline.

"Her hair, Louisa! So blowsy and untidy." She fanned herself as if she might faint from the very thought of such carelessness for one's appearance. "I could hardly keep my countenance."

Their brother shook his head as he poured Darcy a glass of port. "I say, it quite escaped my notice. I thought she looked remarkably well."

"I am certain you observed it, Mr. Darcy," Caroline cooed at him with her best smile.

"I did," was his curt reply.

Dissatisfied with this disinterested answer, she pressed on. "I am inclined to believe that you would not wish to see your own sister take on such an errand."

"I would not object to Georgiana showing such compassion and care for anyone she loved, or even one of my tenants. That is, after all," he added with a pointed look to his increasingly irritated hostess, "amongst the duties of the mistress of any estate. Though I admit I would prefer my sister take a carriage or some other conveyance for so great a distance, and preferably a footman. But they are different creatures and Georgiana is not so great a walker."

"Oh, yes. Yes, indeed," Caroline latched onto that which she felt she could use to disparage Eliza without contradicting Mr. Darcy. "What can she mean by coming all this state, four or five miles, or whatever it is, in mud and filth, just because her sister has a little cold? And *alone*! It does nothing more than highlight an abominable sort of conceited independence. A complete disregard for civilized and sophisticated decorum."

"It shows nothing more than a very pleasing affection for her sister," Bingley sharply retorted. In an undertone he added, "Something I wager you know little about."

After sending her brother a poisonous look but otherwise ignoring this comment, she turned her attention again on Mr. Darcy. "I fear, Mr. Darcy, that this little jaunt *must* have affected your admiration for her fine eyes. No lady who displays such inelegance could possibly continue to garner your good opinion."

"Not at all," he replied and Caroline sat a little straighter until he continued on. "Her lovely eyes were made all the brighter by the exercise. I found Miss Elizabeth to be in exceedingly fine looks when she came upon my daughter and me in the park. And Amelia was quite taken with her, as well."

Sensing her sister's extreme vexation with this answer, Louisa made an attempt to change the subject by lamenting the sad state of the Bennet's situation. They had learnt a great deal at dinner the night previous before Jane had fallen ill; in fact, that had been Caroline's purpose in inviting Miss Bennet to dine. She eagerly informed her brother and Mr. Darcy that Jane had unashamedly told them of an uncle who was nothing more than a country solicitor in Meryton and another in trade who lived in Cheapside, confident in her belief that such people would steer both gentlemen away from every member of the Bennet family; Mr. Darcy in revulsion of such unworthy connections and their brother under his friend's influence.

But Mr. Darcy could not care for any of this. Did he himself not have embarrassing relatives? Was not the woman whom he had been obliged to call mother-in-law for three years far worse than Mrs. Bennet? That lady did, indeed, put her daughters forward most forcefully, but he had learnt of the entail on their estate and he could not but sympathise with her. With five daughters and little means to care for them when their father was dead, she must feel the desperation of their situation. Lady Catherine had forced Anne upon him for no reason other than to dispose of a daughter whom she considered a burden and to retain the illusion of control over Rosings Park.

With a fierce mien which thoughts of his overbearing and unscrupulous aunt always garnered, Mr. Darcy excused himself from the room to seek some way to clear his head. To Caroline, who could not imagine that he would take this information in any other way than that which she had intended, he was the picture of disgust at having to associate with such intolerable company and she rejoiced.

In her anxiety over her sister, Elizabeth had returned above stairs as soon as dinner was finished. Wishing to check on Amelia, Mr. Darcy had accompanied her and she felt some of her worry slip away in his presence. His deep, calm voice was soothing as he asked after Jane's health and offered up some of those remedies which had been employed to nurse Amelia during her illness. He smelled of spicy sandalwood, book leather, and something else she could not identify but it was divine and was quite effective at distracting her from her concerns.

In her sister's room she sat at the edge of Jane's bed, mopping her hot, sweaty brow, and forced herself to put the gentleman from her mind. She was here for her sister, not Mr. Darcy. She would welcome whatever time she was able to spend in his presence, but she must focus her energies on returning Jane to health.

The other set of sisters paid a visit and were everything kind and concerned, sympathising with Jane's misery and lamenting on how very miserable it was to have a cold. Elizabeth would have liked nothing more than to evict them from the room, but Jane seemed to appreciate their efforts and so she tolerated their presence for as long as they would stay. Fortunately, it was not long. After half an hour they excused themselves with every good wish for Jane's swift recovery and Elizabeth breathed a sigh of relief.

Soon, however, Jane drifted off to sleep and Elizabeth felt it would be only proper to join her hosts below stairs. If she harboured any desire to speak with Mr. Darcy, she willfully ignored those wishes. Leaving instructions with the maid that she was to be sent for if Jane should awaken before she returned, she spared one last look to assure herself that her sister was fast asleep and stepped from the room, gently closing the door behind her. She was obliged to stifle a rather unladylike yelp, however, when she turned from the door to find a tall, stately gentleman standing in the hallway behind her.

"Forgive me, Miss Elizabeth," Mr. Darcy bowed his apologies. "I did not intend to frighten you. I saw you leaving as I passed and thought we might descend together, if that was your intent."

"Do not concern yourself, sir. I did not expect to meet anyone out here, that is all." As her beating heart calmed, mostly, she offered a bright smile. "And, yes, I felt it would be proper to join my hosts as Jane is asleep and has no need of me at the moment."

"Then, shall we?" Mr. Darcy held out his arm with a heart stopping smile and she could only nod stupidly as she took it.

As they descended, Mr. Darcy asked after Jane again and, having answered, Elizabeth inquired after Amelia. Mr. Darcy assured her that his daughter was tucked in bed and they continued to converse amiably all the way to the drawing room, both wishing they had any excuse not to enter. Yet, enter they did and Mr. Darcy was immediately solicited by Miss Bingley to join them at the card table. He accepted his hostess's invitation, though Elizabeth felt certain he only acquiesced for a lack of any excuse not to. As he stepped away from her with a quick bow, she caught his pained expression and a hasty roll of his eyes and was required to check her laugh.

The moment Mr. Darcy was seated, Miss Bingley had very little attention for cards, or anything else for that matter, and it was left to Mrs. Hurst to offer a half-hearted invitation for Elizabeth to join their game as well. Elizabeth demurred, citing her intentions to only remain for a short time until she would return to Jane and expressed her intentions to occupy herself with a book. To this, Bingley offered to fetch her anything she might wish from his meagre library.

"I wish my collection might be greater for your benefit and my credit," Bingley lamented good naturedly. "But I confess I am an idle fellow and sadly have far more books than I ever look into."

Elizabeth assured him that she would be well satisfied by those that were stacked on a small table and selected a collection of poetry. The topic which was raised by Bingley's mention of his sad library left her little attention for her book, however. Miss Bingley wondered at her father having left so few books to his son and turned her effusions on Mr. Darcy.

"You must have a great library at Pemberley, Mr. Darcy. You are always reading and visiting bookstores. I confess, I am quite wild to see it."

"It ought to be good," the gentleman replied neutrally as he laid down a card. "It has been the work of generations."

"I am certain it is nothing short of perfect," Miss Bingley cooed.

"I cannot comprehend the neglect of a family library in this age in which we live."

"Oh, I am sure you have neglected nothing which can add to the beauties of your splendid home. In fact, Charles, when you build your home, you must take Pemberley as a model."

"Caroline, you have never even seen Pemberley," her brother reminded her absently as he inspected his cards before laying one down atop Darcy's. "You might not like the house. It is unlikely, I grant you, but you ought not speak until you have been there."

Miss Bingley scowled at her brother then sent a fleeting look of chagrinned annoyance in Elizabeth's direction. "It is true that I have not *yet* laid eyes on that grand estate, but Pemberley's reputation has preceded it. I am convinced that Mr. Darcy's home can be nothing short of exquisite. You have such excellent and refined taste, sir," she finished with a furious batting of her eyelashes at the object of her overt praise.

Elizabeth was struggling to reign in her mirth at this ridiculous display and was forced to turn an escaped snicker into a cough. Mr. Darcy turned to her and she nearly lost all control when he rolled his eyes in an exaggerated manner followed by a brief wink. She raised her book higher to cover her face.

When Darcy showed no intention of continuing this line of discussion, Miss Bingley moved on to expressing her rapturous delight with Miss Darcy and her many great accomplishments. This line of flattery, however was disturbed by the entrance of a woman wholly unknown to Elizabeth, but whom she quickly surmised to be Amelia's nursemaid as she had the teary-eyed little girl by the hand. Elizabeth immediately looked to Mr. Darcy. The gentleman hastily laid down his cards and stood, his face filled with concern. She also noted Miss Bingley's reaction to this intrusion; that lady threw her cards unceremoniously onto the table and folded her arms over her chest with a scowl.

"Mrs. Lawson, what is the matter?" Mr. Darcy addressed the newcomer though he had only eyes for his daughter and was on bent knee at her side in a moment. An irritated huff was heard from the lady who felt herself abandoned at the card table, but it was ignored by the gentleman.

"Forgive me, sir," answered the nurse. "She could not sleep and was quite insistent on seeing you. I tried to calm her but she was so distraught."

"Thank you, Mrs. Lawson. Please feel free to retire. I shall see Amelia back to bed myself." Another exasperated sigh was heard from the card table at this.

Mr. Darcy took his daughter in his arms and sat beside Elizabeth on the sofa, placing Amelia on his lap and pulling out his handkerchief to dry the little girl's eyes. "What is the matter, dearest?"

"I fwightened," replied she as she twisted the hem of her nightgown around her tiny fingers.

"Frightened?" Mr. Darcy asked his daughter gently. "Of what are you afraid, my love?"

The sweet child sniffled and shrugged her tiny shoulders. She looked from her father to Elizabeth and let out a tiny squeak. "Miss Lizzy!" She reached out her arms and Elizabeth happily pulled the little girl onto her lap.

"Did you have a bad dream, Miss Darcy?" Again, the child shrugged. With a knowing smile, she leaned in close to Amelia and asked in an exaggerated whisper, "Did you miss your papa?" Amelia nodded shyly, now fingering the fringe on Elizabeth's shawl.

"I want dolly," she sniffed, her sweet little chin quivering.

Mr. Darcy reached over and gently caressed his daughter's cherubic cheek. "I am sorry, Amelia. Mrs. Lawson could not find dolly tonight."

"I want a 'tory," Amelia pouted, her tiny, plump lip stuck out.

"I read you a story after Mrs. Lawson tucked you in, sweetling," Mr. Darcy gently reminded her.

"May I tell you a story?" Elizabeth asked, eyeing Mr. Darcy for his consent. He gave a single nod accompanied by a soft smile. She forced herself to look away from his tender look before she forgot the words and became entirely useless. "Actually, 'tis a poem, one of my favourites. Would you like to hear it, Miss Darcy?" The girl nodded enthusiastically before snuggling into Elizabeth's arms. Tightening her hold on the small child, she recited:

> "Twinkle, twinkle, little star,
> How I wonder what you are!
> Up above the world so high,
> Like a diamond in the sky.
>
> "When the blazing sun is gone,
> When he nothing shines upon,
> Then you show your little light,
> Twinkle, twinkle, all the night.

"Then the trav'ller in the dark,
Thanks you for your little spark,
He could not see which way to go,
If you did not twinkle so.

"In the dark blue sky you keep,
And often thro' my curtains peep,
For you never shut your eye,
'Till the sun is in the sky.

"'Tis your bright and tiny spark,
Lights the trav'ller in the dark,
Tho' I know not what you are,
Twinkle, twinkle, little star."[1]

"I like 'tars," Amelia yawned. "They pwetty."

"Yes, they are. Just like you," Elizabeth replied with a smile as she gently tapped the sweet girl on her little button nose.

Mr. Darcy reached across and tenderly stroked his daughter's soft curls. "It is time for bed, my dear. Come now."

Amelia clung tightly to Elizabeth. "I want Miss Lizzy take me."

"I would be happy to, if your papa does not mind. I ought to return to Jane in any case." She again looked for consent and was given a single nod and that heart melting smile. Both stood and Mr. Darcy excused himself to remain close to his daughter before escorting the two lovely young ladies upstairs.

Those who remained behind watched with wildly differing feelings. Mr. Bingley pondered smilingly on just how much the departing trio looked very much like a sweet little family and how dearly he hoped to one day know intimately the love of a father. Miss Bingley was seething and contemplating how she might rid her house of the very much unwanted guests. Mr. Hurst hoped that Mr. Darcy would snatch the girl up quickly so that his tiresome sister-in-law would at last realise the futility of her hopes and might soon be wed elsewhere and cease to manipulate his wife. Mrs. Hurst surreptitiously stroked her middle and sighed, whether from contentment or apprehension, she was not entirely sure.

[1] "The Star" by Jane Taylor, 1806

Chapter Six

***

Few of the occupants of Netherfield Park slept well that night. Bingley paced his chambers for hours fretting over the health of his angel. When Miss Elizabeth had come back to the drawing room later into the evening to express her concerns over Miss Bennet's condition, he had been nearly undone. Nothing short of knowing that he would be less than worthless in the sickroom and having no desire to make Miss Bennet any more uncomfortable than she already was had stopped him from storming the stairs and rushing to her side.

He knew what his friends and sisters thought of him. He was ever falling for some or other pretty face and declaring himself in love only for his enthusiasm to cool in a week or two when another lovely lady caught his eye. He had learnt, thanks to his older and wiser friend, to be cautious never to express his feelings too ardently to any young lady for fear of raising expectations and finding himself shackled to a woman who was beautiful but whom he did not truly love, and who did not love him. There was no denying, however, that he did enjoy his little flirtations.

This, however, was different though he could not explain, even to himself, how. He only knew that the moment he laid eyes on Miss Jane Bennet, something within him had stirred and would not leave him in peace. It was as if he had ever been walking the earth with half a heart, searching for the woman who possessed the piece which would fill the void. When Miss Bennet stood before him with her unearthly beauty, her gentle smile, and those kind eyes, his heart instantly recognised her as the woman who would complete that most vital of organs.

His every waking thought since making her acquaintance was of that most excellent woman.

And not only of her lovely face and pleasing figure, though he greatly admired those features. It was Miss Bennet's goodness, her sweetness, how they seemed able to converse easily and at great length on any topic, and the way she smiled and her eyes lit up when she looked upon him. He wanted to see that smile and those bright cerulean eyes every day for the rest of his life. He *wanted* to be cautious with Miss Bennet, not for fear of raising expectations he would not wish to fulfill later, but rather to ensure that what they had was real and pure; and to ensure that he was worthy of such a woman.

Caroline, he knew, wished him to marry some high-born heiress and secure all their places in the highest echelons of society. In fact, she would have him marry Miss Georgiana Darcy fully believing her brother would then magically desire Caroline for a wife. This would never happen, and he wondered if he ought to speak to his sister, as Darcy had suggested. Not only would Darcy never offer for Caroline, Georgiana was only just sixteen-years-old. Even if Bingley were inclined to offer for his friend's sister, Darcy would not allow it for several more years. But he was not inclined; he never had been. He looked upon Miss Darcy quite as another younger, much sweeter, sister.

At the thought of his friend, Bingley's mind turned to that charming scene in the drawing room as Darcy and Miss Elizabeth had left the room together, Amelia held tenderly in Miss Elizabeth's arms, her sweet face resting gently on the lady's shoulder. She looked to be already half asleep. They had looked so much like a beautiful little family as they departed, Bingley was struck strongly with the thought that Miss Elizabeth would be a perfect wife for his friend. She was kind, compassionate, and friendly as well as intelligent, lively, and playful. She would be just what Darcy needed to enliven his spirits and bring some light and joy into his life. And she would be a marvelous mother to that sweet little girl.

Jane will be a remarkable mother, he thought to himself as he at last climbed into bed with a contented smile. With that thought, he was finally able to lay his head down and drift off into a restful sleep filled with dreams of a flaxen-haired angel surrounded by beautiful, golden-haired children.

Across the hall, Caroline was fuming. She knew exactly what that pathetic little country floozy, Eliza Bennet, was doing. She was using Mr. Darcy's brat in order to work her way into the gentleman's affections. She hoped it would not work because Caroline did not know if she could bring herself to spend any more time with the child than she already was forced to do.

She simply could not comprehend why Mr. Darcy wished to spend so much time with the girl. Her own father had never troubled himself overmuch with Louisa and her, nor even Charles until he was much older. In fact, she did not know of any among her acquaintances unfortunate enough to have children who spent any more time with them than was necessary; just a pat on the head in the morning and again before bed. Perhaps they would be brought down to parade before company so that their fineness might be exclaimed over then sent away again. Anything more? That was what nursemaids and governesses were for. It was simply not fashionable to be a doting parent. She was only grateful Mr. Darcy already had a child and she would not be expected to ruin her figure giving him an heir once they were married. At least the brat had that use; though it would not stop Caroline from shipping the child off to boarding school as soon as possible.

The vision of Mr. Darcy leaving the drawing room with Miss Eliza and the child filled her vision. She reached for a pillow from the bed and, holding it to her face, screamed into it, releasing only a mote of the tension she felt. She had been disgusted by the looks of admiration her brother, and even Louisa and Hurst, had donned as they watched the couple—no! The two wholly unconnected people leaving the room coincidentally at the same time. It was sickening. There was nothing endearing about the scene at all and she would have a word with her sister on the morrow.

Oh! And Jane Bennet. They would need to do something to stop their brother from making a complete fool of himself and marrying that insipid country nobody. An alliance with the Bennets would do nothing to raise their social status. She shuddered to think of what her friends and acquaintances would say if they ever learnt that she was connected to somebody so vulgar and stupid as Mrs. Bennet.

As for Eliza Bennet, two could play at this game. If it came down to it, she would grit her teeth and engage Darcy's girl, but until that became necessary, Caroline would be her most charming self. She would do everything within her power to show Mr. Darcy that she was the perfect Mrs. Darcy and, compared to herself, Eliza was nothing but a dirty, impertinent, poor country hoyden.

Armed with a plan, Caroline crawled into bed determined to sleep the night, and her frustrations, away that she might wake refreshed and in her best looks, prepared to charm her way into the role of mistress of Pemberley. Every time she closed her eyes, however, the vision of Eliza Bennet carrying the child with Mr. Darcy at her side gently grasping her elbow filled her mind and she nearly screamed again.

"That was a good dinner tonight, was it not?" Marcus Hurst asked his wife as he settled back amongst the pillows of his wife's bed.

Louisa sat at her dressing table in her night shift and dressing gown, absentmindedly pulling pins from her hair. "Mm-hmm."

"I say, your sister may be the most frustrating, annoying woman in England, but she does set a fine table. Well," he chuckled, "at least when Darcy is to be one of the party!"

"Mmm," was his wife's distracted reply.

Marcus surveyed his wife. "I say, dear, are you well? You have not caught that Bennet girl's cold, have you?"

"Hmm? Oh. Oh, no, dear. I am...I am well." She looked into the mirror at her husband's reflection upon the bed. He was so dear to her and had put up with an awful lot over this first year of their marriage. Caroline was a trying woman who liked very much to have her own way. Louisa had never been able to stand up to her younger sister and she knew it displeased Marcus to see it.

There was little they could do, however; even Marcus saw that. Charles had not his own home until he had taken Netherfield, only rented rooms at a fine boarding house in London. And Caroline had adamantly refused her own establishment with a companion. Louisa could not entirely blame her sister. That was something only hopeless spinsters and old widowed women did.

"Come, dear. You look pale and weary," Marcus called to her gently in that sweet way he did only when they were alone. "I do hope Darcy makes short work of wedding that pretty little Miss Elizabeth. Then Caroline *might* finally see that he will never marry her and settle down with someone who *will* have her and quit plaguing you so." She crossed the room and slid into the bed beside her husband, happily giving herself into his embrace. This was a nightly ritual she hoped Caroline never learnt about. It was not fashionable for husbands and wives to share a bed. But she had slept by Marcus's side nearly from the beginning of their marriage and could not imagine abandoning the comfort now.

Everyone assumed that theirs was a marriage of convenience, but it was not. Not anymore. It was true, Marcus's father had squandered away much of the Hurst fortune and Louisa's twenty-thousand-pound dowry had been essential in preventing the family from falling into genteel poverty. In exchange, the Hurst name was not insignificant and had raised the Bingley's consequence in society—though it had not been enough to satisfy Caroline.

Within the short months of their courtship and engagement, however, Marcus and Louisa had grown close and discovered a true meeting of the hearts. They loved one another, though neither were especially demonstrative people and cared little to display their affection.

"Do you really believe Mr. Darcy will never offer for Caroline?"

Her head bounced slightly where it lay on his chest when he chuckled. "There was never any hope of it, my dear. Did you believe there was?"

"Caroline is so sure of it," she sighed. "I suppose Mr. Darcy has never given her any encouragement. And he would not marry any woman who could not be a good mother to little Miss Darcy, and Caroline does hate children so." She pushed off his chest and peered down at him as the full weight of his words struck her belatedly. "Do you really think he would marry Miss Elizabeth? She has no dowry, and pitiful connections."

"Pah. What need has Darcy for more money or noble relations he can barely tolerate? Besides, the girl is perfect for him. But I imagine he will be slow about it. He will not rush into a marriage as he did the last time, whatever that was about. And, as you say, he will wish to ensure that whomever he marries will be good for the child. As he should.

"Did you see the way they moved together so naturally as they left the drawing room this evening. Like a lovely little family." He gently pulled his wife back down to lay against him. "One day, my dear, that will be us."

"Marcus," Louisa asked softly, "would that please you?"

"Of course. Why? Would it not please you?" her husband asked through a heavy yawn.

"No, it would. Very much," she assured him, relieved to hear his approbation of such a future. Perhaps it was only hearing Caroline's constant complaints against Mr. Darcy's daughter which had allowed the fear and doubt to creep in. Now that she was more certain of her husband's feelings on the matter, there was room no more for anything but joy. "Marcus?"

"Mm-hmm?" he answered sleepily.

"I am with child."

For a moment she wondered if he had fallen asleep and not heard her, so still did he lie there. When, at last, he did respond, it was in a awe-struck murmur.

"A child?"

"Yes, dear."

"Ha ha!" he burst out as he shot up, startling his wife and nearly knocking her off the bed. "A child! Oh, forgive me, Louie! A child!"

For several minutes there was not a coherent word spoken through his laughter and exclaims of joy. Louisa had never seen her husband so jubilant and it brought happy tears to her eyes. If only she could displace that one source of anxiety which lingered. For now, at least, Caroline and her aspersions could be pushed to the side.

"When?" Marcus asked at last, holding his wife tightly against him and pressing joyful kisses to her lips, cheeks, and neck.

"March, I think. Or April. I felt the quickening only yesterday. Truly, you are pleased?"

"Pleased? I could not be happier, my love," the husband assured his wife, pulling her close for a tender kiss. "I will admit to a certain amount of trepidation; I have never so much as held a small child. Seeing Darcy with his girl so much lately, however, has awakened within me a certain stirring, a longing of sorts. Yes, I am very pleased, my dear. My mother will be thrilled. Shall we tell your brother and sister on the morrow?"

"Oh," Louisa mumbled, some of her joy seeping from her at the idea. "I thought, perhaps, we might keep our news to ourselves. At least for a time. You know, cherish it for a while."

"Louie?" Marcus shifted and tipped her chin up to look down into her face, his own expressively displaying his skepticism. "What troubles you?"

Louisa wriggled free and nestled deeper into his side, annoyed that her sister was marring yet another special moment in her life. "Caroline will not be pleased."

"Oh, hang Caroline. This is nothing but a blessing and I will not allow that woman to steal our joy. I think, my dear, when we return to London, we will not be inviting Caroline to join us. We are to have a family and I will not tolerate your sister's interference and ill manners to plague us any longer. It can be your brother's turn to put up with the burden for a time. He has a house now to keep her."

"Truly? You will not allow her to join us?"

"I will not. Does that displease you?"

Louisa glanced around nervously as if afraid Caroline might be hiding behind a curtain or in the dressing room and could hear their conversation. Her reply was spoken at nearly a whisper. "Not at all, my love. It is just what I would wish."

As for the other occupants of the house who had been present in the drawing room that evening, they were very similarly engaged. Each sat over their sleeping charges, thoughts dwelling upon the other and contemplating how sweet and natural it had felt to ascend the stairs and tuck that precious child into bed together. Darcy replayed over and over again the image of Elizabeth pressing a gentle kiss to his daughter's cheek, feeling with every fibre of his being that he would give a good deal and pay any price to repeat that same scene every night for the rest of his life.

There had been a time in his life when he had believed that his wife would be required to bring great wealth and excellent connections to his name. A lady of superior standing in society and impeccable breeding. What need had he of those things? His marriage to Anne, and with such the acquisition of Rosings Park and her substantial fortune, had made him one of the wealthiest men in England and among the greatest landowners in the kingdom. Many would consider him exceedingly fortunate but his extensive wealth and all he owned had brought him little joy. His true delight was in those things which could not be purchased; his love for his daughter and sister, pride in his name and continuing to uphold his family legacy. A sparkling eyed maiden with a musical laugh from Hertfordshire.

He thought of his final promise to Anne as he gently stroked his daughter's silken hair. He had promised he would marry again, that he would love. She had begged him to seek a mother for Amelia and a true companion for himself. For three years that vow had hung about him like chains, a heavy burden he knew not how to free himself from. For the first time since that terrible night, he felt those bonds loosening.

Though their acquaintance had been of a short duration, he now felt a certainty within him that Elizabeth was that woman he had promised to find. Her ease and natural way with Amelia touched his heart and her lively manners and refreshing intelligence delighted him. And she was so very beautiful. He knew society favoured the Jane Bennets of the world; fair, blue eyed, statuesque and impossibly perfect. But Elizabeth's dark, sparkling eyes and rich, chestnut curls captivated and bewitched him in a way no other woman ever had. She was not what most men would define as classically beautiful, but to him, she was a goddess.

Even the tiny imperfections of symmetry he had noticed in her form fascinated him. She was perfectly imperfect and had no care to reshape herself to fit into society's mould as so many ladies of the ton desperately attempted to do. Best of all, she was aware of her flaws, yet had a great deal of confidence in herself anyway. She was exactly the kind of woman he wished for his sister and daughter to emulate.

That thought sobered him. The woman he married would be required to take on some heavy tasks. Already he had a daughter who would need care and love. It would take a very special kind of woman to love another's child as her own. Then there was Georgiana. His sister was so painfully shy and unsure of herself, even more so after this past summer. His wife would have the task of guiding her in society and drawing her out of her reserved nature. Was it fair to ask so much of any woman? When a young woman married, she ought to look forward to nothing more than parties, balls, and running her own home, not the raising of other women's children. Would Elizabeth, so young and carefree, be willing to take on such burdens? Something within him answered, unequivocally, yes; so compassionate and kind, Elizabeth would likely take it on willingly, happily even. But was it fair to ask it of her?

In another room, Elizabeth was engaged in a different but similar reverie. That evening spent with Mr. Darcy and Amelia had burst open the gates of her heart and lodged them both firmly in her affections. It was very natural that she would adore the child; so innocent and sweet, she could not fathom how one could not love such a creature. The depth of her feelings for the father after so short an acquaintance, however, surprised her. After their first disastrous meeting, she had not thought they would even be able to find their way to being friendly. Yet now, with only a few meetings, she had no doubts she was rapidly falling in love with the man.

Oft had she imagined falling in love and the qualities of the gentleman who would eventually lay claim to her heart. He would have to be kind, caring, and generous. She could never abide a man who was stupid or ignorant; she desired a husband who would challenge her mind and engage her in intelligent, lively debate.

Ever had she believed that any man she would love must be as lively and sociable as she, but now she saw how tiresome that would be. Likely, a man such as that would grate on her nerves in very short order. No, what she desired was a husband who could balance her lively spirits with a dignified calm and steadiness yet who was not afraid to joke with and tease her. Mr. Darcy, she now felt, was the man who, in talents and disposition, would most suit her.

Could she suit him, though? she wondered. Mr. Darcy was a very wealthy man with great connections. He was the nephew of an earl, for heaven's sakes! Surely, he would be loath to connect himself to her silly and vulgar family. Her mother, more often than not, was in some fit of hysterics; her youngest sisters were wild about officers and beaux; her middle sister, Mary, was pious and studious; even her father was indolent and could not be bothered to check his improper wife and daughters, preferring by far to laugh at their antics than exert himself to protect their family's respectability. Could a man such as Mr. Darcy ever connect himself with such a family? Only Jane could be credited with ever behaving with decorum and grace. Even Elizabeth herself was always scampering about the woods and fields, muddying hems and obtaining freckles in the sun. Most assuredly she was not what anyone could imagine as the mistress of Mr. Darcy's likely very fine homes.

~~~*✱*~~~

Chapter Seven

₊

When morning fell, Jane's fever had not yet broke though she had slept peaceably enough to ease much of her sister's fears. Even so, Elizabeth was desirous of having her mother come and judge her eldest daughter's condition for herself. Though Mrs. Bennet was no skilled nurse, she had a mother's heart and was likely worried over Jane. If she were to be completely honest, Elizabeth also hoped that seeing what her machinations had wrought on her favourite daughter might temper some of her mother's madness to marry off her daughters to anyone who would have them, though it was likely a futile hope.

She sat at the desk in Jane's room and dashed off a note to her mother then, remembering her encounter with little Amelia last evening, pulled out a second sheet to write a quick note to her sister Mary. She asked a favour of her sister and begged her discretion; the last thing Elizabeth needed was her mother getting excited over her simple idea. She gave the note to Joseph, one of Netherfield's footmen whose sister worked in Longbourn's kitchens and could assure the note made it into Mary's hands with little notice.

Mrs. Bennet arrived, along with the rest of her daughters, shortly after the residents of Netherfield had broken their fast. As her mother at least pretended to assess Jane's condition and Kitty and Lydia exclaimed over the fineness of the room and giggled madly about how lovely it would be to be mistress of such a house, Elizabeth beckoned Mary to join her in her own chamber under the guise of wishing to show her a book she had borrowed from Netherfield's library. No one need know, and certainly none of the present party would ask, that Mr. Bingley's library boasted few volumes that anyone of understanding might boast.

"And just think girls," Mrs. Bennet was crowing as Elizabeth and Mary exited the room, clearly not as concerned over Jane's fever as Elizabeth was, "this is only a guest room. Just imagine how fine the mistress's chambers must be!"

Closing the door on the inane chatter and vainly hoping her mother did not mean to tarry long, Elizabeth turned to her next younger sister. "Did you bring it?"

Mary pulled something lumpy wrapped in a shawl from under her cloak and presented it to her sister with a questioning look. "I cannot imagine why you need it. Is it frightening here? 'Tis a lovely room." Mary surveyed the cheery room with its floral wallpaper and dusky pink bedding. It was a little girlish for Elizabeth's tastes, but it was far from frightening.

"'Tis not for me, Mary," Elizabeth laughed at the thought. Tenderly she unwrapped the parcel to reveal her childhood doll. When each of the Bennet daughters had turned three, their father had presented them with a beautiful China doll which was designed to resemble themselves. The doll which she held had dark chestnut ringlets half tied up in a plum-coloured ribbon which matched the sash tied around the waist of her light green gown. Her dark green eyes were the exact shade of Elizabeth's. "Mr. Darcy's daughter, Amelia, has misplaced her own doll and I thought she might like this one."

"You are going to give away Lizzy Doll? Is that proper?" Mary asked, her voice barely above a whisper as if they might be overheard and chastised.

"It is not as though I am presenting a gift to Mr. Darcy. 'Tis for a sweet little girl who has lost her own. Surely her own doll will be located soon and, if not, it will be well worth it to cheer the dear child. You are certain Mama did not notice?" Lizzy Doll was not particularly small and had created a sizable bulge under Mary's cloak.

"You know Mama pays me little notice." Mary's reply was disinterested but Elizabeth thought she detected a shadow of hurt in her sister's eyes. It was true. Mrs. Bennet was as proud of her daughters as any mother could be, but it was no secret that some were dearer to her than others. Jane, being the eldest, most beautiful, and the one upon whom Mrs. Bennet hung all her hopes for a secure future, was the clear favourite. Second only to Jane was Lydia. Mrs. Bennet doted on her youngest daughter who had the liveliest spirits and reminded her greatly of her own youth.

Mrs. Bennet was largely indifferent to Kitty, who followed everywhere Lydia led thus earning her more notice than Mary. Mary was nearly invisible, being neither especially beautiful nor lively, while Elizabeth seemed often to be the bane of her mother's existence. Willful and obstinate, she had never been afraid to resist her mother's attempts to tame her into some version of herself. Mrs. Bennet simply could not understand her second daughter's penchant for reading anything she could get her hands on and an almost manic need to walk daily.

"Mama loves you, Mary," Elizabeth tried to console her sister.

"She loves me, but she does not like me."

"No less than she likes me, dearest. You must not allow it to trouble you so. Our mother is a simple woman and cannot understand you and me, who care more for what is in our heads than for what we put upon them. You can only be who you are, Mary, and you are a wonderful young woman." Elizabeth kissed her sister on the cheek, realising with some guilt that she had not done so in a very long time and made a silent vow to give more of her time to her unseen sister. "Thank you for bringing Lizzy Doll."

The doll tucked safely within Elizabeth's trunk until she could find an appropriate time to present it to Amelia, the sisters rejoined the rest of the visiting Bennet women in sitting with their hosts in the drawing room below stairs. Miss Bingley greeted them with scant civility and barely concealed disdain but Mr. Bingley was all smiles and asked promptly after Jane's condition. Elizabeth cringed and flushed as she listened with growing mortification whilst her mother blatantly promoted her eldest daughters to the gentlemen of the house.

"Oh, she is very ill I am afraid," the lady exclaimed, "and suffers a vast deal. But she does so with the greatest patience, so sweet is my Jane. My other girls, I often tell them, are nothing to their eldest sister with her superior beauty and sweet temper. Ask anyone around and they will tell you that Jane Bennet is the jewel of Hertfordshire! She will make the perfect wife someday. The sooner some fortunate gentleman snatches her up, the better, I say. Oh, but my Lizzy!" Mrs. Bennet turned an almost hungry look on Darcy. "So caring and obliging! And clever, too! She will make an excellent mistress of a fine estate. And there are many who will declare that she is very nearly the equal to her sister Jane in beauty!" Mary coughed loudly at that moment and Mrs. Bennet started and returned to the subject at hand. "Mr. Jones has said we must not think of moving dear Jane. I fear we must trespass a little longer on your kindness, sir."

To this Mr. Bingley could only reply that he would not hear of Jane's removal until she was fully recovered and assured Mrs. Bennet that both of her daughters were very welcome to remain as long as necessary. Elizabeth could not bring herself to look at Mr. Darcy who stood quietly at the window witnessing her mother's vulgar display.

"Oh! But this is a sweet room you have here, Mr. Bingley! And what a charming prospect over the gravel walk there. I do not know of another place in the neighbourhood that is the equal to Netherfield. I am sure you will not ever wish to leave, though you have but a short lease."

"I confess, whatever I do is often done in a hurry," Mr. Bingley replied. "Should I resolve to quit Netherfield, I should probably be off in five minutes. I am delighted with Hertfordshire, however, and consider myself as quite fixed here."

"That is exactly what I supposed of you, Mr. Bingley," said Elizabeth with a smile.

"You think you comprehend me, do you?"

"Oh, yes! I believe I understand you perfectly, sir."

"I shall choose to take this as a compliment, though I cannot pretend that to be so easily seen through is anything but pitiful!"

"I cannot think that a deep, intricate character is any more or less estimable than one such as yours, sir."

"You are a studier of characters, are you, Miss Elizabeth?" Darcy asked, speaking for the first time and drawing Elizabeth's attention. She was vastly relieved to see a smile on his lips, despite her mother's blatant hints. "That must be an amusing study."

"Indeed." Seeing the good humour in his eyes, she raised one mischievous brow at him. "Though Mr. Bingley's character is everything worthy, I do find that more intricate characters are the most amusing. They have at least that advantage."

"The country can in general supply a very few subjects for such a study," Miss Bingley hissed, not even bothering to disguise her contempt for the present company. "In the country you are limited to such a confined and unvarying society."

"True," Elizabeth replied. "But people themselves alter so much, there is something new to be observed in them often enough to keep me satisfied."

Nothing more could be said, thankfully, before a whirl of bouncing curls and joyous giggles rushed into the room and launched herself into Elizabeth's arms.

"Oh!" Mrs. Bennet cried. "Who have we here?"

Elizabeth looked to Mr. Darcy, uncertain of how he would wish to proceed. The gentleman, with a contented smile gracing his handsome features, stepped forward and stopped next to Elizabeth. "Madam, may I present my daughter, Miss Darcy. Amelia, dear, this is Miss Elizabeth's mother, Mrs. Bennet, and her sisters." Elizabeth placed the child on her feet so she could demonstrate her adorable ladylike greetings, which earned exclamations of delight from all the Bennet ladies. If anyone heard Miss Bingley's scoff at the display, they did not acknowledge it.

"Mr. Darcy, such a lovely child," Mrs. Bennet said softly with a tender look on her face she most often reserved for her youngest daughter. "Oh, she does remind me so of when Lydia was just a small child. Would you like a sweet, my dear?"

"Oh, Mama—" Elizabeth began, but Mr. Darcy placed a gentle hand on her shoulder and shook his head with a smile. Amelia took several timid steps towards Elizabeth's mother, looking back often to her father who urged her on with smiles and nods, until she stood directly before Mrs.

Bennet. That lady had pulled out the ever-present tin filled with paper wrapped chewy caramels from her reticule, being her favourite indulgence. She unwrapped one small sweet and held it out to the child. With one last look to her father in a final bid for permission, Amelia took the treat and shoved it hastily into her mouth.

With a large grin, Amelia curtseyed to Mrs. Bennet again, mumbling a stifled "Fank 'oo!" before climbing up onto the lady's lap. Her sweet devoured, Amelia began babbling away to the lady as Kitty and Lydia, sitting on either side of their mother, gushed and fawned over the beautiful little girl. Even stoic Mary could not disguise her admiration. It was a most endearing scene and Elizabeth could only smile at the tenderness her mother displayed towards the child.

After a surprisingly pleasant quarter of an hour, Mrs. Bennet reluctantly acknowledged that the time had come for them to depart and Mr. Darcy stepped forward to release the lady from his daughter's enthusiasm. Before he could reach her, however, Miss Bingley hurried forward and brusquely pulled the child from Mrs. Bennet's lap with a very forced smile that more resembled a pained grimace. She held the girl under her arms straight out in front of her as if she were something filthy that might soil her gown if she allowed it too near.

"Allow me to return the girl to the nursery, Mr. Dar—"

An ear-splitting scream pierced the air as Amelia began to kick and fight to be released from the lady's grasp. Mr. Darcy dashed to his daughter and wrested her from a violently flushed Miss Bingley. Amelia clung to his neck and buried her face in his shoulder, her tiny body wracked with sobs. Without any forethought, Elizabeth stepped to the little girl and gently rubbed her back, whispering soothing words. A little arm reached out and hooked around her neck, pulling her body flush against Mr. Darcy's. Her eyes locked with the gentleman's and, for a moment, every other occupant of the room was forgot as they gazed upon one another.

The heat and scent from Mr. Darcy's strong body infiltrated Elizabeth's senses and for several moments the whole world faded into obscurity. She had never been so close to a man other than her father. Her hand, which had been poised to straighten the sash of Amelia's dress, rested against his firm, warm chest. She began to feel so many things she did not understand. She wanted to experience more of him; the feel of his arms and shoulders, to touch his neck and cheeks or run her fingers through his thick hair. To stop herself from giving into these wildly improper impulses in front of so many witnesses—and her mother, for goodness sakes!—Elizabeth tightly closed her fingers around the lapel of his coat, without the slightest notion of how very much such a small act affected the gentleman.

Several sounds alerted them to their surroundings at once; Miss Bingley's growl-like harrumph; Mrs. Bennet's excited "Oh!"; Kitty and Lydia's giggling; Mr. Bingley's clearing of his throat. All shattered the moment and Elizabeth made to release herself from the little girls embrace but Amelia clung tight.

"Amelia, dear," Mr. Darcy prompted gently, his voice rather gravely and low, "you must let go of Miss Elizabeth."

Instead, the tiny girl released her father and fell into Elizabeth's arms.

"She seems to like you, Lizzy," Mrs. Bennet noted, a touch of motherly pride laced in her speech as she nodded pointedly to Mr. Darcy.

The gentleman could not stop the chuckle and dazzling smile which her words inspired. "Yes, Mrs. Bennet. Amelia has been quite taken with Miss Elizabeth from the moment they met yesterday."

"Well, fancy that." She flashed them all a rather smug grin before turning to her younger daughters. "Girls, come. We must be going. Thank you, Mr. Bingley, Miss Bingley, for your excellent care of our dear Jane."

"It is our absolute pleasure, Mrs. Bennet," Mr. Bingley bowed his farewell. Miss Bingley said nothing, only fumed in her seat, arms crossed and not even bothering to rise as her guests turned to leave.

"I shall see you out, Mama. Would you like to come with me, dear?" she asked Amelia, then added quickly with a shy glance towards Mr. Darcy, "If your papa does not object."

"Not at all. I shall accompany you," Mr. Darcy answered. "If you are not needed to tend Miss Bennet for the moment, perhaps you might wish to join Amelia and me for a walk in the gardens?"

Mrs. Bennet squealed, "She would be delighted, Mr. Darcy! Of all things, my Lizzy enjoys a good ramble out of doors!"

"Mama!" Elizabeth sighed in exasperation but could do little more than shake her head. "Yes, Mr. Darcy, I would be delighted."

"Yes!" Miss Bingley practically yelped. "A walk sounds like just the thing to ease my spirits after that most horridly distressing display!" Then she reddened again when she realised she had not even attempted to disguise her disdain for Mr. Darcy's daughter.

Elizabeth and Mr. Darcy exchanged worried glances but Mr. Bingley rescued them. "Caroline, I need you to remain. We must look over the ballroom and see what needs to be done to bring it up to scratch. I mean to hold a ball here at Netherfield."

Lydia and Kitty squealed in shared delight which drowned out Miss Bingley's huff of annoyance. They both began speaking at once, begging for details and asking Mr. Bingley to confirm at least three times that he was in earnest. Their raptures could hardly be contained when the amiable gentleman laughingly assured them of his sincerity and incited more excited chatter when he gave them leave to choose the date as soon as their eldest sister was recovered.

~~~*✳*~~~

Chapter Eight

✳✳*

Sweet, childish giggles rang across the grounds as the three walkers meandered their way through the gardens. Darcy and Elizabeth walked on either side of Amelia, each holding one of her tiny hands. Every few steps Darcy would count to three and they would lift the little girl and swing her back and forth while the child squealed her delight. On one such pass, Darcy turned quickly and snatched his daughter from the air, pulling her in tight and spinning her about in his arms. The girl shrieked,

Elizabeth laughed, and Darcy triumphed in having elicited both reactions.

Setting Amelia back upon her feet, he gave her a gentle pat on her backside. "Why do you not go fetch some lovely flowers for the lovely Miss Elizabeth, dearest?" With nary a hesitation, the darling child scampered on ahead to do just that and Darcy offered his arm to his companion. Very naturally, Elizabeth wrapped both hands around his arm affectionately, delighting the gentleman to no end.

"She is such a dear child, Mr. Darcy," said Elizabeth, smiling fondly at the little girl cramming blossom after blossom into her tiny fist.

"Thank you, Miss Elizabeth. I could not imagine my life without her," replied he with a tender smile.

"She has your eyes, but little other resemblance. May I assume she takes more from her mother?"

"Indeed. Amelia looks very much as Anne did as a child, though Anne had blue eyes."

"Would you...would you tell me about her? If it is not too difficult, that is."

"'Tis not difficult," Darcy answered, eyebrows knit together as he turned his gaze into the past.

"Anne was my cousin, the only child of my mother's elder sister. At the age of eight, she contracted scarlet fever and it weakened her dreadfully. Before her illness, Anne was a sweet, rambunctious child, much like Amelia," he chuckled as he watched his daughter twirling down the path, flowers and petals flying about her. "I imagine you would have liked her very much, as I would venture to guess she was little different from yourself." He threw her a roguish wink and Elizabeth did not even bother to temper her smile.

"I know not of what you speak, sir," replied she, lifting her chin and adopting a very Miss Bingley-like tone. "I have ever been a model of perfect ladylike comportment." Raising her nose even higher, she cracked when she cast a gaze at Darcy and saw his highly skeptical expression. She burst into laughter and dropped the pretense. "Very well, perhaps I have not *always* been so very proper and genteel. I have been known to footrace with the neighbourhood boys and have climbed a tree or two in my day, but it has been some time."

"Yes, I imagine you have not found yourself in a tree in at least a week."

Torn between scandalised and amused, Elizabeth swatted his arm and laughed. "I beg your pardon, sir! It has been at least a few months!" They laughed together and walked on in silence for a few minutes until Elizabeth could contain her curiosity no longer.

"I beg you would forgive my impertinence, sir, but I am an incurably curious woman. Mr. Bingley had intimated that you had never intended to marry your cousin. May I ask why you did? I imagine a man such as yourself rarely does anything not of your own choosing."

"Think you I am such a tyrant?" he asked with mock affront. Elizabeth raised a brow and gave him a look which very much said *you know very well what I mean!*

"Very well. You do have the measure of me. After my mother died, my aunt began claiming that it had long been agreed between them that Anne and I had been intended for one another. My father vehemently denied these claims, and I had never heard such a thing. For it to be the favourite wish of my mother, as my aunt was so fond of claiming, she never said a word of it to me.

"It is true, I had no intentions to marry Anne. Neither of us were inclined for the union, Anne wished never to marry at all. She was always frail and often ill and it was widely understood amongst our family that she would not have a long life, and likely never bear children. But Lady Catherine was relentless. I received frequent letters demanding I come to Kent to do my duty and marry my cousin. Every illness of Anne's was blamed on my cruelty and the grief I was putting her through by refusing to marry her."

At this revelation, Elizabeth hugged his arm tighter and Darcy nearly lost his train of thought for the feel of her body pressed against his arm. Shaking away these thoughts, he cleared his throat and resumed his narration.

"After the death of my uncle, Sir Lewis de Bourgh, my father had taken to making yearly calls at Rosings to look over the estate, checking the accounts and the tenants, that sort of thing. My aunt could not bully my father as she did her brother, the earl. In my eighteenth year, he began taking me along. Despite our denials and my continuing not to offer for my cousin, these visits only fanned the flames of Lady Catherine's obsession with the idea of my marriage to her daughter. She seemed to believe that the only reason I accompanied my father was for Anne's sake, never mind that as my father's heir it would likely fall to me to look after Rosings someday.

"On our last visit, the day before we were to depart, I went to Anne's sitting room to visit and bid my farewells—I did have a care for my cousin." He halted their steps and looked out over the garden. "I shall never forget what I witnessed that day."

Regretting her insatiable inquisitiveness at the pained look in his soulful eyes, Elizabeth slid one hand down his arm and grasped his hand. "Forgive me, sir. You need not continue. I ought not to have even asked."

Enveloping her hand in both of his, he looked down into her lovely eyes. "No, I am grateful you did. I have not spoken of this to anyone before. Only my father knew the reason for my marriage. Though I admit it is more difficult than I had imagined it would be, it is something of a relief to unburden myself. I find it very easy to talk to you."

"I am very glad."

Fighting the nearly overpowering urge to lean down and kiss those perfectly luscious lips, Darcy cleared his throat and continued his story. "When I reached my cousin's chambers that day, I heard shouting. My aunt was all but screaming at Anne, berating her for being too undesirable and too frail and not doing enough to entice me to propose. I opened the door just as my rather large aunt brought her hand down across my cousin's cheek." Elizabeth gasped and he squeezed her hand. "I was furious. It was beyond enough that she blamed Anne for my *in*action, but inexcusable that she would lay a hand on her own daughter, frail and sickly or not. I knew Anne would never be safe with her mother if I did not marry her. I proposed on the spot and we were married within the week. Once she had gained her end, my aunt would brook no delays."

"What did your father say?"

"He protested at first, though relented when he learnt of what I had seen. Understand, his objections were never against Anne, per se. He and my mother had a marriage based on mutual love and affection and both desired the same for their children. But he understood why I had to do what I did. He died only a few months after we were wed.

"Our marriage was meant to be one in name only. Anne was removed from Rosings and protected and that was enough. There would be no children to risk Anne's life, and she would carry out what was left of it in peace and as much happiness as I could provide. We were content and lived together comfortably, two cousins sharing a home.

"Nearly two years after we wed, however, Anne came to me in tears, begging me for a child. I refused. I knew that to bring life into this world would be the end of Anne's and I was not prepared to be responsible for that. But she was insistent. At last, I relented, believing that she yearned as many young wives do for a child. How could I refuse her that? When it was learnt that Anne was increasing, she confessed that her mother had been writing her abominable letters, abusing her most cruelly for not providing me an heir. She managed to convince Anne, even from afar, that if she did not provide me with a son, I would send her back to Rosings and that thought terrified her."

"Surely you denied it!" Elizabeth cried, unable to fathom such cruelty from a mother. Her own made little pretense of her preference for any of her daughters before Elizabeth, except perhaps Mary, but Elizabeth could not imagine Mrs. Bennet descending to such acts of malice and brutality.

"I did, of course. It made little difference. Anne had lived an entire life being berated and abused by her mother. I imagine it was exceedingly difficult to shed that burden. Though I know, logically, that there was little I could have done, I cannot help but blame myself for my cousin's death."

"You did not kill your wife, sir."

"I know that," he gave a weak half smile. "I must only convince myself to believe it."

They stood together, gazing into one another's eyes for a long moment until one of them, neither could say who, began to lean in. Slowly, as if time had stopped and they had eternity to savour this one moment, they inched ever closer; hearts beating wildly and the very air between them igniting. With a mere inch separating their lips, two pairs of eyes closed, each prepared to abandon their hearts to one another.

A scream rent the air, breaking the spell, and Darcy and Elizabeth leapt apart. "Amelia!" Darcy breathed, as they both looked about, realising the little girl was nowhere to be seen. Hastening towards the direction the cry had come from, they breathed easier when tiny footsteps sounded from around a curve in the path and, immediately after, Amelia darted into view.

"Papa! Papa, come! Come, Miss Lizzy! Huwwy!" cried she before dashing off again.

Frustrated by the loss of such a blissful moment, yet even more annoyed that he had allowed his control to slip so thoroughly as to nearly kiss a woman to whom he had as yet made no promises, Darcy silently rebuked himself and followed his daughter, Elizabeth close behind. They found the girl bent over a patch of brightly coloured fall blossoms, beaming at the petals.

"Look! A Bufferfry!" she squealed with delight.

The adults glanced askance at one another before bursting into laughter and leaning down to admire the beautiful creature at Amelia's insistence.

Stomping from one end of the ballroom to other, following her brother as she grunted and growled and made various harrumphing sounds, Caroline was excessively displeased. She did not care if the chandelier needed cleaning; she did not care when last the chimney had been swept; she did not care how many couples the ballroom might hold. She simply did not care.

"Think you we can manage?" Bingley asked as he turned in a slow circle, taking in the whole of the room.

"Hmmph."

"I believe the room to be plenty large enough."

A loud, exasperated exhale was the only answer.

"We can easily open the doors between the dining room and breakfast parlour for supper. It should be sufficient to fit the principal families of Meryton. Unless you desire to invite many guests from Town."

This, at least, received a spoken response, unpleasant though it was. "Why on earth would I wish anyone from London to know how far we have sunk? There is not one of my acquaintances whom I would dare to allow witness me in such squalor! Not even Miss Pennywater and she is all but on the shelf! Dear Lord, Charles! Do you mean to ruin us entirely?"

Bingley abandoned his assessment of the room and turned on his sister with a scowl. "What in heavens name is the matter with you, Caroline? You have been in high dudgeon all morning! I thought you would leap at a chance to host a ball and show off your skills as a hostess."

"Yes, in London or Derbyshire!" she snapped at her brother. "Not this backwater county that is entirely devoid of fashion or taste! Why could you not take an estate nearer Pemberley?"

"I thought it would please you to be situated so near Town. We are not a half days journey from London. Derbyshire is at least two days distant. More often three!" He threw his arms up in exasperation. There was simply no pleasing his irascible sister.

"At least there, I can show Mr. Darcy what a perfect a mistress of Pemberley I will be! This house is pathetic and I am wasted here! Do you not wish me to marry your friend? Would you not desire Mr. Darcy for a brother? Why would you send him off with that dirty hoyden?" Caroline spat, gesturing out the doors to the beyond where she imagined that awful Miss Eliza was working on *her* Mr. Darcy.

"Caroline, you must let go of this wish to wed Darcy. He is never going to offer for you." Bingley cried.

With a scandalized gasp, Caroline clutched at her chest. "Of course, he is!"

"You cannot stand his daughter. You despise the country—*where Darcy lives*. You do not even care for the man himself, only his station and wealth. What on earth would induce him to offer for you?"

Caroline counted off her own virtues on her fingers. "I am extremely accomplished, I am highly educated, I am wealthy *and* beautiful—"

"Good God, Caroline. Do you not hear yourself? You are conceited and arrogant and everything Darcy hates about the ton! Darcy does not want just some society wife to parade about on his arm. He desires a true companion. He desires a wife he can love, a mother for Amelia. Have you never noticed how little notice he pays you?"

"How dare you! You will see!" she exclaimed, one bony finger pointed in his face. "Mr. Darcy *will* marry me and I will never invite you to Pemberley. Perhaps I shall just have a little talk with Louisa and return to London with she and Hurst. Then you shall have no hostess for this pathetic ball of yours."

She turned to storm out but his voice stopped her exit.

"They will not have you, Caroline."

"What do you mean? Of course, they will have me. They must."

"Hurst came to me this morning. They plan to return to London after the ball but will not be taking you with them. Hurst is tired of your interference in their marriage." He held up a hand to stall her objections. "Quite frankly, I do not blame him. I mean to marry soon, Caroline, and I shall not have you interfering in my marriage either."

"Interfe—? I do not interfere!"

Ignoring this deliberate falsehood and the fact that she could not even meet his eyes as she uttered it, Bingley squared his shoulders and fixed his sister with a stern glare. "You have but three options, sister. One," —he held up a finger— "you may learn some humility and kindness and remain with me, acting as my hostess until such a time as I marry. After that, your behaviour towards my wife will determine your continued residence in my home. Two," —another finger joined the first— "you may go and live with Aunt Sylvie in Scarborough."

"No, Charles! You cannot!" Caroline gasped in horror, staggering backwards and grasping dramatically at her neck.

"Or three," —he abandoned his count and placed his hands upon his hips— "I shall sign over your dowry to you and you may take up a companion and a residence of your own in Town. The choice is yours, Caroline."

Bingley turned and, shoulders back and chin held high, left his sister fuming in the middle of the ballroom.

~~~*✱*~~~

Chapter Nine

✱

The remainder of Jane and Elizabeth's stay at Netherfield passed quite without incident. Miss Bingley spoke to hardly anyone, which suited everyone just fine. Without the intruding influence of her sister, Mrs. Hurst proved to be a rather sweet, if reserved woman. Elizabeth was strongly reminded of Kitty who followed wherever her younger sister led for lack of her own convictions and wondered if it might be best if Kitty spent less time with the wild and spoilt Lydia. Between herself and Jane, surely, they could spare some time for both Mary and Kitty?

On the third day of Jane's illness, she had begun to feel well enough to join the party below stairs for a short time after dinner. She and Bingley sat close together by the fire in quiet conversation while Darcy and Elizabeth sat on a sofa with Amelia between them, reading stories to the child and laughing at her sweet antics. Mr. and Mrs. Hurst sat nearby, watching the adorable display and holding hands, something neither their brother nor sister had ever witnessed. Miss Bingley sat apart from the group, glowering at everyone before excusing herself to retire early with the claim of a terrible headache.

When Darcy declared it time for Amelia to be off to bed, Elizabeth noticed Jane's heavy eyelids and convinced her reluctant sister that she ought to return to her chambers, as well. She asked if the Darcys would accompany the sisters to their rooms as she had something she wished to give the little girl. Darcy, of course, agreed being as he was rather disinclined to quit her company and the group bid their goodnights to the rest of the party and left the room together.

After tucking her sister securely into bed, Elizabeth slipped into her own room to retrieve Lizzy Doll. When she returned to the hall, Darcy set his daughter on the floor and took a knee beside her with an arm wrapped around her waist.

"I hope I do not overstep, but I asked my sister Mary to bring this when she came yesterday." She crouched as she held out the doll to Amelia and the child squealed with delight. "She was mine when I was a child."

"I luf her! Fank you! Fank you!" Amelia cried, hugging the doll tightly. "She look like you, Miss Lizzy!"

"Yes. My papa had a doll made to look like each of his daughters on the occasion of our third birthdays. I call her Lizzy Doll, but you may name her whatever you please. My sisters had much more traditional names for their dolls."

"No," Amelia stated decisively. "Lizzy Doll is good name."

"Are you sure, Miss Elizabeth?" Darcy asked, torn between a burning warmth for this woman and concern for her parting with such a precious item. "I would not ask for you to part with a treasured gift. I can easily purchase Amelia another doll in London."

"Yes, I know. But until then, or until the missing doll is found, she can keep Lizzy Doll. I am much better pleased knowing she is being loved by Miss Darcy than hidden away in my hope chest."

"I cannot promise Amelia will readily give her up when the time comes."

Elizabeth smiled sweetly. "I know that, too, Mr. Darcy. I am happy to give Lizzy doll to Miss Darcy."

"Miss Lizzy?" Amelia interrupted.

"Yes, dear?"

"Why you call me 'Miss Dawcy'?" the girl asked.

"Oh, well. It is the proper way to address you until you give me leave to use your Christian name."

"I want you call me 'Melia," she pouted adorably.

"I should be happy to, my dear," Elizabeth laughed. "But you must then call me Lizzy."

"Lizzy?"

"Yes, Amelia?"

"I luf you."

"Oh, sweetheart." Eyes misting and heart near to bursting, Elizabeth clasped her hands to her heart. "I love you, too."

Darcy pulled out his handkerchief and pressed it into Elizabeth's hand. Before he released her fingers, however, he gently pulled her to stand. Never removing his gaze from her magnificent eyes, he lifted her hand to his lips and pressed a gentle kiss to her soft skin. "Goodnight, Miss Elizabeth."

"Goodnight, Mr. Darcy," she whispered. "Goodnight, Amelia."

Charles was right, Caroline thought as she sat at her dressing table, gazing unseeingly at her tear-stained reflection. *He is never going to offer for me.* The moment she met Mr. Darcy all those years ago, she had decided that she was going to marry him. He was everything she had ever wanted in a husband; rich, important, nobly connected, and, as more of a superfluous advantage, he was handsome. The only thing he lacked was a title, but she had quickly decided she could live without one for the advantages the Darcy name would bring her. Then he had married his cousin only a few months later and ruined her plans. That had been vexing in the extreme.

How delighted she had been the day she learnt of Mrs. Darcy's early demise! Only now, after a long day of observation and reflection, did she realise how appalling it was to have rejoiced in the death of another. But that had been when her plans had revitalised with a vengeance. She had used the relationship between Mr. Darcy and her brother, or so she had believed, to gain the upper hand over every other lady in London who would sell her soul to capture the newly widowed master of Pemberley, who was now even wealthier than before and surely in need of a mother for his infant daughter. While he had been in mourning for his wife, frustratingly insisting on observing an entire year, Darcy would not attend parties or balls, but he accepted private dinner invitations from his closest friend. When his mourning ended, she had made it her business to know his habits and manipulated conversations to learn to what events he had been invited so she could be sure to be there as well.

Excuses were made for every short answer he gave and every time he moved away just as she drew near. Each season that passed and he did not offer for her, she reasoned that he had likely married too young the first time. Such great men often did not marry until much closer to, or even after, thirty years of age and he had been but two and twenty when he had been ensnared by Miss de Bourgh. Clearly, Caroline convinced herself, the gentleman desired to recapture those years he had been shackled to his sickly wife.

Last season was more difficult to dismiss, but she had. Reasons did not matter. He would see her worth soon enough, she oft repeated to herself, willfully ignoring the mortifying reality that such had eluded him thus far. Only now did it strike her. She had ever intended to marry Mr. Darcy; Mr. Darcy, however, had *never* intended to marry her.

Such was a humiliating epiphany in the extreme. For nearly three years, she had all but flung herself at him full in the belief that he *must* enjoy her attentions. That he had not was now so very plain, she wished for nothing more than a hole in which to crawl and hide away forever. She loved a man who, quite simply, did not love her.

No, she thought. *Charles was correct about that, as well. I do not love him. I never did.* She loved that he was rich. She loved that he was the nephew of an earl. She especially loved that he had already his inheritance and she would have stepped straight into her place as mistress of his grand estate. She loved that doors opened to her due simply to her association with him. The man himself? He was reserved and withdrawn and cared not for society and attending parties and events; all the things Caroline adored. She knew next to nothing about him. Not his birthday, his favourite foods, nor even how he drank his tea. No, she did not love him and, for the first time, she realised she likely would not have been happy with him. When had that begun to matter to her?

As she sat in the drawing room that evening, watching the couples around her, she had felt alone in a way she never had before. It was not simply that the others had excluded her—or rather, she had excluded herself. Staring into her own red-rimmed eyes in the mirror, she pictured the scene again in her mind: Charles and Jane Bennet, seated together before the fire, scarcely aware that any others existed in the world, let alone the room. Louisa and Hurst, hand in hand on the sofa, gazing adoringly at little Miss Darcy. And Mr. Darcy and Miss Elizabeth. The tender looks and sweet smiles shared between them had not been lost on Caroline; neither was the blinding truth that the gentleman had never looked upon her in such a way or anything even nearing such tenderness. They truly had appeared every bit a family as they read to his daughter. They, all of them, were happy—and she found she envied them.

A soft knock upon Louisa's bedchamber door the next morning gave her pause. Marcus was still abed, Charles rarely came to her door, and

Caroline was never awake this early and *never* knocked. Who else could possibly come to visit her here? Miss Elizabeth, perhaps? Though she could not fathom why. They had begun a tentative friendly relationship, but surely, she was tending to her sister at this time, or enjoying an early breakfast with Mr. Darcy.

"Who is it?" she called.

"Caroline. May I enter, Louisa?" came the muffled reply.

Louisa stared at the door for nearly a full minute, wondering if perhaps she had heard wrong. It was so very unlike her sister who typically barged right in, as free as she pleased, caring not for what she might be interrupting or whom she might disturb. It truly was something of a miracle she had not yet discovered the Hurst's sleeping arrangements. Wrapping her dressing gown tighter around herself, more to hide the nonexistent bulge of her belly than for modesty, she stood and went to the door, easing it open just a crack. Sure enough, there stood her sister, her tawny braid draped over her shoulder and fine dressing gown pulled over her nightshift. It had been an age since Louisa had seen her sister thus. Since the age of fifteen, Caroline had been excessively fastidious about her appearance, even amongst family.

"Caroline? What are you doing here?" She cast an uneasy glance towards the bed where Marcus still lay, barely covered by the bedclothes.

"I need to speak to you. May I come in?" Though the woman standing before her had all the appearance of her younger sister, Louisa could not quite reconcile the quiet demeanour and polite deference with the Caroline she knew who rarely asked and just did; who was loud and demanding and did not speak with others but rather just talked at them. "Louisa?"

"Oh, forgive me. Ah…why do we not go…to…your chambers?" She was not prepared for a diatribe about her husband sleeping in her bed and how they would be ruined if anyone of their acquaintance were to find out that Louisa actually cared for her spouse, let alone loved him. She was, however, surprised when Caroline gave no objections nor demanded a reason, but capitulated and led the way down the hall to her rooms.

Ensconced within, Louisa looked expectantly, and not a little apprehensively, at her sister waiting to hear whatever it was she would complain about today. Likely it was Marcus's decision to exclude her from his homes or Charles admission that he had handed their resentful sister an ultimatum. Truthfully, Louisa was quite proud of her younger brother. She liked Mr. Darcy a good deal, yet it was not to be denied that Charles had depended far too much upon his friend's guidance in his younger years. That gentleman's marriage, and subsequent withdrawal from society had been a good thing for her brother. It had forced him to learn to make his own decisions and trust more upon his own judgement.

Concern began to take place of anxiety when Caroline remained silent, sitting on the edge of the sofa, shoulders slumped and staring at her hands clasped in her lap. It was a far cry from the customary ramrod straight, entirely self-assured carriage Louisa was used to expecting from her sister.

"Caroline, what is it you wished to speak to me about?" Louisa prompted.

With a deep, steadying breath, Caroline spoke. "I just...I wondered, well. Are you happy, Louisa?"

Whatever she had expected, this was not it. Louisa stared at her sister a moment or two, eyebrows knit in perplexity, trying to find the challenge in the question. When she found none, she sought clarification. "I do not understand."

Caroline looked up and, for an instant, looked her old self again as she eyed her sister as if she were completely addled, so simple had been the question. It passed quickly, and was replaced with as near a look of contrition as Louisa had ever seen on her sister's face. Caroline had never shown an ounce of concern for another human being's happiness, least of all her siblings who could do little to further her social aspirations but to marry well; and in that, Louisa had fallen short so far as Caroline had ever been concerned.

"In your marriage, in life. Are you happy?"

Without thought, Louisa placed a hand on the gentle swell of her abdomen. "Yes. Yes, I am," she answered almost defiantly.

"And, Hurst? Do you love him?"

This was far more disconcerting than her first question. If Caroline had never cared for another's happiness, she most assuredly had never placed any importance on the notion of love! For years she had hounded Mr. Darcy for no reason other than that he was rich and better pleasing to look upon than many of the single titled men Caroline could have set her cap at. That she should *love* her husband, Louisa was certain, had never entered her sister's mind.

"I do. I know you do not think very highly of Marcus but—"

"No, Louisa, please," Caroline stopped her, twisting her hands together. "I am glad. You ought to be happy, and I am pleased you love your husband. I have never seen you so content as you looked last evening. I am sorry for how I have behaved these many years. It was truly never my intention to make you so...so miserable." She turned dejected eyes towards the window, though Louisa was sure her sister saw little of the view. "Truthfully, I never concerned myself with anything beyond my own selfish ambitions to even notice or care how my actions affected my family."

"*What* did Charles say to you?" Louisa asked, dumbfounded.

With a watery laugh, Caroline shrugged and wiped away her unshed tears. "Only what I desperately needed to hear. Perhaps if he had done so sooner, I would not have made such a fool of myself before Mr. Darcy for all those years." She released a rueful huff. "No. I doubt that is true. If I had not seen the way he looked upon Miss Elizabeth last evening, I would never have recognised how he has never shown even the slightest regard towards myself."

Caroline described the epiphanies of the night before, from the deplorable way she had treated and disregarded her own family to the realisation that, in spite of her wealth and an unprecedented popularity for a tradesman's daughter, she was not happy, not truly. Most surprising, however, was the acknowledgement of Mr. Darcy's indifference to her and her surprising lack of disappointment. In fact, she was now quite convinced that she and Mr. Darcy were not at all suited and could never have been happy in marriage. The greatest source of pain flowed from the years wasted chasing futile dreams.

In light of her sister's newfound clarity, Louisa could not but be moved to some sympathy and sought to soothe her hurt. "Oh, Caroline. Perhaps, with this altered attitude, he might be made to see—"

Caroline interrupted her with a laugh. "I do not wish for Mr. Darcy's addresses, Louisa. Not anymore. He is rapidly falling in love with Miss Elizabeth and I am happy to see it. Truly, I am. They will do well together and she will be a lovely mother for Miss Darcy. I still do not desire children. I suppose there are some things that will never change. What is it?" she asked when Louisa bit her lips together and looked away. It was quite the attestation to her newfound attitude that she would ask after her sister's disquiet, let alone notice. "I have offended you. Is it possible you do wish for children?"

"I do, Caroline. In fact," —she took a deep breath, entirely unsure how her sister would take the news— "I am with child."

"Oh." Caroline looked as if she knew not whether to be pleased for her sister or offer her condolences. "Congratulations, Louisa. Truly. If you are happy, I am happy for you. And Hurst?"

"Thrilled!"

The two sisters sat in confederation for much of the morning, the longest they had ever conversed without bickering over some trifling thing or another in many a year. Caroline was surprised to learn how little she knew of her sister and Louisa was pleased to begin establishing a sisterly bond she had believed lost and long despaired of. She had watched the fond attachment between Miss Bennet and Miss Elizabeth with a great deal of righteous envy.

At last, they separated to dress and rejoined to walk arm in arm to breakfast. They spent much of the day with the Bennet sisters, both acknowledging the budding relationship between their brother and Jane Bennet. It was, perhaps, not the union they might have wished for—good society was still a commodity they enjoyed and connections to a country nobody would do little to raise their status—but it was becoming ever clearer that Charles cared for the lady, more so than any other 'angel' he had obsessed over, and they ought to at least acquaint themselves with her. Besides, if Mr. Darcy married Miss Elizabeth, Jane Bennet would become his sister; and *that* was nothing to sniff at.

When their guests departed the following morning, genuine remorse was felt by all. Promises to call were given, delight in Jane's recovered health was expressed, and the sweetest farewell witnessed between Elizabeth and Amelia.

Chapter Ten

***

"I hope, my dear," said Mr. Bennet over breakfast the morning after Jane and Elizabeth arrived home from Netherfield much sooner than their mother felt they ought to have, "you have ordered a good dinner tonight for I have reason to expect an addition to our party."

"Of what are you speaking, Mr. Bennet?" Mrs. Bennet asked. "I know of no such company, unless Charlotte Lucas should happen to call. I certainly hope my dinners are good enough for her.

I cannot believe the Lucases enjoy as good a table as we."

"The addition, Mrs. Bennet, shall not be a lady."

Clutching her napkin and waving it excitedly before her face, Mrs. Bennet squealed in delight, looking between her two eldest daughters. "Oh! Mr. Bingley and Mr. Darcy! Of, course! Oh, they shall always be welcome here, I am sure! I do hope Mr. Darcy will bring that adorable girl of his. Oh, dear! Not a spot of fish to be got! Lydia, love, ring the bell for Hill. I must speak with her at once!"

Elizabeth looked across the table and shared a joyful smile with her dearest sister as her mother continued in her raptures until Mr. Bennet abruptly put an end to her delight and his eldest daughters' eager anticipation. "It is neither Mr. Bingley," –he glanced at Jane then Elizabeth— "nor Mr. Darcy. It is a gentleman whom I have never laid eyes on in the whole course of my life."

Safe in the knowledge his family would never guess, he indulged in a moment of amusement as they speculated on the identity of their surprise guest. When his entertainment had been exhausted, particularly by the increasing exuberance of his youngest daughters as they became excessively animated with each officer's name they threw out, Mr. Bennet raised a hand to silence the table.

"I received a letter from my cousin, Mr. Collins, expressing a desire to pay a visit and meet my daughters." With great amusement, he looked around his table. Mrs. Bennet looked on with horror, Kitty and Lydia had already turned back to their breakfast, his news having nothing to do with officers and, therefore, of little interest to them. Mary showed signs of polite interest while his two eldest daughters shared identical looks of concern.

"When did you receive this letter, Papa?" Elizabeth asked, knowing full well the habits of her father.

"Oh, not more than a month ago. And," said he with a sardonic grin, "it being a matter of great delicacy and import, I allowed it to sit on my desk for no more than a fortnight before answering it."

"Oh! Mr. Bennet!" wailed his wife. "Do not mention that odious man! Why you have never done anything about that dreadful entail is the cruelest thing in the world! Now you shall die and your widow and children will be forced from our home into the hedgerows to starve by that horrible man! I wish you would not mention him at all!"

"It is a sad affair, indeed," —her husband nodded in feigned solemnity, having long ago given up trying to explain the nature of an entail to his wife— "but I think you will be comforted by his manner of expressing himself."

He then proceeded to read aloud the most ridiculous letter Elizabeth had ever heard. Every word exuded simultaneous self-importance and obsequiousness while demonstrating very little sense. He apologised for the iniquitous sin of being next in line to inherit Longbourn; something entirely out of his control and, she supposed, nothing he would alter even were he able. He made mention of wishing to make amends to his cousin's daughters, which gave her great uneasiness to imagine his meaning. Most surprising, for Elizabeth at least, was the mention of Mr. Collins' patroness, Lady Catherine de Bourgh. Supposing there were not two such named ladies in the country, this must be the aunt Mr. Darcy had told her about.

"Well," said Mrs. Bennet with more composure than any of her family might have expected, "if he means to make amends and proves to be an agreeable sort of man, I, for one, shall be glad to welcome him to Longbourn."

As nobody else seemed inclined to further the discussion of their imminent guest, Mr. Bennet excused himself to his bookroom, Elizabeth invited Mary to join her in the music room to practice duets, while the rest of the ladies retired to the drawing room. Jane sat near the fire with a blanket and enticed Kitty to sit with her to look over a book of watercolour drawings, the younger sister being fond of art and quite talented.

Mr. Collins arrived promptly at four o'clock, as indicated by his letter and the family gathered in the drive to greet their guest. A young man of greater than average height, Mr. Collins stood on long, thin legs which supported a large barrel chest, stuck out in an air of superiority. Far from handsome, though not quite grotesque, he was simply plain with dark, lank hair which covered *most* of his head. He surveyed his surroundings with great interest and spoke with a good deal of formality.

He was invited into the house and had much to say on the elegance of the furnishings, the practical arrangement of the rooms, and general splendor of the house. He offered many compliments to Mrs. Bennet on having so fine a family and divulged having heard much of the beauty of her daughters—from where he might have had such a report, one could only imagine— but that their fame had fallen far short of the truth. Much to that lady's pleasure, he assured her of his opinion that they would all, in time, make fine marriages; one, perhaps, much sooner and far greater than the others.

"I am highly sensible that my good fortune should be a source of unease and discomfort for my fair cousins and yourself, madam, and I assure you that I am most heartily grieved at being the means of injury to your most amiable daughters and come eagerly prepared to admire them. I ought not say more, though I could go on, but shall, perhaps, wait until we are better acquainted. I am confident that my overtures shall not be unwelcome when I have revealed the purpose for my coming to Longbourn."

To the relief of all—for, despite his words, he showed no sign of stilling his tongue and seemed very much as if he wished they would ask after his secret purpose, which he mentioned a further four times—Mrs. Hill appeared at the drawing room door and announced Mr. Bingley and Mr. Darcy. The effect this had on the occupants of the room was great. The previous guest was nearly forgotten in the presence of the newcomers as Mrs. Bennet welcomed them with much enthusiasm. Jane and Elizabeth each composed themselves admirably as they tamped down identical waves of excitement at the sight of the two gentlemen. Even Kitty and Lydia could appreciate having someone else to listen to besides the dull, long-winded parson. Mary seemed the only one unaffected by the gentlemen's arrival.

"Mrs. Bennet," Bingley addressed the matriarch, "we meant not to intrude when you already have a guest. But we could not satisfy ourselves until we could ascertain that Miss Bennet had received no harm from her journey home from Netherfield yesterday."

"Oh, you are so very good, Mr. Bingley! And most welcome! As you see, my Jane is quite recovered, no doubt from the excellent attentions received from her good, kind friends. Oh, you both must stay for dinner! Indeed, you are very welcome anytime, you know."

After ensuring that they would not be inconveniencing the family in any way, to which Mr. Collins opened his mouth as if to object but was preempted by Mrs. Bennet's assurances, both gentlemen accepted with gratitude. They were then introduced to Mr. Collins who, upon learning Mr. Darcy's identity, dropped his offended countenance at once and fell into a near apoplectic state of excitement.

"Mr. Darcy?!" he exclaimed, fluttering his hands and visibly trembling. "*The* Mr. Fitzwilliam Darcy of Pemberley in Derbyshire?!"

Darcy looked to Elizabeth and was surprised to see her hands cover her mouth and her eyes widen in heightened alarm. He silently questioned her with a raise of his brow and was answered with a slight shake of her head. There was naught he could do, however, but to confirm his identity and was immediately acquainted with the cause of her discomfort.

"Mr. Darcy," Mr. Collins gushed, "I am indeed honoured and delighted to make the acquaintance of my noble patroness's son. I am the rector, sir, of her most excellent ladyship, Lady Catherine de Bourgh! And such an honour it has been to serve and counsel your most excellent mother. I am most gratified to assure you that her ladyship was in the best of health when I took my leave of her most august ladyship only yesterday."

Stiffening at the mention of his late wife's vile mother, Darcy made a slight nod to the parson. Elizabeth saw a muscle ticking in his jaw as he replied coolly, "I am...glad to hear it."

"Mr. Darcy," Elizabeth addressed the gentleman in an attempt to rescue him from her bothersome relation, "may I inquire after Amelia?"

With a gaze so tender Elizabeth nearly melted into a puddle at his feet, Darcy smiled his gratitude. "I thank you, Miss Elizabeth. Amelia is very well. Although, she has not stopped asking for you since you left yesterday. You shall be obliged to pay her a visit soon, I am afraid." He threw her a covert wink which inspired a bright smile in response.

"Such would be not be an obligation in the least. It would be my great pleasure, sir, as you well know."

"Amelia is...?" Mr. Collins interrupted the sweet moment.

"My daughter, sir," Darcy answered and attempted to step away to join Elizabeth but Mr. Collins persisted.

"Oh! Yes, her ladyship has told me all about your marriage to her most excellent daughter. Allow me to offer my heartiest condolences for your loss. I am assured by Lady Catherine that Mrs. Darcy was, without contest, the brightest jewel in the kingdom. Such a glorious match, Lady Catherine says, has never been seen! Her ladyship has extolled greatly on the excellence of her granddaughter. Nothing else could be expected, of course, from the offspring of two such illustrious personages of rank and such impeccable birth!"

"That is most extraordinary, Mr. Collins," Mr. Darcy said through gritted teeth, "as my aunt has never deigned to exert herself to even meet her daughter's child."

If Mr. Darcy had expected Mr. Collins to find this information disturbing, he was to be disappointed. Instead, the toadying fool ploughed on as though the very thing was expected.

"I am sure, Mr. Darcy, that her ladyship means no slight. She is, as you must know, exceptionally busy with the management of her impressive estate and my humble parsonage. Her wise and excellent counsel is sought by those both near and far! But I can assure you that Miss Darcy will receive every attention from her ladyship when the time comes for her to reside with her most illustrious and noble grandmother at Rosings which her ladyship is greatly anticipating."

Mr. Darcy fixed the parson with an icy glare. "Mr. Collins, you seem to be operating under some very grievous misapprehensions. Allow me to correct them. Since my marriage to Anne de Bourgh, Rosings Park belongs to me, not Lady Catherine. I am not best pleased to learn that the living at Hunsford fell vacant and was filled without my knowledge and shall discuss it with my aunt at a later time. But, be assured, my daughter will *never* reside with Lady Catherine. Now, if you will excuse me, I should like to speak with Miss Elizabeth." Ignoring Mr. Collins stammers and stifled snorts of indignation for his revered patroness, Darcy turned and stalked away.

Seated before the window and as far from Mr. Collins as could be managed, Elizabeth furtively reached across and squeezed Darcy's forearm. He exhaled forcibly and turned an apologetic smile on her. "Forgive me. I meant not to offend your guest."

"You need not apologise, sir. He has been here barely an hour and already I have had my fill. I am so very sorry you were given no notice. Had I known he was coming, and from whence he came, I would have sought a way to warn you. As it is, Papa only told us this morning of his intended visit and I had not expected to see you so soon."

"Bingley was rather impatient to be assured of the health of your sister," Darcy explained with an indulgent glance towards his friend and her sister seated together on the settee, giving no notice to any others in the room.

"And you, sir?" she asked with a saucy smirk. "Are you so concerned for Jane, as well?

"I readily confess," he smiled, flashing his irresistible dimples at her, "I was scarcely less eager to ease my own worries that you had taken no ill effects from the journey."

"Oh! Yes, indeed! Three miles in an excellent carriage. I can hardly account for how we managed the arduous trek," she teased.

Dinner was then called and some confusion arose as it would have been most proper for Darcy, as the highest-ranking gentleman in attendance, to offer his escort to his hostess into dinner. Reluctantly, he stood to do so when Mrs. Bennet waved him off.

"Oh, posh on propriety. 'Tis nothing more than a family dinner. Stay with Lizzy, sir. I am sure you will enjoy her conversation a good deal better than my own." When Mr. Collins made to hasten towards Jane, she pointedly encouraged Bingley to remain at her side, as well, where he had been since he entered the house. "Mr. Collins, why do you not escort Mary to dinner? You will find much you have in common, I am sure."

With one last longing look towards Jane, Mr. Collins turned an assessing gaze on Mary. With a shrug of his shoulders, he offered his arm and escorted his plainest cousin to the dining room. All the way there, he waxed poetic on the delightful situation of the house, the hall, the carpets, the paintings. Nothing was too small to be below his notice. Dinner was much of the same. Every dish was magnificent; the settings not so elegant as those used at Rosings, but very fine nonetheless; never had he had a more delightful boiled potato, but for those served at Lady Catherine's table. The lighting, the chairs, the linens were all perfectly suited to his tastes. When the second course was laid, he ignited a touch of Mrs. Bennet indignation when he inquired as to which of his fair cousins was to be congratulated for the excellence of the meal.

"Mr. Collins! We are perfectly able to keep a cook! My daughters have nothing at all to do in the kitchens," the lady cried, looking nervously towards the other end of the table where her eldest daughters sat with their impressive beaux.

This set off a seemingly never-ending monologue of apologies and begging of pardons for the affront and his gladness that the estate was so profitable as to be able to afford such comforts. Mrs. Bennet assured him of being not the least bit offended, in fear of offending *him* away from her middle daughter, but still he waxed long his regrets. It was fortunate, therefore, that both Elizabeth and Jane had such agreeable dinner partners; Mr. Collins' plentiful conversation was all but lost on at least four diners that evening.

When the gentlemen had rejoined the ladies after the separation of the sexes, Mr. Collins was greatly vexed to see Mr. Bingley still firmly attached to his fairest cousin's side. He had come to Longbourn, under strict instruction from Lady Catherine, with the intent to marry one of Mr. Bennet's daughters as an offered olive branch to lessen the sting of his own good fortune of being next to inherit their home upon the death of their father. It had been but the work of a moment for him to set his sights on the eldest Miss Bennet. She was far and away the most beautiful of her sisters and, to his mind, that obviously meant she would make the most excellent wife for a man of his lofty station.

Quite convinced that once his desires were made known, his own claim as family and the future master of Longbourn, and his respected position as a rector in the church, especially one who enjoyed the condescension and patronage of so important and noble as Lady Catherine de Bourgh, would certainly take precedence over some relative stranger.

Satisfying himself that there could be no danger from the hopeful, if doomed, rival, Mr. Collins set himself to one last task before crawling into bed that night. Veritably trembling with excitement, he pulled out a sheet of paper from the desk in the guest room and penned a letter to his most esteemed patroness to divulge the glad tidings of having made the acquaintance of her highly respected son-in-law to be sent by express first thing in the morning.

~~~*✲*~~~

Chapter Eleven

✲

When morning dawned, Mr. Collins awoke with the sun and slipped off to Meryton to ensure his letter would be sent with the utmost alacrity. There was a jaunty skip in his gait as he retraced his steps back to Longbourn as thoughts of Lady Catherine's joy at his receiving his letter and the anticipation of becoming engaged to the beautiful Miss Bennet buoyed his spirits.

At the conclusion of breakfast, Mr. Bennet excused himself to his library as the ladies prepared to venture out of doors to enjoy the crisp fall day. Attaching himself to Mrs. Bennet's side, Mr. Collins took the opportunity of informing her of his decision, full in the belief that she would be nothing short of honoured as well as delighted.

"Mrs. Bennet," he began as they walked together in the garden, "I must compliment you on the excellence of your daughters. I find I am quite overcome by their charms and beauty. You must be inordinately proud."

"Indeed, I am, Mr. Collins. They are sweet girls, though I say it myself."

"Quite so, quite so. The eldest Miss Bennet, in particular, is most exquisite. A lady eminently suited to the position of a parson's wife." He stopped and faced the lady to ensure she had taken his meaning.

She certainly had and would do naught to encourage him. Indeed, Mrs. Bennet set to work disabusing the man that there was any hope in that quarter. Heir to Longbourn he may be, but his consequence was nothing to that of Mr. Bingley. "Oh, Jane is certainly the loveliest of her sisters and will make a fine wife for any gentleman, as will all my daughters. I am exceedingly gratified by the attentions she has received from Mr. Bingley. We expect a proposal any day."

"I do not think you understand, Mrs. Bennet." Mr. Collins gripped the lapels of his jacket and puffed out his massive chest. "I am prepared to make Cousin Jane an offer this very day."

"I am sorry, sir. Were it not for the prior attachment between my daughter and Mr. Bingley, there would certainly be no objection. But, as they say," —she smiled at her own rare show of wit— "the early bird does get the worm."

"Mrs. Bennet," cried he, the volume and unnaturally high pitch of his voice attracting the attention of all the ladies and they made their way towards the pair to stand in support of their mother should the need arise. "My situation in life, my connection to the family of de Bourgh, and my relationship to your own are circumstances highly in my favour! It ought to be considered that, despite her manifold attractions, it is highly unlikely another offer may ever be made to Miss Bennet. Your daughter's portion is so insignificant that it is likely such will greatly diminish the effects of her loveliness."

"It is fortunate, then," replied the lady with no little indignation, "that Mr. Bingley has wealth enough that her lack seems to be of little concern to him."

With a petulant huff, Mr. Collins folded his arms across his chest, looking every bit the overgrown child. "Though I am by no means prepared to relinquish my claim to Miss Bennet, if you insist on continuing in this misguided obstinacy, I may be persuaded to take Cousin Elizabeth in her sister's stead."

"I am afraid, Mr. Collins," Mrs. Bennet informed him, endeavouring to maintain her composure and only moderately succeeding, "that I cannot satisfy you there either. Lizzy has lately been the object of Mr. Darcy's attentions. His daughter has taken quite a liking to my Lizzy and I am sure she will make a splendid mother to the darling girl."

"You must be mistaken, madam." The agitated clergyman looked to Elizabeth in alarm. "Mr. Darcy is far too illustrious, elevated, and important to pay his addresses to a lowly country maiden such as my cousin. Besides, he is, himself, engaged to be married."

This proclamation sent a shock through the very air as mother and sisters exchanged glances. Jane took up Elizabeth's hands in her own and whispered assurances in her ear, while Mr. Collins looked on with smug triumph.

Undeterred, Mrs. Bennet raised her chin in defiance. "And to whom is he engaged?"

With a dismissive wave of his hand, as if such information was everything trivial, Mr. Collins rolled his eyes. "Lady Catherine is even at this moment seeking his bride. His mother is most anxious to ensure his next wife is worthy to occupy the position her daughter held." With these words, he cast a disdainful glare at Elizabeth, apparently forgetting that he had, only moments ago, declared his own willingness to take her to wife.

To this Elizabeth released a hearty laugh of relief. "Lady Catherine is Mr. Darcy's aunt, sir, not his mother. Even so, she has no right to choose his bride. And I would not marry you in any case!"

"Lady Catherine is not a lady to be gainsaid. You are not worthy of such a gentleman!" he snarled.

"Enough, sir," shouted Mrs. Bennet. "*You* are not worthy of *my daughters*! Come, girls."

"You cannot be serious!" Mr. Collins cried as the young ladies gathered about their mother and followed her away from the gardens towards the house. "Very well! I shall know how to act! Do not think any of you shall have a home here when your father is dead!" he called after them. If any of them heard, they made no indication as they left him to his brooding.

Tension was thick within Longbourn all the rest of that day and into the next. Mr. Collins continued to assert his superior claim to whichever daughter he chose; that choice vacillating constantly between Jane and Elizabeth, and, at one point, he demanded them both. Mrs. Bennet, in an attempt to preserve a place in their home at the demise of her husband, at first allowed that he may pay his addresses to Mary but insisted, in a move which shocked her entire family, that the decision to accept would be Mary's. When Mr. Collins expressed his disgust at such a notion, angering all the ladies and inspiring an unprecedented united front of loyalty and affection for that sister, Mrs. Bennet reneged her approbation altogether and again declared he could have none of her daughters.

By no means discouraged, Mr. Collins decided in his confidence as future master of the house that he required not that lady's support nor her permission and determined to proceed to offer his hand to Jane anyway. It proved to be no easy task, as none of her family would leave her alone for even an instant in order for him to corner her, and, in the end, he followed Jane and Elizabeth to the stillroom on the third morning of his stay. Ignoring the presence of her sister, Mr. Collins snatched Jane's hand and dropped to one knee.

"Cousin Jane, from the moment I entered the house, I singled you out as the companion of my future life!" He then proceeded to spew forth a barrage of such ridiculous verbal sewage as to render both sisters stunned. He expounded long on his own perceived advantages; his relationship with his noble patroness, Lady Catherine de Bourgh, being mentioned no less than four times.

"And so, there is nothing left to do but to assure you of the violence of my affections," he concluded his lengthy speech seemingly as an afterthought. "I am perfectly aware that you are worth nearly nothing—"

"Mr. Collins!" Elizabeth exclaimed in disgusted anger but was ignored.

"—and shall make no claims on your father for anything more than the one thousand pounds to which you are entitled at the death of your mother. On this subject, I shall be uniformly silent and can assure you that I shall make no ungenerous reproaches on the matter once we are married."

The sisters exchanged a bewildered look before Jane gently extracted her hand from her cousin's sweaty grip as he made to pull it to his lips. With as sweet a smile as she was able to muster under the unpleasant circumstances, she replied, "I thank you, sir, for your compliments but am afraid I must refuse. Excuse us."

"One moment!" cried he, stepping in their path to halt their escape and dropping again to one knee. "Cousin Elizabeth, *almost* as soon as I entered the house, I singled *you* out as the companion of my future life!"

"I also refuse!" Elizabeth preempted him, having already heard his deplorable proposals and being in no humour to hear them again. Grabbing Jane by the hand, she swept past him and out the door.

Just as they gained the front of the house, hoofbeats were heard on the drive and the ladies turned to see who had come. As if by design to brighten their day after the unpleasantness of the morning, Mr. Bingley and Mr. Darcy came into view, seeming every bit their knights in shining armour atop their valiant steeds. The gentlemen were welcomed with beaming smiles and enthusiastic greetings.

"Shall we not walk in the lane?" Elizabeth suggested, having no desire to meet with Mr. Collins again nor to subject Darcy to the man, especially not in an enclosed room with little chance for escape or distance.

"Oh," Bingley hesitated and glanced at his friend. "We would be delighted. But first, we have come on purpose to extend an invitation to your family."

"Of course, sir," Jane replied, quieting Elizabeth's further protests with a look. She then accepted Bingley's arm and led him inside.

"Is aught amiss, Miss Elizabeth?" Darcy asked, proffering his own arm.

Elizabeth accepted it with a heavy sigh. "'Tis nothing more than the presence of a bothersome clergyman whom I had desired to shield you from. I shall tell you all about it later, however. With any luck, he has finally seen sense and will not enter the house, though I do not have high hopes."

In the parlour, Mr. Bingley wasted little time in announcing his ball to be held on Tuesday next and extended an invitation to the whole of the family. This news was met with rapturous delight by Mrs. Bennet and her youngest daughters, and much more decorous appreciation by the eldest sisters. Mary merely smiled and returned to her book.

"Mr. Collins is, of course, included in the invitation," Mr. Bingley, in his unending amiability, assured them.

Rather than expressions of delight and gratitude, as one might have expected, this statement was met with a very pregnant silence as the ladies exchanged looks which displayed the entire gamut of emotion. Kitty and Lydia sneered in derision, Mary heaved a somber sigh and shook her head. Jane pressed her lips together as if afraid she might for once say something ungenerous and Elizabeth looked as if she might laugh.

At last, Mrs. Bennet, who appeared nothing short of greatly vexed, forced a smile and said, "You are...very kind, sir. We shall see."

Bingley turned to Darcy, entirely unsure where he had erred and his friend proposed embarking on the walk Elizabeth had suggested. The gentlemen led their ladies outside where Darcy and Elizabeth quickly outstripped their companions. For some time, neither spoke, each revelling in the nearness of the other and the loveliness of the day. When at last they each began to speak at the same time, Darcy begged her to continue.

"I was only going to say, sir, how good it is of Mr. Bingley to hold a ball for the neighbourhood. But for our little assemblies, we rarely have such opportunities for elegant gatherings."

"He is a good man and eager to please his neighbours. I am prodigiously proud of my friend."

At Elizabeth's questioning look, he expounded. "There was a time when I worried a good deal over Bingley, he was so unsure of himself. He sought my advice in everything." He chuckled lightly as he looked towards where Jane and Mr. Bingley were walking. "When first we met, he was completely at sixes over what colour horse a gentleman ought to purchase, he begged me to accompany him to Tattersall's to advise him.

"But with my marriage, and subsequent absence from society, Bingley has learnt to rely on his own judgement and truly has become his own man. I could not be happier for him."

His confessions served to heighten Elizabeth's admiration for this man. She knew there were men a plenty who would have liked nothing better than for their peers to admire and emulate them, seeking always their approbation and approval. But Darcy, she perceived, was genuinely pleased with who his friend had become in the void of his company and resented not that Mr. Bingley had done so without his aid.

"I do not think, sir, that you can be absolved of all credit. I am quite certain you have laid an admirable example for your friend. I have heard him express a desire to be as devoted and loving a father as you. While I can agree that it is important for a man to learn to stand on his own, he learns to do so by watching those worthy examples around him. Mr. Bingley, if I may say so, chose an excellent man to be his guide."

"Thank you, Miss Elizabeth."

"Now, what was it you were going to say?" she asked sweetly.

"Say?" he asked. Truth be told, he had forgotten all in the wake of her generous praise and was struggling to focus on anything but how lovely she looked standing in the sunlight surrounded by the beautiful fall colours. He shook his head and forced himself to look away to recall his purpose in accompanying Bingley today, other than it simply being an excuse to see Elizabeth again. "Oh, yes. Forgive me. I was hoping that I might have the honour of securing your first set for the ball on Tuesday."

Attempting to regulate the ridiculous smile that tugged at her lips, Elizabeth took several slow breaths before answering with her customary playfulness. "I am astonished, sir. Mr. Bingley had informed my sister and I that you never danced the first set with any lady. That you were quite famous for it."

"Perhaps I have only been waiting for the right lady to ask."

Unable to procure a teasing response for such a statement, Elizabeth's answer came out in a breathy murmur. "It would be my pleasure, Mr. Darcy, to grant you that set."

"And, if I may be so bold, I would very much like to dance the supper set with you, as well," he asked, hoping he had not pressed his luck too far.

"You *are* bold, Mr. Darcy, dancing the first *and* claiming two whole sets in advance!" she teased with a beaming smile, recovering nicely and no longer caring if he were to interpret her secret hopes; hopes she was beginning to believe she could give wings to. "Am I to be allowed to dance with any other gentlemen at the ball?"

"If it would not cause a scandal, I would happily claim all your sets, Miss Elizabeth. But, if you would rather not grant me your favour for the supper set, I understand." He raised his chin and looked casually away as if he were not bothered in the least to give up such an opportunity as a whole hour of her undivided attention at the ball. "Might there be another you would rather pass the dinner hour with? Perhaps I might summon Mr. Collins? I have a feeling he might be willing to do the job and I suspect he has conversation enough to pass the time."

She fixed him with as fierce a glare as she could manage through her amusement. "You would not dare!"

"Would I not?" Darcy challenged, a roguish half grin tugging at his lips. He turned to see the very subject of their lighthearted discussion rounding the corner of the house, looking disapprovingly at Jane and Bingley. "Ah, the man himself. Ought I call him over? I might hint that you would be pleased to pass an hour or more in his company if that be your desire."

"No!" she laughed, tugging at the arm he had begun to raise to flag down Mr. Collins. "Very well, you may have the supper set! I yield! I yield!"

"Oh, no. 'Tis too late. I am cut to the quick and withdraw my request, madam."

"A gentleman would do no such thing, sir," she chastised him. Dropping all pretenses, she stepped close and looked up into his handsome face, stating boldly, "There is no other gentleman in all the kingdom to whom I would rather promise my dances to, Mr. Darcy."

"I am inordinately pleased to hear it, Elizabeth." Darcy reached up and gently tucking a loose curl behind her ear. They stood in silence, mutely communicating much between one another, daring not to move or speak for fear of breaking the spell.

~~~*✳*~~~
Chapter Twelve
✳

It did not take a great deal of time—though longer perhaps than was warranted, for thoughts ran through his mind as quickly as a one-legged man might run through molasses—for Mr. Collins to persuade himself that his fair cousins could not be serious in their refusals. His hand was certainly not unworthy of their acceptance. He was a respectable clergyman, more so as he was so fortunate as to enjoy the patronage of the noble Lady Catherine de Bourgh! He was the heir to their father's estate and would be in a position to offer whichever lady he settled upon to remain in her home as well as her widowed mother and sisters. If neither Cousin Jane nor Cousin Elizabeth accepted his hand, they could not really expect him to offer them sanctuary when that day came that Cousin Bennet made that sojourn from his mortal existence. It was absurd! He *must* remove the family from Longbourn if one of them were not his wife!

What, then, could they be about? Aha! Had not Lady Catherine herself educated him in the way of elegant females? Oh, he was so fortunate in his patronage! That great lady must have the right of it; they wished only to assure themselves of his fervent love by first rejecting the offer they truly meant to accept. He would not disappoint his cousins. He would prove his constancy to his fairest cousins by continuing to offer his hand until one of them accepted; he did not, at this point, care overly much which one it was. Jane was assuredly the most handsome, but Cousin Elizabeth was quite pretty as well, and so lively! That was rather enticing. But Cousin Jane was so demure and complying; that would certainly suit him well. Really, he could not go wrong either way and whichever could be first convinced, or rather, assured of his violent affection and unending devotion would be the victor!

His course at last decided on, Mr. Collins left the stillroom to seek out his fair cousins. Upon entering the house, however, neither lady was in the drawing room. He wandered through the music room when he heard feminine voices chattering excitedly in the adjoining parlour. *They must be exclaiming their good fortune of having both been singled out by the future master of the estate to their mother and sisters!* He lumbered towards the door between the two rooms and listened, dismayed at first that he was not overhearing the joyous raptures of his two eldest cousins, but rather inane chatter from the two youngest and their mother.

"A ball!" squealed the youngest, Lily or Laura or something of that nature; he really could not care less. He would worry about their names when he married one of their sisters. "Can you believe it! A real ball here in Meryton!" Someone excitedly clapped their hands together.

"Oh, yes, my love! How exciting for you girls!" Mrs. Bennet agreed. She then continued to blather on about dancing and gowns, officers and other such unimportant topics for which he had no interest.

But a ball! he thought as he stepped away from the door to go in search of his other cousins. How serendipitous! He would seek out Cousin Jane and solicit her first set; surely Cousin Elizabeth would understand, Jane being the eldest and loveliest. But he would not leave Cousin Elizabeth in suspense for long; he would claim that lady's supper set. Or, perhaps it would be pleasanter to spend that time looking upon fairest Jane? Ought he begin the ball with Elizabeth? Would that offend dear Jane? Oh, goodness! This was proving to be an arduous task indeed! Perhaps he ought to write to Lady Catherine to inquire as to what he had best to do? Yes, that was, perhaps, the best course. Her ladyship was always happy to give her excellent advice and would certainly wish to have a say in which lady he brought back to Hunsford with him. Yes, he would write to Lady Catherine, laying out in minute detail, each of his fair cousin's feminine qualities and attributes and his reasons for wish to marry each one. Then he would explain how each lady would be an asset to his parsonage, his parish, and, most importantly, to Lady Catherine herself. Finally—oh!

He was halfway through composing his letter to his most excellent patroness when he turned the corner around the house and was faced with a sight which brought him no joy at all and a great deal of concern. To one side of the garden, her arm linked through the gentleman's, stood Cousin Jane smiling brightly up at Mr. Bingley. *Well, she really does smile too much in general,* he snarled inwardly. *That must be why Mr. Bingley persists in his futile attentions.* Mr. Collins turned his feet towards his eldest cousin to claim his set and possible future bride when bright peals of laughter reached his ears from the opposite end of the garden.

Turning towards the sound, he was nearly knocked off his feet by the sight of Cousin Elizabeth clinging to Mr. Darcy's arm as he tried to pull free from her cloying attentions and standing far too close to the gentleman, no doubt in an attempt to lure him in with her arts and allurements. Or, even more disturbing, attempting to entrap the man by luring him into a compromising position!

For several moments he stood in shock, looking between the two parties, unsure of what he ought to do. If he went to Elizabeth, he would be giving up the most beautiful lady he had ever set eyes upon for his wife. Yet, if he went to Jane, he would be leaving Elizabeth free to continue working on Mr. Darcy. Oh, Lady Catherine would never forgive him if ever she were to learn that he had witnessed her illustrious son in such danger and done nothing to interfere!

With one last wistful look after the beautiful Jane Bennet, Mr. Collins set off across the lawn in the opposite direction with all haste.

"Mr. Darcy!" he panted, clutching at his chest and trying desperately to catch his breath. "Mr. Darcy, if you...you would be so...so kind...as to...to step away from...phew!" With a final deep breath, he pulled himself up to his full height, though he still stood several inches below Darcy. "Step away from my betrothed!"

"I beg your pardon," Mr. Darcy growled, looking between Elizabeth and Mr. Collins.

"I am not your betrothed!" Elizabeth cried. "I refused your proposal, sir!"

With a wave of his hand, Mr. Collins dismissed her denial with a scoff.

Darcy turned incredulous eyes on the lady by his side. "He proposed to you?"

"Aye, not half a moment after he was refused by Jane. Mama has denied him the pursuit of any of her daughters but he has persisted."

"He has only been here all of two days!"

"It is of no matter," Mr. Collins insisted. With an air of great superiority, the clergyman clung to the lapels of his coat and stuck out his beefy chest. "Cousin Elizabeth, I have come to solicit your hand for the first two dances of the ball, and inform you that I intend to remain near you for the whole of the evening."

The lady blinked and looked up at Darcy a moment before turning back to her cousin with a polite, if rather strained, smile. "You must excuse me, Mr. Collins, but I cannot oblige you. I have already promised the first set."

All bravado forgotten, Mr. Collins visibly deflated as he blustered, "That is impossible! Who could have possibly begged your first set so quickly? The invitation has only just been extended!" He looked about them as if expecting hordes of hidden gentlemen lying in wait to claim ladies' dances to appear from the hedgerows.

"I have claimed Miss Elizabeth's first set," said Mr. Darcy in a voice that brooked no opposition, yet oppose Mr. Collins did and their conversation had now attracted the attention of Jane and Mr. Bingley, who ventured near.

"Impossible, sir! You are engaged!"

"I am? To whom? Please enlighten me, sir," Darcy asked with a surprising degree of equanimity. "I cannot recall offering my hand in marriage to any lady in more than five years."

Elizabeth snickered behind her hand as Mr. Collins floundered. "I...well, that is...surely you know it is your mother's greatest wish—"

"My mother's greatest wish was that I find true happiness and mutual affection with the woman of my choosing as she informed me on her deathbed, sixteen years ago. If you refer to the woman whom I have the great misfortune of acknowledging as my former mother-in-law," –Mr. Collins gasped and took several scandalized steps backwards— "I have heard enough of Lady Catherine's greatest wishes to last me a lifetime. Thankfully, I am no longer beholden to my aunt for anything. I ask again, to whom am I betrothed?"

Raising his chins, Mr. Collins adopted his best Lady Catherine tone and replied, "A specific lady has not, as yet, been chosen but I have it from Lady Catherine de Bourgh herself that she is even now seeking a bride worthy to replace her most excellent and accomplished daughter and she is not a lady to be gainsaid!"

"Darcy," Bingley interjected, "is everything alright?"

"Mr. Bingley!" screeched Mr. Collins, all thoughts of conveying impressive dignity completely discarded at the sight of Jane's hands wrapped affectionately around that gentleman's elbow. "Unhand my betrothed at once, sir!"

"Your betrothed?" exclaimed Bingley at the same moment Jane cried out as her sister had, "I am not your betrothed!"

"Sir, not five minutes ago you declared Miss Elizabeth to be your betrothed," Darcy reminded him. "I cannot think you hope to marry two ladies at once. I am no clergyman but I am quite certain such a thing goes against God's will. Are you not a parson?"

Again, the pompous idiot grasped his lapels as his chest swelled. "I have not yet decided which lady I would prefer to have for my wife. Therefore, as heir to Mr. Bennet and future master of this estate, I reserve the right to claim them both until such a time as I have made my decision."

"We both refused you, Mr. Collins!" Elizabeth cried in exasperation.

This was not going at all as Mr. Collins had anticipated. Why, her ladyship had advised him that all his fair cousins would be exceedingly grateful to receive his attentions and the assurances which his proposal would provide to their family. He had the power to turn them all from their home on the event of their father's death, yet this seemed to give them very little concern.

In fact, this entire visit had not proceeded as he had envisioned. He had expected to be received as something akin to a saviour. The next master of Longbourn to be their guardian and protector. Until that day, he would remove one of them to his humble yet excellent parsonage to bask in the condescending glow of Lady Catherine de Bourgh! His chosen lady would, of a certainty, be the envy of her sisters. The wife of William Collins, humble clergyman yet, as such, equal in station to the noblest in the land.

"Hold your tongue, Cousin Elizabeth. Men are speaking. Now, Cousin Jane, you will dance the first set of the ball with me and, Cousin Elizabeth, the supper set."

"No!" both sisters cried out in unison.

"I fear Miss Elizabeth cannot satisfy you in that corner, either, sir, were she of a mind to," Mr. Darcy informed him, a small smile playing at the edge of his lips. "I have also secured her supper set and, having worked so hard for it," −he sent a cheeky wink Elizabeth's way— "shall not release her from that obligation."

"You have claimed two dances, Darcy?" an incredulous Bingley inquired.

"Aye. Why, have you only secured one? Come now, Bingley!"

Bingley gaped at his friend a moment before turning to his walking companion. "Miss Bennet, might I be so bold as to also claim *your* supper set? And the last set of the evening?" he added quickly.

"I would be happy to grant you those dances, sir," Jane laughed sweetly.

Bingley turned to his friend, looking every bit the cat who got the canary. "Ha!"

"Very well, Bingley, I concede victory to you." Darcy acknowledged his defeat with a mocking bow. "I shall not be so bold as to claim three of Miss Elizabeth's sets at this time as she has already indicated two would be more than enough to spend in my poor company."

"Lizzy!" Jane admonished her sister.

"Mr. Darcy!" Elizabeth laughingly scolded.

The gentlemen laughed and the ladies joined them in their amusement. Mr. Collins was at a complete loss as to what was happening. He had come to Longbourn, asserting his dominance as Lady Catherine had instructed him and yet his cousins continued to refuse him. Now here they all stood, laughing; at him he was beginning to suspect. Had he asserted his dominance incorrectly? Perhaps he ought to give it another go? But *more* assertive?

"Cousin Elizabeth," he all but shouted over their mirth. "I *will* lay claim to your first two dances for the ball. I had thought to offer my hand for that set to my Cousin Jane, she being the loveliest of the Bennet ladies, but I believe Lady Catherine de Bourgh would prefer if I extend my condescension to you, thereby preventing you from throwing yourself at this illustrious gentleman like some common trollop and protecting her ladyship's most august family. Therefore, I relinquish my claim to Jane's hand in marriage in favour of yours that I might protect my noble patroness and her family from your taint and—"

"Mr. Collins!" Darcy barked, all signs of diversion gone, replaced by a look which would make much braver men than the toady parson quake. "You will not speak of Miss Elizabeth or any of her family in such a way again. If you would excuse us." He gently took Elizabeth by the elbow and began to steer her away but, despite the tremor in his voice, Mr. Collins persisted.

"M-Mr. Darcy! I m-must object on behalf of, of your noble mother!" Mentioning that lady seemed to restore some of Mr. Collins fortitude for he soldiered on, raising his chin to ridiculous heights. "She would not be best pleased to know you are associating with such common, low-born, improper—"

Having heard enough against her family, Elizabeth now cried out, "Mr. Collins! You will cease your abuse this instant!"

"Cousin Elizabeth, allow the men to handle this. I will not tolerate such behaviour when we are married."

"I will not marry you, as I have already told you!"

"Sir," Darcy scowled at the parson, his face as hard as stone, "you have offered your hand to Miss Bennet and Miss Elizabeth and have been refused. A gentleman does not persist where he is unwelcome."

The sweaty parson looked on Mr. Darcy and shook his head with a look of such arrogant sympathy as if he were addressing a child who had made a simple arithmetic error. "I have been informed of the nature of your marriage to the late Mrs. Darcy, sir, and understand that you may not be familiar with the mechanics of a traditional courtship being, as you were, intended for your wife from infancy but allow me to flatter myself by being assured that Miss Elizabeth, even Cousin Jane for that matter, cannot be serious in their refusals. Her ladyship, Lady Catherine de Bourgh, has herself informed me that it is the usual practice of elegant females to refuse the hand of the man whom she secretly means to accept as many as three or four times as a means of increasing his love by suspense. Therefore, I am by no means discouraged and am confident that I shall be leading my cousin to the altar ere long. You need not worry that Miss Elizabeth shall importune you any further, sir."

"Enough! You have been refused, sir."

"That is impossible. Neither of my cousins could possibly refuse me. They have no fortune, no prospects. I am to inherit Longbourn!" he shouted as if this settled everything. "My patroness, Lady Catherine—"

"Has absolutely no say in the matter whatsoever," Darcy growled. "Furthermore, she is not your patroness as Rosings Park belongs to me. After this display, you leave me with little choice but to write to your bishop to inform him of the officious and inappropriate behaviour which I have witnessed this day. You demand the hand of not one, but two unwilling ladies and refuse to accept their answers. You have insulted and denigrated a good family, your own family no less! You are a disgrace to the collar you wear.

"Now, *you* will not importune Miss Elizabeth or any of her sisters further. If I learn that you have so much as asked any of the Bennet ladies for a dance, you will answer to me. In fact, you will not attend the ball at all. You will remove yourself from this house and cease to harass the Bennet family immediately."

Mr. Collins sputtered and blustered for several moments before he seemed to be able to form a coherent sentence. When he did, he seemed to have forgotten all his previous deference for Mr. Darcy and swelled with indignation. "You cannot evict me from this place nor bar me from offering my addresses to my cousins! You have no authority here!"

"But I do," Mr. Bennet calmly interceded, crossing the lawn. "Mr. Collins, you are no longer welcome at Longbourn so long as I am master. You will make no further offers of marriage to any of my daughters as you are not worthy of any of them. Mr. Hill," the Bennet patriarch addressed his man, "please assist Mr. Collins to the guest room to gather his things. Then see that he is removed from the property. Should he set foot on Longbourn's grounds again, be so good as to set the dogs on him."

As lanky Mr. Hill, who he guessed to be older even than his cousin, approached, Mr. Collins smirked. "I should like to see this man remove me!" He planted his fists defiantly on his hips.

His sense of self-satisfaction wavered when both Darcy and Bingley stepped forward, ostensibly to offer their assistance but Mr. Bennet raised a hand to hold them back. "Thank you, gentlemen. But Mr. Hill can manage."

Mr. Collins' indignation was now raised. That Mr. Bennet would dare set his servant against one such as *he*! Why, he was a clergyman; a clergyman in the service of her noble ladyship, Lady Catherine de Bourgh no less! That practically made him as good as noble, as well! These people ought to be bowing and scraping before him; he had the power, after all, to evict the ladies from their home as soon as word reached him of his cousin's death—and he would! In fact, perhaps he was too good for Longbourn, this tiny estate which was nothing to the condescension and notice he received at Rosings!

Mr. Hill took a step nearer and Mr. Collins raised a fat hand to stall him. "Hear me now, Cousin Bennet. If your man so much as lays a finger on me, you will regret it!"

"Oh? How so?"

He gestured towards Mrs. Bennet and her daughters. "These ladies will be destitute when you are gone! I refuse to inherit Longbourn! I shall march straight down to the solicitor's office and denounce my claim on this pathetic estate!" Mrs. Bennet gasped her indignation at the insult to her home. "With no master, there will be no home for your widow and daughters! Do not think for one instant I will give them sanctuary at my parsonage nor will my most noble patroness pay them the slightest notice!"

"That would be grievous, indeed, Mr. Collins," Mr. Bennet conceded with a twist of his lips and a nod. "Mr. Hill?"

"What?!" cried the parson. "You would be the means of leaving your wife and children in poverty and destitution?! You would deny them the one and only means of a respectable future?! You would—"

He felt himself lifted by the seat of his trousers and the back of his clergyman's collar by the servant who had crossed the yard with surprising agility and taken hold of him. He was half-carried, half-dragged across the grounds and down the drive by Mr. Hill who showed no sign of being taxed by his hefty burden. Once across the boundary of Longbourn's drive, Mr. Hill unceremoniously dumped the vile parson on his seat in the road and brushed his hands together to rid himself Mr. Collins filth.

"I' be sendin' yer things along ta th' inn. *Sir*," he informed the man before turning on his heel and walking away, signaling to Jimmy the groom, who had followed, to close the gate. He turned and nodded to Mr. Bennet. "Fo'give me, sir. I knew ya said to take 'im inside ta gather 'is things, but I would'na hear 'im speak so about our 'ome and th' ladies. I' pack 'is things and send 'em on."

"Thank you, Mr. Hill. I quite understand. When Mr. Collins' things have been removed, I would like you to take the rest of the day to yourself. Lord knows, you deserve it!"

Mr. Hill beamed at the man he had served since his boyhood and, tipping his hat, went off to finish the job, already dreaming about the pint of ale that awaited him at The Merry Rooster.

"Oh, Mr. Bennet! Mr. Bennet! Is it true? Are we doomed? Is there nothing you can do?" wailed Mrs. Bennet.

"Mr. Collins is free to do as he wishes," Mr. Bennet confirmed, glancing around seeing a look of knowing in Darcy's eye and confusion on all others. "Do not fret, Fanny, my love. I believe all will turn out well." Then, taking his flustered wife, whom he had not called Fanny nor 'my love' since before Mary's birth, by the hand, he led her inside.

~~~*✱*~~~
Chapter Thirteen
***

The ladies of Longbourn waited in the drawing room in a tense and very unusual silence. Mr. Bennet had been summoned to the office of his wife's brother, Mr. Phillips who was the town's solicitor, regarding the entail on his estate. It seemed Mr. Collins had been good on his threat and paid the man a visit, though they were not, as yet, privy to the details of what had come of it or what such action would mean for their family.

Each lady sat at an occupation, but gave it little attention. Kitty and Lydia sat before a table strewn with ribbons, silk flowers, buttons, feathers, and lace to make over their bonnets; yet each only sat staring at the hat in her hands. Mary sat at the pianoforte gazing at the sheet music but not a note had been played. Jane held an embroidery hoop in her hands, her needle stuck in the linen haphazardly, but never pulled through. Elizabeth was perched in the window seat with a book she had yet to open on her lap. All the while, Mrs. Bennet sat in her chair, twisting her handkerchief, too nervous even to fret about her nerves.

Every creak of a floorboard as a servant passed through the hall caused them to turn and watch the drawing room door expectantly; the clock striking the hour made them all jump and Jane to stab her palm with her needle. This, at last, created some distraction for the tip of the thin needle broke off in her flesh and Elizabeth rushed to her dearest sister's side. Mary fetched some cotton and a penknife as Kitty and Lydia sough to distract Jane who had never been much able to stand the sight of blood and had very little tolerance for pain. Elizabeth ran to her father's study for a thimble of whiskey to ease Jane's nerves; the needle tip was embedded deeply in the fleshy part of her palm.

In little time, a deep cut was made and the metal removed from Jane's hand. Elizabeth was applying plaster to the wound when Mr. Bennet returned from his brother's offices. He entered and sat heavily in his chair, looking around at his girls who looked nervously back at him.

"Well?" Mrs. Bennet prompted him at last, her knuckles positively white from clenching her handkerchief so tightly.

Instead of answering his wife, Mr. Bennet sighed and rested his chin in his hand. "I ought to have done better by you girls. I am heartily ashamed of myself. Though I can happily say I have not done nothing, I have not done as I should."

"Papa, what happened at my uncle's?" Elizabeth asked.

"Well, you may all breathe easier. Mr. Collins, it seems, is truly as witless as he has always presented himself to be. He has, in fact, renounced his claim to Longbourn and signed away his rights to it. He seems to believe that with no one to inherit the estate, ladies will not be permitted to remain without a man to act as master. I wonder what he will do when he realises that his *most noble patroness* inhabits Rosings with no master in residence."

Elizabeth left Jane's side and knelt at her father's knee, taking his hands in her own. "So, what does that mean, Papa? Is the entail broken? May Jane have the estate?"

"I am as yet uncertain," he responded with little ceremony. "My brother Phillips is looking into the language of the entail as we speak. A search must be made for any other heirs, though I am positive none exist. When no heir can be found, it may be that Longbourn must be sold on my death."

"Sold?" Mrs. Bennet shrieked.

"Yes, my dear, but you must not fret." Mr. Bennet reached over and took up his wife's hand. "'Tis not yet certain. The entail may very well be broken and I may do with it as I wish. However, in the event Longbourn must be sold, Phillips and I have had some room to ensure your security, and that of our girls. Since my brother is the attorney in the case, he may hold off the sale of the estate. And he will ensure that whomever purchases is made aware of the situation. Preference will be given to a purchaser who might allow you and any unmarried daughters to remain, perhaps a gentleman seeking only an investment rather than a home. However, in case such a buyer cannot be found, Mr. Darcy has agreed to assist me in making some improvements on the estate. Such improvements will be beneficial in either case; either by demanding a higher price or to bring in a greater income in the interim which can be saved for your futures."

Silence fell over the room as the ladies took in this information, each deciding how this news would affect them. Were they better off? Worse off? Mrs. Bennet could not decide how to feel. Being rid of Mr. Collins was certainly to be celebrated, but now their fate may lay in the hands of some other unknown stranger. Jane, in her eternal optimism, could naught but feel all would be well. Uncle Phillips would ensure that whomever purchased Longbourn would be kind to them. Elizabeth felt little had changed. Whether Mr. Collins inherited or their home were sold, it would no longer be theirs. Mary did not think on it overly long, feeling God would provide one way or another. Kitty and Lydia could not be bothered to care too much; Mr. Collins was gone and that could only be a good thing.

As they considered these new possibilities, the door opened and Mrs. Hill entered to announce Bingley, Darcy, and Amelia, held in her father's arms.

"Ah, gentlemen," Mr. Bennet stood and greeted them. "Good of you to call. You are always welcome. Mr. Darcy, I thank you for your willingness to assist me. Good afternoon, Miss Darcy," he cooed at the little girl with a little finger wave. She smiled at the old man but quickly buried her face in her father's shoulder.

"'Tis my pleasure, sir," Darcy replied to his host as Bingley made straight for Jane. "I hope I am not imposing but it is Mrs. Lawson's day to herself and Amelia begged to come along to see Miss Elizabeth. Might I beg your indulgence in entertaining her whilst I speak with your father?" he asked Elizabeth.

"Of course! I would be happy to, sir. Amelia, dear, would you like to walk with me in the gardens, if your papa does not mind?"

The little girl turned large, brown eyes on her father. "Please, Papa? May I go wif Lizzy?"

"You may, my love." He set the girl down and she ran for Elizabeth's outstretched arms, wrapping her own around the lady's neck and pressing a sweet kiss to her cheek.

"Oh, Lizzy," cried Lydia, "may we join you? Please? I should like to play with Miss Darcy, as well."

It was soon decided that all the young ladies, accompanied by Bingley, would venture outside while Mr. Bennet and Darcy discussed business in the library. While he was genuinely pleased to offer his assistance to the older gentleman, Darcy rather felt that he had drawn the short straw this time as he watched Elizabeth beaming at his daughter. But it filled his heart with incomprehensible joy to see his darling girl surrounded by so many who adored her. His family circle was so small and there were so very few ladies to fuss over his little girl. The Bennets were not the most proper nor fashionable people, but they had unreservedly welcomed he and his daughter into their family. For that, he could be naught but grateful.

Darcy saw the ladies out before following Mr. Bennet to his library where he was offered a glass of fine brandy. They sat in comfortable silence for several minutes, enjoying the excellent liquor before Darcy put his glass down and surveyed his host. Mr. Bennet looked placidly back, his hands linked over his chest. As he had when first they met, Darcy recognised something in the elder gentleman's eyes, a certain twinkle which he had seen in Elizabeth's eyes whenever she was about to tease him. Only, this time, he believed he knew the source of Mr. Bennet's amusement.

"Mr. Bennet," he began, "as you know, I have been aiding Mr. Bingley in learning estate management. In doing so, I have looked over all of Netherfield's books for the last several years. About a week ago, I came across something that interested me."

"Did you now? And what was that?" Mr. Bennet asked, though Darcy was convinced the man knew already exactly what he had found.

Darcy's lips quirked up in a lazy half smile; the man enjoyed his games. "Five years ago, Sir Reginald Denton sold some one hundred acres of Netherfield's lands to his nearest neighbour. Oh!" he exclaimed in mock surprise. "That would be you, sir."

With a chuckle, Mr. Bennet nodded. "Aye, I seem to recall something of that nature taking place."

"I have heard it reported by some of your neighbours that Longbourn brings in about two thousand pounds a year."

"A *little* more than that, but that is close enough."

"But that does not include the lands from Netherfield, does it, sir?"

"It does not." Mr. Bennet took a sip of his drink and peered into its amber depths. "My neighbours have also likely told you that I am a negligent father and an indolent estate manager who cares more for his books and brandy than the well-being of his family."

"Mr. Bennet—"

"And, at one time," he continued on, the twinkle gone to be replaced with a shadow Darcy thought might be something akin to shame, "they would have been correct. For the longest time I could not see the purpose in maintaining an estate that would not benefit those I would leave behind when my time upon this mortal coil came to an end. I despised my cousin's father and feared his son would be just like him—a fear I have recently seen realised. So, I did only what was necessary to feed and clothe my family and little else, all to spite my heirs.

"Then, seven years ago, Jane went to visit my wife's brother and his family in London, as my two eldest daughters are wont to do from time to time. She met a gentleman there who, if you were to ask my wife, was so in love with her an offer seemed imminent. He wrote Jane some awful poetry and called nearly every day. Then, with no warning, his attentions stopped. Now, Jane was but fifteen at the time and that may likely have been what deterred him—and I would not have given my blessing when she was so young in any case, but do not dare tell my wife that.

"However, my brother confided that the gentleman had sought an audience with him and was told the extent of Jane's meagre dowry which was, at that time, only her share of my wife's five thousand pounds upon Mrs. Bennet's demise. Gardiner informed me that the worthless young man could not depart the house quick enough. For the first time, I realised what my inaction could cost my daughters. As you can see, Jane is more than uncommonly lovely and quite likely the sweetest girl in all of England. Yet it is not enough to secure her future, no matter what Mrs. Bennet might believe. Well," he laughed, "it was not. I had not counted on some young, wealthy gentleman as good and amiable as Jane to stumble into our little neighbourhood. So, I began to save. It was not much, my wife is a talented shopper, but little by little I was able to put something aside. Then I began to make improvements. I am quite proud to say that Longbourn estate now brings in just over three thousand pounds per annum."

"That is an impressive improvement, sir."

"Ha! Or a testament to just how miserably I was failing. If I had been the master and father I ought, had I begun saving the day Jane was born, she might not have remained unmarried long enough for your amiable Mr. Bingley to come and completely lose his head over her. But she is happy, so I cannot repent that.

"When Sir Reginald approached me about the sale of his lands five years ago, I leapt at the opportunity. I was saving what I could, but also using much of that extra income to enact more improvements. The purchase of those lands cost me dearly, but has proven to be a wise investment. What is more, the lands from Netherfield were purchased in such a way that they do not belong to Longbourn estate but to Thomas Bennet, squire. When I am gone, the land will fall into the keeping of my brothers Phillips and Gardiner, or anyone I should so choose, to continue providing an income for my wife and any unmarried daughters."

"I rode over those fields, sir. Correct me if I am wrong, but it is my estimation that you ought to be earning at least two thousand pounds from those lands."

"Nearer three. And I have saved nearly every farthing since that time. The first year was not so profitable, the fields had not been worked properly in years. But I am pleased to say, should you come seeking the hand of any of my daughters at some future point," he said with a wink, "she will come with a little more than twenty-five hundred pounds. Not much to you, I daresay, but more than her considerable charms and more than my daughters are aware of. And that is in addition to her share of Mrs. Bennet's money."

"Mr. Bennet, *when* I come seeking Miss Elizabeth's hand, I shall not accept her dowry."

"Mr. Darcy—" It was his turn to be cut off.

"Sir, at the risk of sounding excessively arrogant, I have little need for more money. I was already one of the wealthiest men in the country before my marriage. My late wife's fortune made me wealthier than I have any right to be. I would be very pleased to know that the money has been distributed amongst her younger sisters. And I believe I can safely say Bingley will feel the same.

"I should also like to request first rights to purchase Longbourn should the day come it must be sold."

Darcy followed the sound of bubbling laughter outside after finishing his discussion with Mr. Bennet. They had gone over several options for further improvements on Longbourn and discussed methods Darcy employed at Pemberley which had proved profitable for both tenant and master. Now he was eager to be with Elizabeth and Amelia. He rounded the corner of the house and spotted the two most important ladies in his life across the garden. Elizabeth was perched on a swing hung from an oak tree with Amelia held firmly on her lap. For a moment, he only watched. Though Elizabeth did not swing high, each time they glided forward Amelia squealed with glee crying out "Higher, higher!" It was among the most beautiful sights he had ever seen.

Unable to stay away any longer, Darcy crossed the yard and his heart did a somersault when Elizabeth looked up and broke into a radiant smile when she spotted him. She slowed the swing and waited for him to approach but Amelia was impatient and wriggled down to run to her father.

"Papa!" she squealed, jumping into his arms. "Me and Lizzy fly!"

"Yes, I saw. We must have a swing hung at Pemberley. Would you like that?"

She answered with a bright smile and wide eyes as she threw her arms around his neck. There was nothing he would not do for this precious child. He set his daughter back on Elizabeth's lap, feeling only slightly jealous at her privilege to be so close to that magnificent woman, and stepped around the swing to offer a gentle push. They continued thus, Darcy living for each moment he was allowed to gently lay his hands against Elizabeth's back, until

Amelia called out for him to stop. When the swing halted, the girl leapt off of Elizabeth's lap and ran to where Kitty and Lydia were weaving small flowers together to make crowns.

Assured his daughter was in safe hands, Darcy held out an arm for Elizabeth to take and led her on a walk through the gardens in the fall sunshine. They walked in companionable silence, Darcy boldly laying a hand affectionately over the delicate one holding his arm.

Elizabeth blushed and bit her lips together to temper the brilliant smile that threatened to burst forth at his touch and hoped he could not hear the pounding of her heart when he began gently stroking the back of her hand with his thumb. Even through two layers of gloves, his touched burned into her skin and it was heavenly.

Seeking to turn her mind from the exquisite torture he was wreaking on her senses, Elizabeth sought a topic and chose that which would most likely bring a dazzling smile to his handsome face.

"I must tell you again, sir, what a darling little girl Amelia is." *Ah, yes. There it is,* she thought as he beamed down at her.

"I thank you. Though I am biased, I cannot but agree. I do adore her so."

"She is a very lucky little girl. You are a wonderful father." She rather delighted in the faint blush that crept across his cheeks and hoped she did not embarrass him too much.

"I begin to think you are a flatterer, Miss Elizabeth."

"Not at all! I speak only the truth. As a daughter who is the not-so-secret favourite of her father's, I can attest that it is a special relationship. Not many young ladies have such a closeness with either parent. 'Tis not *fashionable* to be a doting parent." She wrinkled her nose and he laughed.

"I take it you have no desire to be a *fashionable* mother?"

"Oh, dear me, no!" she laughed. "My children will be hugged and kissed every day! They will, all of them, know what it is to be dearly loved."

"I am exceedingly glad to hear that, Elizabeth." He stopped their motion and turned to look down into her beautiful eyes. "For neither do I wish to be such a father."

The sound of her given name in his deep, rich timbre sent a wave of sensations through her body and she shivered at the tender way he gazed upon her. She chanced a quick glance around and saw that they had walked to a secluded part of the garden behind the roses and wondered that she did not feel at all nervous or worried about being alone with him. In fact, she rather wondered if they might be able to walk a little deeper into the foliage.

Taking a small, bold step nearer him and looking back up into his dear face, Elizabeth felt a strong sense of peace and belonging with this man. *I love him*. Gathering her courage, she slowly tipped her chin a fraction of an inch higher and waited. She was not to be disappointed as he slowly closed the distance between them and, with only a second's hesitation to allow her to protest, tenderly touched his lips to hers.

The kiss was brief but indescribably sweet. He did not wish to frighten her with his passions and so pulled away before he could lose himself completely in her perfect lips. Pressing his forehead against hers, he released a ragged breath.

"Dearest Elizabeth," he whispered, reaching up to stroke her cheek. He could not stop himself from gently caressing her bottom lip with his thumb and wanted nothing more than to kiss her again.

"Lizzy! Mr. Darcy!" Lydia's voice pierced the air and the two lovers quickly stepped apart. Darcy held out his arm to her and led her back to the lawn where her sisters were. "There you are! Look, there is someone here to see you, Mr. Darcy. He is rather dashing! Who is he? Might we be introduced?"

Darcy looked across the yard and there, standing tall in his bright red regimentals, Amelia in his arms, was his favourite cousin.

"Richard? What do you do here?" Darcy asked, incredulous.

"'Tis good to see you, as well, Darce. Need I an excuse to seek out my favourite cousin who I have not seen in many weeks?" said he with a look which plainly said he did, indeed, have a reason for this intrusion. "And my goddaughter." He tickled Amelia under her chin and she giggled and squirmed.

"Of course not, but how did you find me?"

"I went first to Netherfield and from thither was directed here. Come, introduce me to these lovely ladies."

"Of course. Cousin, may I present Miss Catherine Bennet, Miss Lydia Bennet, and," –he looked fondly down at the lady on his arm— "Miss Elizabeth Bennet. Ladies, this is my cousin. The Honourable Colonel Richard Fitzwilliam of his majesty's Fifth Dragoons Cavalry and the second son of the earl of Matlock."

The ladies all curtseyed at the dashing soldier with sandy blond hair and friendly dark blue eyes, Kitty and Lydia giggling and batting their eyelashes all the while. He bowed as well as he could with Amelia still in his arms.

"We have two other sisters, sir," offered Elizabeth, "but Mary must have returned inside and Jane is there," —she nodded across the garden— "walking with Mr. Bingley."

The Colonel smiled at each of the ladies before addressing his cousin. "I know you will claim Derbyshire to be the loveliest of all counties, Darce, but it is clear to me that true beauty resides here in Hertfordshire."

"Richard," Darcy growled a warning as all three sisters blushed at the flattering words then raised a brow to his cousin in question.

Darcy watched his cousin switch subtly from charming gentleman to war-hardened soldier in a flash. "In fact, there is something I would like to discuss with you, Darcy, if I may steal my cousin for just a moment, Miss Elizabeth."

"Of course. What say you to a trade?" She smiled at Darcy before stepping forward and taking Amelia from the Colonel. "Would you like to swing some more, my dear, or shall we seek out some lovely flowers?"

"Flowers!" Amelia cried and the two set off on their search.

Darcy led his cousin away and was just about to step behind the same rosebush where he had kissed Elizabeth only a few moments before but stopped just short. That spot was sacred now and he would not violate it. At last, coming to stop near a small stream just within sight of the ladies, Darcy turned on his cousin. Before he could raise any questions, however, Richard anticipated him with a mischievous glint in his eye that Darcy knew all too well.

"Georgie will be quite vexed when she hears that I have met your Miss Elizabeth before her!"

Caught entirely off guard, Darcy started and stared at his cousin in bemusement. "Georgie? What can she know of Elizabeth?"

"Oh, 'tis just Elizabeth already, is it?" Darcy fixed his cousin with his sternest glare, little good though it did. Richard had gown immune to Darcy's intimidating glower many years ago. "Come now, you have written to your sister of Miss Elizabeth Bennet no less than six times. In one such letter, you droned on and on about the lady for near a whole page! I hope you are serious, for Georgiana has grown quite attached to the idea of your bringing her home a sister. Come now, tell me about her."

Ignoring Richard's smirk when a broad grin stretched across his own features, Darcy sighed and shook his head. "She is...she is...I have not the words. She is everything."

"She is...everything?"

"Everything."

"What the bloody hell does that mean, Darce?"

Darcy's smile only grew and he turned the subject, knowing his cousin simply would not understand; not until he, himself, felt the overwhelming sensation of falling in love with the right woman.

"You know I am always happy to see you, Richard, but what are you doing here?"

"Fine, but you will tell me more of your lady later. I come bearing a warning. Lady Catherine came to London, paid a visit to my father. She is looking for you."

"What? Why?"

"She had word from some parson that you were here paying court to some tart." Darcy clenched his fists and drew breath to defend his Elizabeth but Richard held up a hand to forestall him. "Her words, not mine. She claims to have found your next wife."

Darcy huffed at this. "Dear God, will I never be rid of that woman? Why does she not plague you to marry for a change?"

"There is more, Darcy. She is at Netherfield, terrorizing Miss Bingley and Mrs. Hurst, this very minute."

~~~*✳*~~~

Chapter Fourteen
✳*✳

Perhaps he ought to have been focused on why his belligerent aunt had tracked him down and infiltrated his friend's home or how she had done so. Mayhap he ought to be considering what he would say to her to be rid of her as soon as possible. Instead, Darcy was thinking, as he barreled across the fields between Longbourn and Netherfield, that he must pass on his compliments to Mr. Bennet for the magnificent animal he had lent him. Unwilling to allow his daughter anywhere near Lady Catherine until he knew what she was about, Darcy had asked the Bennets if Amelia might remain at Longbourn until he could return for her and borrowed a horse. He knew his daughter was in good hands; the Bennet ladies doted on his girl and Elizabeth loved her as if she were her own child. That thought brought a beaming smile to his face as the stallion positively flew over the last fence.

Skidding to a halt on Netherfield's drive, Darcy dismounted and tossed the reins to the groom who came running from the stables.

"Walk him, will you. Give him a good rub down and then some oats. I shall be returning him to Longbourn later."

"If it please ye, sir, I could—"

"No," Darcy cut off the boy. Softening his tone, he added, "Thank you. I must collect my daughter in any case. Just look after the animal."

Richard reined his mount in a moment later and Bingley a moment behind him. Both dismounted and handed over their animals, as well.

"Good God, that is a magnificent beast!" cried the Colonel, eyeing Mr. Bennet's stallion appreciatively.

"Is it not?" Darcy agreed.

"The way you cleared that gate in the first pasture." Richard whistled his appreciation. "Amazing."

"I doubt Bennet would sell him to me, but perhaps I might bring one of my mares down from Pemberley. Perhaps I shall demand it in lieu of Elizabeth's dowry."

"Dowry? Well, well, Cous. My congratulations!"

"I have not asked yet, but I intend to."

"Truly? I imagined that must have been what you were doing in the rosebushes." Darcy felt the heat creeping up his neck and avoided his cousin's impertinent gaze. "Oh, ho! You have much to tell me, I can see! No more of this 'everything' bollocks! She is a lovely lass—"

"I do not mean to be rude, gentlemen," Bingley interjected, "but I have just left my own Miss Bennet for the sake of your aunt imposing on my sisters. So, shall we?"

"Of course. Forgive us Bingley. Come, let us see what the dragon wants." Darcy led the way into the house, wondering if this was how Richard felt each time he prepared to face the French. He made a note to ask his cousin when the smoke had cleared.

They were directed to the drawing room by the butler who showed no signs that he would follow them. Darcy could not blame the man. If it were not required of him, he would certainly not choose to go, either.

As they neared the specified room, his aunt's unmistakable squawking could be heard loud and clear. Darcy shuddered at her blatant display of such ill-breeding. *This woman was my mother's sister?* It never ceased to amaze him. Lady Anne Darcy had been so gentle and kind; he had never heard an unkind word from her lips. Even when she corrected his behaviour or was required to chastise a servant, she did so with compassion and understanding. Pemberley's staff had adored Lady Anne and often went out of their way to please her. In stark contrast, Lady Catherine struggled to keep servant's positions filled and those who had little choice but to remain were terrified of their mistress and took great strides never to cross her. To do so often ended in harsh punishments and lost employment.

"...tradespeople!" Lady Catherine's screeching pierced his thoughts. "That *my son* would be brought so low! 'Tis disgraceful! You," she barked as Darcy appeared in the doorway. Lady Catherine was pointing at a cowering Miss Bingley as she sat on the sofa clutching her sister's hands.

"Where is my son?! Where has my nephew gone? Who is this lowly trollop who dares to attempt to entrap my noble son?"

"That is enough, Lady Catherine!" Darcy bellowed in his most authoritative voice. "Who on earth do you think you are to come into another's home and berate your hosts?"

If she felt the shame of his words at all, Lady Catherine showed no signs of it. "*I* am the daughter of an earl. These tradespeople are not even worth my notice!"

"These are your hosts and my friends! You will not speak to them in such a manner. Miss Bingley," —he turned to the ladies on the sofa— "Mrs. Hurst, I apologise for my aunt's appalling behaviour."

"Darcy!" Lady Catherine began to protest but he halted her words with a withering look.

"Bingley, might I beg the use of your library?"

Lady Catherine drew herself up, indignant, and banged her stick on the floor. "I beg your pardon? I am not moving. They may go!"

"This is not Rosings, Lady Catherine. I will not chase my friends from their own drawing room." He turned back to Bingley. "The library?"

"Of course, Darcy," Bingley replied and Darcy was proud of how bold and unaffected his friend appeared, yet saw the apprehension on his face when he asked, "Shall we have a room prepared?"

"I will require—" her ladyship began but Darcy cut her off.

"No. My aunt will not be staying. Lady Catherine?" He stood back and gestured out the door. In an act of defiance, his aunt lowered herself onto the edge of a nearby armchair, looking away and raising her chin high in the air. "Richard, may I ask your assistance, please?"

"My pleasure, Darce," Richard replied, a spark of glee in his eye.

Together, they flanked their aunt and, each taking an arm, lifted her to her feet and steered her from the room, Lady Catherine shrieking her indignation the whole way to the library. When they had reached that room, her ladyship was dropped unceremoniously upon a sofa in the middle of the floor. Richard sauntered to the sideboard to pour himself a drink and sat back to enjoy the show. Darcy stood, shoulders square and arms crossed, before his aunt.

"I have never been thus treated in my life! Have you no respect for your own mother?" cried she as sniffed and she wiped at nonexistent tears. But Darcy was not moved; Richard choked on his brandy as he tried to stifle his laughter.

"You are *not* my mother, Lady Catherine. You are the mother of my wife who is dead. You are nothing more to me now than an odious aunt whom I must endure."

All pretenses of tears forgot, her ladyship's face screwed up in anger. "I ought to have been your mother! I would have been had not my spoilt sister turned George Darcy's head just when he was about to come to the point!"

"You are delusional, Lady Catherine," Richard scoffed. "Uncle George had been in love with Aunt Anne since they were children. My father told me all about it. They were best friends after all. He even told me how you tried to sneak into his bedcham—"

"Enough!" shrieked Lady Catherine. Her eyes were wide, her nostrils flared, and cheeks flushed as her breath came in great noisy huffs.

"Lady, Catherine," Darcy interjected. "What are you doing here?"

For several minutes, Lady Catherine said nothing, chin raised as she gazed stubbornly about the room, clearly torn between demanding the respect she felt she was owed and accomplishing that which she had come to do. In the end, the latter won out.

"I have several complaints. Firstly, what is this I hear of you dallying with some vile upstart trollop who has turned your head and distracted you from your duty?"

"I beg your pardon?" he growled through clenched teeth. "I have *never* dallied with any woman in my life. I do very much hope you are not speaking of Miss Elizabeth Bennet for I will not hear her spoken of in such an insulting manner again."

"She is meant to marry my rector!"

"Mr. Collins made his proposals and was rejected. A lady has the right to refuse where she does not wish to marry."

"Not if she knows what is good for her!" cried Lady Catherine hotly. "She would be mistress of her family's estate, save them from poverty and destitution. But no, she has cast that future aside and set her sights far above her station. No doubt she foolishly believed she could do better once you came to this godforsaken county. Sought to entrap you and raise herself."

"Lady Catherine, Bingley and I had come to Meryton and began courting the Misses Bennet weeks before Mr. Collins ever came to Hertfordshire and made his ridiculous, and rather insulting, addresses."

"You cannot possibly be serious about this girl! She is nothing, no one! She is penniless and improper! I know it all!"

"I assure you, madam, I am very serious and you know nothing. I fully intend to take Miss Elizabeth as my wife."

Lady Catherine waved her hand dismissively. "Take her as a mistress, if you must, but I have found your bride."

Darcy fumed, trying to hold on to his temper in the face of such an offensive suggestion. "Miss Elizabeth is a gentleman's daughter. I would never dishonour her, nor any woman, in such a manner."

Again, her ladyship flapped her hand as if to waft away his words. "The Duke of Dorchester's youngest daughter has just come out in society. You will wed her and further increase the Fitzwilliam family's standing. I have already spoke to the duke. And she is not so frail as Anne. She will provide you a proper heir. Which leads me to my second purpose. Lady Prudence is full young. Therefore, my granddaughter will come to Rosings. Georgiana as well. They will not be in the way of your wife there. I shall take charge of their education."

"No."

"What did you say?" Lady Catherine looked on her nephew with furrowed brows and a gaping mouth as if he had spoken an imprecation.

"You have no say in who I marry, nor the education of my daughter and sister. When I remarry, it will be to a woman of my choosing, a woman I can love and who will be a good mother to my daughter and a capable guide for Georgiana."

As if to banish his words from her hearing, Lady Catherine gave her head a shake and then pressed forward. "Where is Catherine? It is time for her to come to Rosings and begin her education. Where is she?"

Darcy shared a dumbfounded look with his cousin. "Of whom are you speaking?"

"Do not be stupid, Darcy. I am speaking of my granddaughter. Where is she? The girl is five now, it is time to begin."

"My daughter is but three, Lady Catherine. And her name is Amelia."

"Of course, her name is Catherine! It must be! She must have been named for me!"

"And yet, she was not," Darcy replied calmly. "She was named for my Grandmother Darcy and her own mother. Amelia Anne. If you had deigned to visit at any time since her birth or bothered to read the letter I sent upon that occasion, you might have known that."

"You would ignore my daughter's wishes?!"

"I ignored none of Anne's wishes. Before my wife died, she was very specific about the naming and christening of her daughter. She was adamant that her child would not be named for the woman who berated, belittled, and abused her." It was becoming more and more difficult keep his temper in check and it folded completely at her next words.

"How dare you?!"

"How dare I?" Darcy shouted. "How dare you? Have you forgotten the manner in which I found you and Anne the day I proposed? Because I assure you, madam, I have not! Amelia will never set foot within Rosings Park so long as you remain."

"That is preposterous, Darcy! She needs a woman's guidance. The girl will come to Rosings where she belongs and I will oversee her education. And Georgiana's."

"As Georgiana's co-guardian," Richard piped in, "I shall be withholding my consent."

"Hold your tongue, Fitzwilliam," Lady Catherine barked. "Nobody asked you. Now bring me my granddaughter this instant! I must return to my estate."

"May I remind you, madam," Darcy said in a voice as cold as ice, "that Rosings Park belongs to me? I was not best pleased to learn that you had assigned a rector without consulting, nay, without so much as informing me. And what of Mr. Malvern? Why did the steward I hired not inform me of the need for such an appointment?" Lady Catherine did her best to fight the wicked grin which began forming at these words but could not fool her nephew. "I see. And how much do you pay him to disregard my directions and follow your orders instead? No more, Lady Catherine. I am through dealing with you. I have obligations to see to here, but as soon as I am finished, I will be coming to Kent. You will remove to the de Bourgh London townhouse which I will sign over to you along with what remains of your widow's portion from Sir Lewis's will. Then we are finished, madam. Any further assistance or needs can then be addressed to Lord Matlock."

Lady Catherine's face was contorted in utter horror as she listened to Darcy's edicts. "You cannot!" she shrieked.

"I can and I will. This is what you wished, is it not? Why you pressed, schemed, lied, and abused your daughter? So that I would become master of Rosings and unite two of the largest estates in England? Congratulations, Lady Catherine," he said with a mocking bow, "you have succeeded. If you believed, however, that I would ever be a passive and absent master, you were sorely mistaken. I have done nothing up to this point because, quite frankly, I much prefer not to deal with you at all. But I will not ignore your coming here and insulting my acquaintances, attempting to take charge of my life, and trying to take my daughter and sister."

"Fitzwilliam! Talk some sense into your cousin!"

"Do forgive me, your ladyship. I seem to recall having been told to hold my tongue. I should not like to be considered disobedient." He raised his glass to his aunt with satisfied smirk and took a leisurely sip of the amber liquid.

"Lady Catherine," –Darcy stepped forward— "we are finished. You will return immediately to Kent and begin packing your things. I will be writing to my solicitors to have all funds held until I can come to Rosings myself. I shall also be writing to Mr. Malvern to release him from his position. I shall be generous and give you one month to pack what you will and remove yourself from *my* estate to your London house. I care nothing for any of Rosings belongings. If you have not done so in that time, I will come and remove you myself." Darcy crossed the room and stepped out into the hall and beckoned a waiting footman. "Please have Lady Catherine's carriage brought round as quickly as possible."

"Darcy! My brother will hear of this!"

"Indeed, he will. I shall write to him myself. You ought to know that my uncle is already aware of my intentions. I had informed his lordship when I married your daughter that I would take such steps if ever you attempted override my authority as master of Rosings. Though he will not be best pleased that the task of managing you will now fall to him, he will understand my reasons."

"Fitzwilliam!" Her ladyship turned to her least consequential, therefore least favoured, nephew. "Do something!"

"Of course, Lady Catherine." Richard stood and came to the lady's side. "Darcy, if you would?"

Together, they took their aunt under the arms in the same way they had before and began marching her from the room.

"You cannot! This is insupportable! You insolent, unfeeling brutes! Darcy! I am your mother! I am your aunt! I have never been so insulted in my life!"

"Then I daresay you ought to get out more, your ladyship," said Darcy.

Unrelenting, the gentlemen led the lady through the halls and out of the house to her waiting carriage. A footman opened the door then leapt out of the way, as if fleeing a rabid wolf. Darcy and Richard stopped before the open door to allow her ladyship the option to board with some dignity. She whipped around to face Darcy.

"This is your final resolve?"

"It is. I wish you safe travels," he replied with little sincerity.

"Very well! Do not think I shall ever give way! I shall know how to act!"

"Goodbye, Lady Catherine," Richard said in a singsong voice and the two men lifted her into her carriage a gave the driver the word to be gone.

~~*✱*~~

As her carriage sped towards Town, Lady Catherine fumed within. Never, in all her life, had she been so ill-used. How dare that insolent boy threaten her in such a way? She! Who stood as his very own mother! Well, it would not stand. She would not allow him to humiliate the Fitzwilliam name by marrying some impudent upstart with no name and no connections. And she absolutely would not be removed from Rosings Park.

Lady Catherine rapped her stick on the roof of the carriage. When it came to a stop and a footman stuck his head in, she demanded to be taken to de Bourgh House in London. She passed the remainder of the journey ruminating on how ill-used she was by all her ungrateful family.

When the carriage pulled up before de Bourgh House, a fluttering of curtains in a ground floor window was the only indication that the building was inhabited at all. Paint was peeling on the walls, the windows were dirty, and the walk was littered with leaves. As her ladyship lighted from her barouche and approached the house, the front door was slowly opened with a creak to reveal a crotchety old woman in a wrinkled black housekeeper's gown. She was stooped over a crooked cane and one eye was pinched closed and covered with an angry red scar.

"Mrs. Bell," Lady Catherine addressed the woman as she entered the house. "This place looks awful."

"Then ye's ought to pays me be'er ta keep up," replied the housekeeper with a deep gravelly voice.

If her ladyship took any offense to the disrespectful statement, she made no indication. Instead, she swept passed Mrs. Bell without removing any of her outer things and made quick work of touring the principal rooms. She wrinkled her nose at the faded and peeling paper on the walls, the threadbare rugs, and the cobwebs in the corners. It had been some years since she last stayed in this house. When she came to London, she preferred to stay with her brother, the earl, and his family at Matlock House. It gave her immense pleasure to insert herself into their lives and remind them of her importance to the family.

But this time, she had business to attend to and had no wish for her brother's family to interfere.

"Mrs. Bell, fetch some tea then join me in the parlour."

The housekeeper made no attempt to hide her eyeroll and shuffled off, grumbling the whole way. Ordinarily, Lady Catherine would never countenance such ill-manners in her servants, but the woman had her uses. There was nothing Mrs. Bell would not do for a few extra coins, and her nephew had been of use to her ladyship on multiple occasions. Lady Catherine also knew that the old housekeeper knew far too much to ever allow her to leave de Bourgh employ.

Still murmuring under her breath, the housekeeper returned with a tray laden with a teapot and two cups in saucers. She set the tray down and helped herself to a cup of tea, leaving Lady Catherine to pour for herself.

"Are there no biscuits or cake?" Lady Catherine demanded.

"Yer ladyship didna' ask fer none," Mrs. Bell stated with a shrug. "Even iffin ya did, we didna' know to es'pect ya. Thar's none ta be 'ad."

With an annoyed huff, Lady Catherine poured herself a cup of tea and took a sip. She made a face at the poor quality of brew and set down her cup.

"Mrs. Bell, send for your nephew straight away. I have a job for him."

Again, the brassy servant rolled her eyes. "I dunnut know 'ow many times I mus' say it, 'e ain't my—" She stopped short at the look on her employer's face and sighed. "Iffin you insist. As it is, 'e mightin' be eager fer the work. Las' we spoke 'e 'ad some nasty creditor's breavin' down 'is neck. Gettin' desperate, 'e is. Some ridiculous talk 'bout takin' a commission in th' militia, the bloody fool."

"I hardly care about that, Mrs. Bell. I have an important task for him to fulfill. And, this time, he will not fail me."

Chapter Fifteen

***

Had they not the upcoming Netherfield ball to look forward to, the ladies of Longbourn might have easily been driven to distraction. In the final days preceding the ball an unrelenting rain fell which kept everyone indoors. There were no walks to Meryton to visit their Aunt Phillips to glean any news, no officers with whom to flirt, and no calls from two certain gentlemen neighbours.

Each night, Jane and Elizabeth commiserated together under the covers of Jane's bed. They felt rather silly, much like their two youngest sisters mourning the absence of their favourite beaux, but there was nothing to be done for it. They were two ladies very much in love and would not repent of it. Jane's modesty would only allow her to acknowledge Mr. Bingley's having shown a decided preference, but Elizabeth had no such reservations. Mr. Darcy loved her; of that she was certain. She was equally certain that he would have declared himself had Lydia not interrupted their rendezvous in the rosebushes the other day.

Much time was spent dwelling on that memorable moment. Long after Jane's breathing slowed and her legs ceased twitching, Elizabeth's mind wandered down to the garden where Mr. Darcy had bestowed upon her her first kiss. Butterflies danced in the pit of her stomach as she recalled the tender way he had looked upon her, his deep brown eyes expressing clearly what he felt without the need for words. *"Dearest Elizabeth,"* he had called her and the memory of the way he caressed her name with his lips made her heart race and spine tingle. In her heart, Elizabeth believed that he would soon offer her his hand in marriage and nothing in this world could make her happier than to become his wife and Amelia's mother.

Three miles away at Netherfield Park, Darcy was often in similar contemplations. Whenever he sat with Amelia, he could not help but remember the times Elizabeth had held his sweet girl and how obviously she cared for his daughter. As he lay in bed at night, his mind would recall that tender kiss and imagine sweeter moments in her embrace. He had only ever been with one woman, and that had been Anne and only for the sake of duty. It had been awkward and excruciatingly embarrassing for them both. They had not even removed most of their clothing; only that which was necessary to do the job.

How a man could lie with a woman he did not love for nothing more than his own selfish pleasure, Darcy could not fathom; yet he knew many who did. He could never lay himself so bare, quite literally, and vulnerable with a woman whom he did not trust with his entire being. Even lying with Anne, whom he had known his entire life, was stressful—which did not help matters in the slightest—and left him feeling as the vilest of cads knowing it would likely bring about the end of her life. Perhaps the nature of their relationship had made it all the more mortifying.

Ah, but to hold the woman for whom his heart beat and was the reason for his every life-giving breath; Darcy could not imagine a more beautiful paradise. To wake up each morning to her radiant smile, magnificent eyes, and loving kisses would be nothing short of heaven, he was sure. Elizabeth embodied everything he had ever imagined his wife would be. She was beautiful, alluring, and tempting. But more than this, she was kindness and compassion personified. Her selflessness knew no bounds and the love she showed to Amelia never failed to tighten his throat and bring moisture to his eyes.

Not only was she intelligent, witty, and lively, she was wholly unabashed about it. Intelligence in a woman was not fashionable in his world. He had known many smart women, but they endeavoured to quell their intelligence for fear it would turn potential husbands away. Elizabeth cared not. She would not accept a husband who did not value her superior mind and that made her extraordinarily special. She demanded respect and love from any man who would seek her hand and damned be the consequences of refusing a suitor who had naught but wealth or position to offer.

This meant, also, that she would give no less. Elizabeth would wed only a man to whom she could give her whole self; body, heart, mind, and soul. Which made it all the more exhilarating when she looked upon him and he could see, without the slightest trace of doubt, that she loved him. Elizabeth saw not the wealthy landowner with noble relations who occupied the highest echelons of society. Elizabeth saw Fitzwilliam Darcy, the man and the father. She saw his flaws and weaknesses yet did not condemn him for them, but accepted them and would seek to help him overcome them. He could ask for no greater gift than the love of Elizabeth Bennet.

Much to everyone's delight and relief, the morning of the ball dawned bright and sunny; nary a cloud in the sky, though the ground was still soft and muddy from so many days of rain. Every gentry household in the neighbourhood spent the day preparing for the ball; trimming gowns and trying different hairstyles, consulting with valets and maids, or practicing dance steps in their parlours. Ladies giggled and tittered together over which gentleman they most hoped to dance with; the gentlemen were scarcely less giddy about their hopes for certain fair maidens.

Jane and Elizabeth helped one another to ready for the ball as ever they had. They each took great care in their preparations, both eager to be in their best looks for the gentlemen who owned their hearts. Elizabeth braided Jane's hair and twisted it into an elegant knot atop her head, weaving a string of crystal beads throughout. Jane was absolutely resplendent in her soft pink gown.

253

Switching seats, Jane twisted Elizabeth's thick curls into a lovely chignon, leaving a few delicate ringlets hanging over her shoulder. A light green bandeau across the crown of her head to match the ribbon at the waist and neckline of her ivory silk gown and several sprigs of tiny white flowers strategically placed left Elizabeth feeling radiant.

The ladies carefully piled into the carriage when the time came, while Mr. Bennet climbed atop so as not to crush any gowns. Mrs. Bennet showered her girls with compliments, saving the most effusive for Jane; though she was uncommonly excessive in her praise for her second daughter, as well.

Netherfield Park was nothing short of a dreamland with glowing torches lining the drive, leading guests towards the large, beautiful building. A long swath of white linen had been laid out where guests would alight from the carriages to the front doors, saving dancing slippers and hems from the effects of the rains. More torches lit the front steps and tall, potted evergreen shrubs flanked the grand double entry, adorned with flowers and crystals sparkling in the fire and moonlight.

When at last they reached the entrance and were released from the carriage, Elizabeth linked her arm through Jane's as they began to climb the steps. Glancing up, her heart began the night early by engaging in a reel of its own when she spied Darcy beaming down at her from one of the many windows, Amelia in his arms waving excitedly. He gave a nod in greeting before turning from the window, no doubt to come meet her in the hall. She was not disappointed in the least when, indeed, he was waiting for her at the bottom of the grand staircase as her family approached the receiving line.

Elizabeth greeted her hosts but had little attention to give for anyone but him and made her way across the hall as soon as she was able.

"Miss Elizabeth," Darcy sighed contentedly, taking her outstretched hand with his free one and placing a soft kiss on the back of her glove. "You look magnificent this evening. Does she not, Amelia?"

"Lizzy! You so pwetty!" the little girl cried then leaned away from her father, reaching for Elizabeth.

"My dear, we do not want to upset Miss Elizabeth's gown before the ball even starts, do we?" Darcy chided his daughter. She pouted but nodded sadly.

"Oh, Mr. Darcy. I would happily ruin my gown for one of Amelia's delightful hugs. Come here, dearest." She held out her hands to take the sweet child who beamed happily as she left her father's arms. "And how have you been, my dear. I have missed you so!"

"I miss you, too, Lizzy. And Papa!"

"Indeed, Miss Elizabeth," Darcy agreed quietly. "You have been greatly missed." The two stood, smiling at one another, saying not a word but communicating much until the moment was disturbed by Mrs. Bennet.

"Oh, Mr. Darcy and Miss Darcy! It is so lovely to see you this evening, my dear. But you are not bringing Miss Darcy to the ball?" Mrs. Bennet eyed the young girl's loose curls, nightgown, and doll clutched in her arms. "Is that Lizzy Doll?"

"It is, Mama. Amelia has lost her own so I have given her Lizzy Doll," Elizabeth explained, waiting for the scolding for giving away such a treasure but was pleasantly surprised by her mother's reply.

"That was very kind of you, Lizzy dear. I am sure Miss Darcy appreciates it greatly. Did you know, dear," she asked Amelia, "that was Miss Lizzy's doll when she was your age?"

Amelia nodded and hugged the doll and Elizabeth tighter. "I luf Lizzy."

"Oh, is that not the most precious thing?!" Mrs. Bennet sighed.

"Mrs. Bennet, I had only brought Amelia down so that she might greet Miss Elizabeth. She has missed your daughter very much these last few days. Now, however," –he turned to address Amelia— "it is time for bed, poppet. I promise you will see Miss Elizabeth again, soon."

"Of course, my dear," Elizabeth assured the little girl with a squeeze. "Perhaps I shall call on the morrow and tell you all about the ball. Would you like that?"

Amelia nodded but continued to look subdued and pouty. With a thoughtful expression, she looked to her father then back at Elizabeth. "Are you gonna dance wiff Papa?"

Smiling brightly and casting a glance at the gentleman in question, Elizabeth nodded. "Yes, dear. Your papa has asked me for two dances. Can you believe it?"

"Of course! Papa lufs you!"

To this, Mrs. Bennet squeaked and fluttered her fan while it was quite the contest as to who blushed deepest; Darcy or Elizabeth. Thankfully, Mr. Bennet took hold of his wife's elbow at that moment and led her away to the ballroom, flapping and sputtering the whole way. Darcy turned to the staircase where Mrs. Lawson awaited to take her charge above stairs.

"Mrs. Lawson, would you be so kind as to take this imp off to bed, please?" He placed a kiss on Amelia's cheek and Elizabeth did the same before the nursemaid took the girl away. Darcy held out his elbow for Elizabeth and she took it with trembling fingers. As they made their way across the hall to the ballroom, he leaned down and whispered in her ear, "I ought to be embarrassed but she speaks the truth."

Elizabeth bit her lips together to contain the exultant smile which threatened. She swallowed her nearly overwhelming excitement down before looking adoringly into his eyes and replied, "I know."

It was the most beautiful night in Elizabeth's remembrance. Though it took her away from Darcy more than she liked; she danced every set, returning to his side after each one. Not insensible to her younger sisters' silly antics, it was difficult to give them much thought when she was on the receiving end of Darcy's most tender gazes.

The dances she enjoyed the most, of course, were those which she shared with him. For those precious hours there was no one else in the world but she and the man she loved. As they opened the ball together, they spoke little for there was little that needed to be said. They both knew what lie in one another's hearts and were fully aware that they stood upon the precipice of the rest of their lives.

Through Elizabeth's encouragement, Darcy danced with other ladies, as well. She was exceedingly gratified when he led her middle sister to the floor. Mary often spent balls sitting to the side with a book or simply watching the dancers, praying for the end of the evening.

Cautiously, he asked Miss Bingley for a dance. It was his duty, after all, she being his hostess. For the first time ever, he rather enjoyed his time with that lady. Not once did she bat her eyelashes at him or titter flirtatiously. In fact, most of the set passed in silence. It was broken only when Miss Bingley uttered the words that surprised him greatly.

"I must apologise, sir," she said.

"For what, Miss Bingley?" asked he.

She smiled a smile he had never seen before. It was small, but genuine, perhaps even a little self-depreciating. "I had never stopped to consider that you could not love me. I never even stopped to consider you would *wish* to love your wife. It is simply not how things are done amongst the ton."

"Oh, Miss Bingley. I..." What was he to say to that? Fortunately, she saved him from having to respond at all.

"No, Mr. Darcy. Do not try to placate me. I have had quite the revelation and have come to see that you and I would never suit. I would have been pleased to have your wealth and name, but for how long? I am sure we would both be miserable within a fortnight. No, sir. I shall now bow out gracefully."

"I do not know what to say, Miss Bingley," he admitted truthfully. "May I ask what has inspired these reflections?"

Miss Bingley threw her head back and laughed, the feathers in her turban bobbing with her mirth. It was a full, hearty laugh he had never heard from her before. As he watched, he was struck for the first time since the very beginnings of their acquaintance with the thought that she was a very handsome woman. Perhaps, if she had not always been so grasping and mean-spirited in the past, he might not have been always so indifferent to her. He was in no danger from her now, but it was an interesting thought.

"Did I not ask you the same thing when first we came to Hertfordshire? 'Fine eyes in the face of a pretty woman,' you had been contemplating." She paused and looked down the set where Elizabeth was dancing and laughing with his cousin. "Yes, she does have remarkable eyes. Now that I have ceased to despise the lady for the grievous crime of your liking her better than me, I rather like your Miss Elizabeth. Be good to her, Mr. Darcy."

"I fully intend to, Miss Bingley."

"Good. Then all whom I care about shall be happy. All is as it should be."

"And what about you, madam?"

"I shall seek the same. I shall wait for a man whom I can love and who will love me in return while keeping me in the style I have come to enjoy. Do not mistake me, sir." She tilted her head and eyed him pointedly. "I still desire an advantageous match. I do so enjoy the parties and soirées of London. But I shall endeavour to seek out a gentleman who will enjoy them with me."

The music ended and Darcy bowed to his partner. "I truly wish you every joy, Miss Bingley."

"And I you. Now, if you will excuse me, Charles has asked for my assistance on an important matter." She turned a significant look to where Jane was standing with Elizabeth. "I must get the lady to the balcony. If you would be so good as to distract her lovely sister for me, sir. I know it must be a great imposition."

"I shall do as I must for my friend," replied he in a tone of forbearance. Before he knew what he was doing, Darcy winked conspiratorially at her. His initial feelings of horror at such a display to *this* woman gave way to relief and then amusement when she laughed and wagged a finger at him. The two made their way to the sisters where Darcy wasted no time in capturing Elizabeth's attention— for his friend's sake, of course—as Miss Bingley begged a private word with Jane.

The engagement of Charles Bingley and Jane Bennet was announced just before the supper set to everyone's delight and no one's surprise. Elizabeth beamed up at Darcy before rushing to her dearest sister to wrap her in a warm embrace. When the dancing recommenced, it was with renewed energy and joy all around.

As Darcy led his lady to the floor, Elizabeth's good humour and pure happiness would not allow her to be silent. She circled around the man who lay claim to her heart, smiling saucily up at him.

"This is one of my favourite dances."

"I confess, it is quickly becoming one of mine, as well," replied Darcy with a heated look that made her cheeks flush and her heart race.

She was grateful for the next steps which took her away from him that she might recover from the effect this gentleman had upon her. When they came together, she addressed him again. "I believe it is your turn to speak, Mr. Darcy. I said something about the dance. You might remark on the size of the room, or the number of couples."

"Be assured, my dear, I am prepared to say whatever you most wish to hear." That response was rewarded with her musical laughter which he was quite certain he would never tire of. Indeed, he found himself spending and inordinate amount of time thinking of new ways to draw forth that beautiful sound from her perfect lips. Such thoughts always led to dreaming of silencing her laughter with his own lips.

"Very well," Elizabeth replied with a smile. "That response will do for the present. Perhaps I shall soon comment that private balls are much pleasanter than public ones. But we may now be silent, I suppose."

"Are there rules to speaking whilst dancing that I am unfamiliar with? I daresay, I might not always have dreaded the activity so much had I been privy to such information."

"Of course," Elizabeth laughed. "One must speak a little, you know. It does look odd when two people are entirely silent for half an hour together."

"Our first set must have looked utterly ridiculous, in that case."

This elicited such a burst of tinkling laughter from the lady's lips that she clapped a hand over her mouth to contain it. Though she attempted to chastise him with a look, her smile could not be smothered and Darcy followed the next steps of the dance looking inordinately pleased with himself.

"What think you of books?" he asked when they stood across from one another at the top of the set. Though he wanted nothing more than to see her smile and hear her laugh again, he decided to have mercy on her.

"Books? Oh, no! I cannot talk of books in a ballroom. My head is always full of something else."

The music ended at that moment and Darcy stepped forward to offer his arm. When she wrapped her hands delightfully around his sleeve, he slyly manoeuvred her closer. Leaning down, he said in low growl, "My head is full of you, Elizabeth."

Unable to conjure a single response to such a statement, Elizabeth looked about her before pressing herself into his side and squeezed his arm affectionately. Both felt quite as though they walked on air as they made their way to supper.

Caring not at all for the stir it would cause, Darcy did solicit Elizabeth's hand for the final dance which would be a waltz, Miss Bingley had confided in him.

The world around them melted away as Darcy held Elizabeth in his arms and twirled her around the ballroom. They gazed into one another's eyes, neither able nor desirous of hiding what they felt. Had either been of a mind to glance about them, it would have been clear that their secret was out. Despite the engagement of Bingley and Jane, all eyes were for his friend and her sister.

When the last strains of the music had died, the lover's remained in one another's arm a moment longer than was proper, yet no one could bring themselves to raise any fuss, so beautiful a picture did they paint.

By the contrivance of Mrs. Bennet, the Longbourn carriage was the last to be brought round, but no one complained, even as the youngest Misses Bennet hid yawns behind their gloves and Mr. Bennet nodded off for a spell as he leant against a large column. Miss Bingley and Mrs. Hurst stood with their brother and his newly betrothed; Mr. Hurst had disappeared upstairs some hours ago. Darcy pulled Elizabeth a little away from the group and held her gloved hands, gently stroking his thumb over her knuckles.

"Bingley has invited Miss Bennet to join us for luncheon on the morrow, well, later today," he said with a grin. "I would be pleased if you might be able to join her. There is something particular I would very much like to speak with you about."

Biting her lip to contain an exultant smile, Elizabeth took a few calming breaths before reverting to her customary teasing. "I would be most happy to come, sir. But, what could you possibly wish to speak on that we could not canvass at this moment, I wonder?"

Revelling in the magnificent sparkle of her eyes, Darcy almost blurted out a proposal right then and there but stopped himself with the words on the tip of his tongue. No, this glorious creature deserved such a moment to be done properly; not hurriedly uttered in hushed tones as her mother looked on, verily bouncing on her tired toes. Besides, if he asked now, he most assuredly would not be able to kiss her to seal their betrothal.

"I very recently finished Mr. Milton's latest work and wished to discuss it with you. Would you indulge me?"

A laugh escaped her lips at his serious demeanour but for the twinkling merriment mixed with tenderness in his eyes. "I would be most pleased to, sir, but I am afraid I have not yet had the opportunity to read it for myself. It would not make for a very lively debate."

"Ah, that is a pity. Then you must come on the morrow so that you might borrow it. Then we may discuss it properly."

"I shall look forward to it, Mr. Darcy."

~~~*✱*~~~
Chapter Sixteen
✱

Jane's bed creaked under the weight of all five Bennet sisters gathered to happily chatter and laugh over the events of the ball. Elizabeth reflected with some amusement how five vastly different ladies could so easily put aside their squabbles and frequent vexations in the face of their eldest and most deserving sister's happiness.

"Oh, Jane," sighed Kitty. "'Tis so romantic! Do you love him so very dearly?"

"I do, Kitty, dear. I love him with all my heart," was Jane's serene but heartfelt answer.

"Did he kiss you?" Lydia demanded boldly.

"Lydia!" Jane and Elizabeth cried together, but Jane's deep blush answered her sister's brash question.

"Oh! He did! He did!" Lydia giggled and kicked her feet, nearly sending Mary off the side of the bed. "What was it like? Is it just like in the novels?"

"Very well," Jane said with a sigh, no doubt as relieved by this question as Elizabeth. It indicated, at least, that Lydia had not yet given away any favours that she ought not. "I will tell you all, but you must promise me that you will follow my example and only ever allow a man to kiss you after you have the promise of a betrothal." Mary gave her solemn vow as Kitty and Lydia agreed impatiently, eager to hear all the sordid details. Elizabeth pressed her lips together and said nothing, hoping none of her sisters noticed her blush as she recalled how Darcy's lips had felt against her own only a few days ago. Oh, her Jane would be so ashamed of her! But for herself, she had not yet learnt to regret allowing him the liberty.

"Yes, Mr. Bingley kissed me *after* I accepted his proposal. It was very sweet. Miss Bingley said she needed to speak with me on a matter of some importance and led me to the balcony. Charles," – Kitty and Lydia giggled to hear their sister use a gentleman's Christian name— "was waiting for me when we got there. I do not even recall Miss Bingley leaving us, so happy was I to see him there.

"Oh, it was so romantic with the moonlight and the stars! He took up my hands and held them to his heart." Jane clasped her hands together against her own breast as if remembering her beloved's touch. "He looked deeply into my eyes and told me that he knew he loved me from the moment he laid eyes on me. He then asked if I would do him the honour of allowing him to love me all the days of his life and begged me to make him the happiest of men and consent to be his wife."

A collective "Aw!" sounded from each of her sisters at her recital only for the moment to be broken by Kitty and Lydia's giggles.

"And then he kissed you!" Lydia squealed.

"Yes, Lydia," Jane smiled as radiant a smile as any of her sisters had ever seen. "Then he kissed me. No, it was not like in the novels. It was tender and sweet. Little more than a brush against my lips." She closed her eyes and touched her fingers to her lips as she breathed, "It was perfect."

"And what about you, Lizzy?" Kitty asked. "Did Mr. Darcy propose as well? I was watching you as we waited for the carriage. You were certainly very pleased about something he said!"

"No, Kitty," Elizabeth answered honestly. "Mr. Darcy did not propose to me tonight."

"Truly?!" Lydia cried. "After the way you looked at one another as you waltzed, I was certain he would ask! What on earth could he be waiting for? You do suppose he will ask, do you not? He has been ever so attentive to you. And I could not imagine a man so dull and rigid as he being a cad."

"Lydia!" Elizabeth scolded her youngest sister a second time. "Mr. Darcy is not dull and rigid. He is disciplined and proper. A true gentleman. But he can be very amusing and playful."

"Then he will ask you?" Mary asked quietly as she stifled a yawn.

Elizabeth hesitated only a moment as she thought back to when he had asked her to join him for luncheon, and recalled the tender way he had looked on her and the delicious way he had stroked her hand as he told her he had a particular subject on which he wished to speak. Quite unaware of the beaming smile which lit up her face she answered, "Yes. Yes, I think he will."

"But you will be a mother right away, Lizzy, and to another woman's child," Lydia stated, not quite able to hide what she thought of this idea. "I have always imagined that when I married, my husband and I would spend time together before children came, enjoying parties and balls and perhaps travelling. What if you cannot love his daughter?"

Elizabeth did not even hesitate with her answer. "Oh, but I already do, Lyddie. I do not know that I could love Mr. Darcy so well if I did not love his child. I confess, dear sister, I am quite as anxious to be Amelia's mother as I am to be Mr. Darcy's wife."

The talking and giggling continued until the sky began to lighten outside their window and Jane and Elizabeth shooed their sisters away. They wished for at least a few hours rest before they returned to Netherfield and their gentlemen. How they would manage to fall asleep, however, with the way each of their hearts fluttered and their minds so full of the men they loved, neither lady could imagine.

Several hours later, Jane and Elizabeth began the three-mile journey to Netherfield Park, perhaps not as rested as they might have wished, but eager and delighted all the same. Elizabeth watched the familiar scenery pass by without truly seeing it. Preparing for luncheon had been an inexplicably stressful affair! She changed gowns no less than four times, wanting to look perfect for this day, yet also desiring not to look over-dressed. Jane styled her hair, but Elizabeth could not decide if she would rather a bandeau or ribbons in her curls. In the end, Lydia had traipsed in with the perfect suggestion; two ribbons tied across the crown of her head, bandeau style. She felt incredibly foolish, but could not help it. She held every expectation of returning to Longbourn an engaged woman and wanted to inspire Darcy to truly wish to propose her.

She could not fathom how it had happened, but Darcy was everything she had ever hoped to find in a husband. Besides being obscenely handsome and wealthy, he was kind and responsible. She loved her father dearly, but was not blind to his faults and had long known that she would not be happy with a man who did not take his role, whether it be landowner or merchant, seriously and jeopardised the security of his wife and children.

Darcy was also a wonderful father, and that thought filled her with such warmth. He doted on sweet little Amelia so and she knew he would treat any other children with which they might be blessed with exactly the same devotion. They would be a truly loving family, not one of those fashionable couples of the ton who left the rearing of their children to servants and governesses while they enjoyed parties and balls. Elizabeth could not even fathom such a thing. She imagined sleeping in on lazy mornings, half a dozen children cuddled all around, some with her dark green eyes and freckles, some with their father's strong chin and devastating dimples. No, Elizabeth smiled to herself, she wanted all her children to have Darcy's heart-fluttering dimples.

"Lizzy," Jane interrupted her musings.

"Hmm?" Elizabeth half answered as she fought to pull her thoughts from her vastly pleasing imaginary future.

"You cannot fool me, you know."

"Fool you? I should never attempt it."

Jane took up her sister's hand and pressed her lips together before she spoke. "I noticed how you did not answer last night. When I made our sisters promise to wait before bestowing their favours on any gentlemen?"

Elizabeth opened her mouth to speak but could not find the words to defend herself and so remained quiet.

"He has kissed you already, has he not? Mr. Darcy?"

Again, there was nothing she could say. Elizabeth focused her attention on her hand wrapped in her sister's and nodded ever so slightly. To her utter amazement, Jane neither scolded nor tsked her disapproval, but laughed lightly.

"Yes, I thought so."

"Are you terribly ashamed of me, dear sister?"

Jane laughed again. "Of course not, dearest! It would be exceedingly hypocritical of me." Elizabeth looked up at her sister at last, her brow furled in question. "Charles kissed me last week, the day Colonel Fitzwilliam arrived. In the hermitage."

"Jane! But you said—"

"Yes, I know. I was untruthful and I am sorry for it. But I do so fear for Kitty and Lydia, Lydia especially. She is so fond of the officers and love and flirting. I mean not to speak disparagingly of our youngest sister, but I fear it would not take much for her to bestow her favours on some unworthy gentleman for naught but a lark. If she knew I had allowed Mr. Bingley to kiss me without a true understanding, she would certainly run out and kiss the first man to give her a chance.

"But Charles and Mr. Darcy are not like the officers. Our gentlemen are good, respectable men who would not go about kissing young ladies for sport. And I am positive Mr. Darcy invited you today to make you an offer, Lizzy. They are to be our husbands and some liberties may be allowed."

The carriage rolled to stop and the ladies looked out. They had reached Netherfield without noticing. Bingley and Darcy were making their way down the front steps to greet them, while the Colonel trailed behind, and arrived at the carriage just as a footman opened the door. Bingley reached in a hand and helped Jane to disembark, then stepped aside to allow Darcy to hand down Elizabeth. He gazed tenderly on her for several moments, raising both of her hands to his lips for a kiss each before tucking one in the crook of his elbow and covering it with his own.

"I am so pleased you could come," he said quietly, stroking the back of her hand.

"As am I," answered she. "I am excessively keen to see Mr. Milton's latest publication. Tell me, did you enjoy it?"

For a moment, Darcy looked on her in bemusement until he was able to tear his thoughts away from how lovely she looked in the morning sun and how he hoped this day would end and could recall their earlier conversation. "Ha! Yes! Yes, I enjoyed it immensely. I am hopeful you will be just as pleased with it as I."

"I am quite certain I shall be."

"Do not mind me," said the Colonel. "I am of no consequence to anyone here!"

"Only in comparison to such superior company, Cousin," Darcy teased him. "But the ladies cannot remain forever." He leaned over and in a low voice verily growl in Elizabeth's ear, "Not yet, anyway."

Colonel Fitzwilliam ambled behind as the gentlemen led their ladies into the house where Miss Bingley and the Hursts awaited. Bingley's sisters greeted Jane with enthusiasm, and even had a kind welcome for Elizabeth. The party was soon called in for luncheon and enjoyed a pleasant meal together. Miss Bingley and Mrs. Hurst found great enjoyment in talking over wedding plans with Jane, discussing trousseaux and wedding gowns. The sisters good naturedly teased their brother about finally seeking out a London townhouse for his bride, for they could not forever be living with the Hursts. Bingley agreed with enthusiasm, declaring he would gladly take Carlton House for his wife if she so wished and the prince regent could be convinced to give it up.

When the meal was finished and the courses cleared away, Bingley and his sisters proposed taking Jane on a tour of the house of which she would become mistress. Elizabeth declined to join them and instead chose to remain with Darcy and his cousin. Mr. Hurst found a comfortable, out of the way sofa to settle as his lunch digested.

As pre-arranged, Mrs. Lawson soon brought Amelia down to see Elizabeth that she might fulfill her promise of telling the young girl all about the ball. As the very reliable nursemaid had not been feeling well that morning, Darcy relieved her of any further duties for the remainder of the day to rest. The lady dipped a grateful curtsey and returned to her rooms.

"Shall we venture out? It is a fine day," suggested Darcy and all agreed.

After gathering their outerwear, they had no sooner stepped out onto the front steps when an express rider bolted up the drive and skidded to halt at the bottom of the stairs. He leapt from his horse and took the steps two at a time.

"I beggin' yer pardon, sirs, miss. Might'n one of you's be Mis'er Darcy?" the rider asked the two gentlemen.

"I am Mr. Darcy," answered he.

"Then this'll be for you, sir." The rider held out an envelope and exchanged it for the coins Darcy pulled from his pocket. He was then directed to the side entrance where he might access the kitchens for refreshment before returning to London.

"From the earl," Darcy said distractedly as he looked over the seal.

"Lady Catherine," replied the Colonel. "I would bet my life she has gone straight to my father to complain of your *insolence*."

"If you gentlemen would like to see to your letter, Amelia and I can walk to the gardens and wait for you there. Can we not, dear?" Amelia beamed at the suggestion and agreed happily.

"Thank you, my lo—ah. Ah, Miss Elizabeth," Darcy stumbled, blushing from the edge of his cravat to the roots of his hair, matching Elizabeth's crimson-stained cheeks. Elbowing his cousin, who had made a valiant attempt to turn a hearty guffaw into a violent cough, Darcy cleared his throat as he tugged at his neckcloth. "We will join you ladies shortly."

Darcy placed a lingering kiss on the back of Elizabeth's hand, looking extremely reluctant to release her. Another kiss for his daughter and he and his cousin returned indoors to determine what kind of trouble their aunt was causing.

"Come, sweetheart. Shall we find some lovely flowers to pick for the table?"

"Yes!" cried Amelia. "Purper ones!"

Laughing at the sweet girl, Elizabeth hugged her tightly. "Purple ones it shall be."

With not a care, the two young ladies skipped along the path, Amelia jabbering gaily about how this flower was prettier than that and which were her favourites. When Elizabeth informed her that yellow and blue were her preferred colours, the little girl determined she would find all the flowers of those colours for her dear friend.

They had only just reached the edge of the formal gardens when they heard footsteps approaching. Elizabeth bit down on her lips to tamper the excitement she felt at Darcy's enthusiasm to return to her and turned to greet him.

"That did not take lon—" she began to tease until her eyes landed on a man she had never seen before. "Oh, excuse me."

The man before her was tall and slender, dressed in gentlemen's clothing that looked to be good quality except they were wrinkled and thinning at the elbows and knees. Buttons were missing from the coat that hung off his thin frame. He had long, dark blonde hair pulled back in a queue and might have been very handsome were it not for a disconcerting wild look in his icy blue eyes and a gaunt quality to his unshaven face. He stood stock still, staring at her with an almost predatory grin stretched across his lips. His eyes raked over her body, down then up again, before turning on Amelia. Elizabeth instinctively stepped closer to the child and took her up in her arms.

"Excuse us, sir." She took a few steps to the right, intending to give the man a wide berth, but he moved to block her path with surprising speed.

In one quick, fluid motion, his hand pulled a pistol from under his coat and he held it out before him. "Give me the girl," he demanded in a voice that was surprisingly smooth and almost sounded friendly but for the terrifying words he uttered.

"No," Elizabeth replied without thought. She knew not from where it came but every fibre of her being tensed in preparation to protect Amelia.

"Do not be foolish, woman. Give me the girl and I need not harm you."

"I will not. Now, let me pass."

The man seemed not to hear as he stared silently at her, looking her over once again. At last, a wicked smile crossed his face and his eyes seemed to light up with feral anticipation. It was this which most frightened her. "Ah, Miss Elizabeth Bennet, I presume. I have only yet seen you from a distance. Yes, I can see why Darcy likes you. Oh, this is even better. Very well, you may keep the girl. If you scream, however, or make any attempt to run, I will kill you and the child." Much quicker than he appeared capable of, he crossed the yards that separated them and grabbed her by the elbow, pressing the barrel of the gun between her ribs and pulling her close.

"Please let Amelia go. I will go with you, but let her go. I beg you."

"Sorry, love. But it is the girl I have come for. You," –he pressed his nose into her hair and inhaled deeply— "are a fortuitous happenstance. I had expected the nurse to bring little Miss Darcy out, but this," he cackled. "This will work much better in my favour. Now, move. Your carriage awaits."

He forced her to walk at a brisk pace, keeping to the edge of the drive near the trees, all the while pressing the gun into her side just enough that it was uncomfortable and ensured she could not forget it's presence. She kept herself between Amelia and the man, whispering calming words to the sweet girl, promising that everything would be well; trying to convince herself as much as her charge.

Just before they reached the stables where Elizabeth had hoped they might garner some attention, the barrel of the pistol pressed sharply into her ribs, forcing her to step off the drive and onto a path in the trees nearly hidden by brush. It was over grown and narrow, likely a game trail used by deer and foxes. If this had been the woods that separated Netherfield and Longbourn, Elizabeth might have had an advantage, so oft did she traverse those paths. But they were on the opposite side of the estate, in forests she did not know as well.

As they marched through the woods, Elizabeth's mind raced through various possibilities. She had to protect Amelia at all costs. Eyeing the man askance, taking in his thin frame and gaunt features, she imagined he did not see a good deal of exertion. He was taller than she and probably stronger, but Elizabeth was no wilting daisy. She walked miles every day and was strong and quick. Under the pretense of adjusting her hold on the child, she raised Amelia higher on her waist.

"Amelia, dear," she whispered to the frightened little girl, "when I put you down, run to the house."

"But—"

"Silence!" the villain growled.

"Just do as I say. Stay on the path. Run to Papa." She looked meaningfully into the dear child's eyes, so deep and intelligent just like her father's, and Amelia nodded.

Taking a deep breath, Elizabeth spun around, checking the man with her hip and knocking him off balance. She quickly released Amelia on the ground nudging her back the direction from whence they came. Using her body to block the man who had begun to regain his balance, she screamed, "Run, Amelia! Run!"

Thankfully, the girl did not hesitate but scrambled back along the path as quickly as her tiny legs would carry her. Their kidnapper cursed and moved to go after her but Elizabeth threw herself, elbow first, into his abdomen. He stepped back with an "Oof!" and bent over double, dropping the pistol. Thinking she might make her own escape, Elizabeth turned to run but her wrist was caught in a strong, bony grip. He yanked on her arm, causing her to spin around and the back of his other hand met sharply with her cheek. Stars burst across a field of black in her vision and she felt herself fall to the earth.

Pushing all thought of her own pain away in favour of ensuring Amelia got away, she opened her eyes just as the man turned to chase after his runaway target. Elizabeth kicked out her foot, catching him about the ankles and he fell unceremoniously across her legs. She felt a sharp pain course up her leg when his knee landed hard on her ankle but could only focus on keeping this scoundrel from pursuing Amelia.

Breathing heavily, the man looked after Amelia, who had disappeared into the trees, and cursed again. Then he turned a menacing glare on Elizabeth. She watched as thoughts raced through his mind until he seemed to come to a decision.

"Right, change of plans. Darcy can keep his brat. I have no doubt he will pay handsomely for his pretty little tart." Picking up the pistol, he jumped to his feet and reached down, grasping her by the upper arm, and pulled her roughly to her feet.

Elizabeth was half marched, half dragged down the narrow path, her cheek burning and ankle throbbing with every step. They burst out of the trees not ten feet from the end of Netherfield's drive and she spotted a large, handsome carriage waiting just at the end of the lane. It was towards this carriage she was pulled, then shoved inside and thrown against the backwards facing bench. Her abductor sat heavily beside her and shouted orders for the driver to go.

~~~*✳*~~~

Chapter Seventeen

₊

"What? Who is this? This is not my granddaughter!" shrieked an older, unpleasant looking woman who sat across from Elizabeth. She wore a very fine black satin gown under a heavy velvet pelisse. Grey curls, smattered with a few still dark strands framed the lady's face under a very large, ostentatious bonnet. Her shoulders were broad and her features sharp and severe. Even sitting, she was quite tall and Elizabeth thought she looked as a woman whom bitterness and anger had aged beyond her years.

"How very astute of you, Lady Catherine," the villain replied, rolling his eyes. Elizabeth gasped at the name. This was Darcy's late wife's mother?

"Catherine is a child!" her ladyship spat. "Only five or six years of age!"

Offended on Darcy and Amelia's behalf that this woman would descend to such malicious behaviour as to try and steal her granddaughter away, and yet not even know the girls name or age, Elizabeth crossed her arms and fixed the woman who had caused the man she loved so many years of grief with a steely glare. "*Amelia* is but three."

Other than sending a contemptuous glare her way, Lady Catherine did not acknowledge Elizabeth's words and turned her ire back on the man sitting beside her. "Why have you brought this woman? I need my granddaughter! Darcy must be made to marry the duke's daughter!"

"You are fool, woman." Lady Catherine huffed and pulled herself up in indignation. "Darcy will never bow to your wishes. He need only storm Rosings with a few dozen men and take his daughter back. This," he gestured with his pistol at Elizabeth, "is Darcy's ladylove. I imagine my old friend will pay anything I ask to get her back."

"You," Lady Catherine sneered at Elizabeth, "are Miss Elizabeth Bennet?"

"I am," answered Elizabeth with her chin held high and as much disdain as she could muster in her look.

"You are the jezebel who thinks she can turn *my* son from his duty? Upstart, pretentious girl! My clergyman told me you had the temerity of aiming so high above your station. I would not injure my dear son so much as to suppose the truth of it possible, but I will make my sentiments known to you."

"If you believe it impossible to be true, I wonder that you would take the trouble of disabusing me. What could your ladyship propose by it?"

"At once to have such notions universally contradicted!"

"Your kidnapping me and taking me away from my family will rather be seen as a confirmation of the basis of your fears."

"Do you deny that Mr. Darcy has taken an unnatural fancy to you?"

"I do not pretend to possess equal frankness with your ladyship. You may ask questions which I shall not choose to answer."

"This is not to be borne, Miss Bennet! I insist on being satisfied! Has he, has my son made you an offer of marriage?"

Elizabeth crossed her arms defiantly over her chest. "It was my understanding you had no sons, only a daughter."

"You know very well what I mean, you insolent girl!" Lady Catherine shouted, shaking the cane she held at Elizabeth. "Has Darcy made you an offer?!"

"Your ladyship has declared it to be impossible."

"And so it ought to be! But your arts and allurements may have made him, in a moment of infatuation, forget what he owes to me. You may have drawn him in."

"If that were the case, I should certainly be the last person to confess it."

Striking her cane on the floor of the carriage, Lady Catherine fumed. "Miss Bennet! Do you know who I am? I have not been accustomed to such language as this. As his late wife's mother, I am the nearest relation he has in the world and I am entitled to know all his dearest concerns."

"But you are not entitled to know mine. And you are mistaken, your ladyship. Mr. Darcy's nearest relations are his daughter and sister."

"Let me be rightly understood. This match to which you have the presumption to aspire, can never take place. Mr. Darcy is engaged to Lady Prudence Caldwell! Now what have you to say?"

"Only this, that if he is so, you can have no reason to suppose he would make an offer to me."

An angry flushed crossed Lady Catherine's face as she looked on Elizabeth. "The engagement has not yet been made official. I have spoken with the Duke and Duchess of Dorchester and informed them of Darcy's intent. It will be a spectacular match which will further raise to consequence and importance of the Fitzwilliam family!"

"But what is that to me? If there is no other objection to my marrying your *nephew*, I shall certainly not be kept from it by knowing you wish for another arrangement. You have done what you could in promoting the match. Its completion, however, is dependent on others. If Mr. Darcy is neither by honour nor inclination bound to Lady Prudence, why is he not to make another choice? If I am that choice, why may I not accept him?"

"Obstinate, headstrong girl! I am ashamed of you! I am determined to carry my purpose and I will not be dissuaded from it. I have not been used to brooking disappointment."

"That will make your ladyship's situation at present more pitiable, but it will have no effect on me!"

"Oh, shut up, the both of you!" the man holding the gun cried out when Lady Catherine opened her mouth to argue. Elizabeth had very nearly forgotten his presence as she argued with the odious woman seated across from her. "I have had just about enough of your bickering! We will take Miss Bennet and if Darcy wants her back, he will have to pay."

"No!" Lady Catherine screeched like petulant child, her face contorted in fury. "He must marry Lady Prudence! You are ruining everything! I do not need this trollop! I need my granddaughter! We must go back!"

"We cannot go back. The child has likely reached the house by now and they will know we have taken the lady."

"You let her go? You are utterly useless! I ought to have sent Collins to do the job. He may be a complete idiot, but he at least follows my instructions to the letter! Do not think I shall give you the rest of your ten thousand now. I suppose this is what I get for trusting a filthy steward's son.

You could not even deliver Georgiana to me last summer. Why I thought you could handle this is beyond me!"

"I told you, I had Georgiana all but secured. Then," —he gestured impatiently with his gun— "Darcy had to go and show up in Ramsgate."

As the two argued back and forth, Elizabeth took in her surroundings. The carriage was moving quickly, but she wondered if she might be able to open the door and jump before either of her captors could stop her. She would not escape injury, but she might yet live and get to safety. Slowly, she inched nearer the door, waiting for an opportunity to act when her arm was seized by the man.

"Not so fast, my dear." He pulled her back against him on the seat. "Lady Catherine, I tire of this and I can see you are only going to be a hindrance." He lifted his pistol almost lazily, taking aim at the lady's chest and pulled the trigger. Lady Catherine's body slumped sideways, her surprise still evident on her lifeless face.

All thought of escape drained from Elizabeth's mind as she looked on the dead woman. She wondered if this man would hesitate to kill her as callously as he had killed Darcy's aunt. There would be no ransom if she died, but he might very well decide it was not worth the trouble if she fought him. Pushing those thoughts from her mind, she reminded herself that Amelia was safe and took comfort in that.

"Do not even think of trying anything courageous," he warned her before crossing to the other bench and seating himself beside Lady Catherine's body. Tossing the spent pistol aside, the man rummaged through her ladyship's reticule and person, removing a heavy looking coin purse, several bank notes, and a large, gawdy gold and ruby necklace from around the woman's neck. Looking extremely satisfied, her kidnapper leaned forward and opened the door.

With a bit of effort, he shoved Lady Catherine's body across the bench and out the door of the speeding carriage. Elizabeth was just contemplating following the body or perhaps shoving this vile man out after it when he snapped the door shut and reached under the bench, producing another pistol.

"There, is not this nicer?" he asked when he had settled himself across from her, looking not the least concerned that he had just killed a noble woman in cold blood then unceremoniously shoved her body out onto the road.

"Who are you?" she demanded with more bravado than she felt.

The man smirked and casually inspected the fingernails of the hand not brandishing the weapon. "Just an old friend of Darcy's."

"What do you want with Miss Darcy?"

"The girl? Nothing. That was all the old bat's idea. I was merely meant to retrieve her." He shrugged lazily as if this were an everyday occurrence for him. Perhaps it was. Once, whilst visiting her relations in London, she had heard of men who could be hired to commit crimes others could not, or would not, enact themselves. Was this just such a man? He clearly had little moral fibre. "However, you, Miss Bennet, are going to make me rich and help me exact my revenge on Darcy."

"How do you know my name? I have never seen you before."

"No, you have not. But I have seen you." He raised a single brow as he again raked her body up and down with his eyes. She wrapped her arms around her middle, as if to protect herself from this man's lecherous gaze. He only laughed. "And I know a lot. I have been in Meryton for several days now, watching my old friend, Darcy. Waiting for the right time to act. Gathering whatever information might be useful. I have spoken with several of your neighbours. It is wonderous how easily free ale will loosen a man's tongue.

"Darcy," he said as though he were one of Mrs. Bennet's fellow matrons sharing a juicy bit of gossip at tea, "has been in Meryton for nearly two months now. I was exceedingly surprised to learn that he has become quite friendly with the locals. My old chum is rarely so sociable. Even more astonishing, he has paid an inordinate amount of attention to one particular lady. The second of five daughters of a minor country gentleman, one Mr. Thomas Bennet. You ought to be flattered, Miss Bennet. I have never known Darcy to give so much attention to any one young lady, and I have known him all my life. Even his wife was nothing more than a sickly, pathetic cousin who was easy enough to bend to his will. He does like having control, our Darce.

"Now, about those sisters. The eldest is quite the beauty. I almost wonder that Darcy did not set his cap at her. But, then again, he is honourable to a fault," –this was said with a slight sneer as though it were a vice rather than a virtue— "and would not dare encroach on his friend's territory. I am not so squeamish. 'Tis quite the shame the lovely Miss Jane Bennet was not out walking with you. I do like to have my choice. Then there is you followed by Mary, I believe. Poor thing. She is not near so lovely as the rest of you. But those ladies who are not blessed with good looks, I find, are often the most eager to prove themselves worthy of a man's affections.

"But the real liability, I think, are the two youngest. Kitty, she is quiet and stupid, but easily biddable, I understand. Then there is Lydia. Ruining her would not even be a challenge. I have seen her about town. Had I come to this insipid town on any other business, I might have made a pretty penny wagering how easily I could coax her into my bed."

Elizabeth knew he was intentionally trying to intimidate her and would not give him the satisfaction of seeing her discomposed. She raised her chin and met his gaze with a hard stare.

"Oh, ho! Yes, I definitely see the attraction. Darcy is not a fan of those weeping violet types. I almost hope he chooses not to pay the ransom I shall ask. You would be a fun one to break." The disgusting man laughed as his eyes turned to glance out the window. Instantly, his face transformed from smug delight to burning anger. He pulled the hammer on his pistol and pressed his face to the glass. "Damn it!"

Shouting could be heard outside just before the carriage gave a violent lurch and Elizabeth was thrown from her seat, across the well, and into her captive's lap. For a moment, everything was a confusion of whinnying horses, flying gravel, angry shouts, and the deafening crack of gun fire.

Mrs. Lawson had just settled into her bed, anxious for a good, long nap and thankful her employer was such a good man and a doting father, when her throat began to tickle and itch. Try as she might, no amount of coughing would dislodge whatever it was that was plaguing her so and every breath seemed to agitate it further. She rubbed her throat hoping to assuage the offending scratch to no avail.

Knowing there would be no sleep until the itch was soothed, she rose from her bed and crossed to the small table set under the window overlooking the front drive where the water pitcher was kept. She poured a glass and swallowed it greedily. The cool liquid and a few more forceful coughs seemed to do the trick and she set the glass down, anticipating nothing but the glorious anesthesia which awaited her in her bed.

As she turned from the table, movement outside caught her eye and she nearly fainted from what she saw. Moving quickly down the long, sweeping drive, Miss Elizabeth and a tall man she did not recognise were carrying Miss Darcy away!

"Miss Elizabeth!" Mrs. Lawson screamed as she burst into the library where the master was most often found. "Miss Elizabeth has Miss Darcy!"

"Yes, Mrs. Lawson," Darcy answered, eyeing the normally sedate woman warily. "She has taken Amelia to the gardens for a walk whilst the Colonel and I address an express which has just arrived from the earl."

"No! With a man! I saw them from my window! She had Miss Darcy and they were running down the drive towards the stables! They've kidnapped Miss Darcy!"

Darcy bolted from the room, his cousin hot on his heels. They tore the front doors open and flew down the steps just as a carriage was whipping passed the end of the drive and out of sight in a cloud of dust.

"My horse! Now!"

"I will check the gardens," he heard Richard shout.

The wait for his horse was excruciating. Pacing about while the carriage pulled further and further away felt like nothing short of torture. He had to get to Amelia. Nothing else mattered. After what felt like an eternity, Darcy ran to the stables, hellbent on saddling his horse himself if the groom could not go any faster.

For the space of mere seconds, he allowed a fragment of hope to flicker to life that Richard would find his daughter and the woman he loved picking blooms in the garden, laughingly anticipating his joining them. Perhaps Mrs. Lawson had been incorrect. Who the hell else she might have seen running down Netherfield's drive with a man and a child he could not even begin to imagine, but Elizabeth could not have taken his precious girl. He was in love with Elizabeth and she would not do this to him. They were in the garden, picking flowers. They had to be.

The groom brought Cerberus around, followed by another groom leading Richard's horse, and handed over the reins.

"Have you a pistol?" he asked the man as he swung himself up into the saddle. He would waste no time sending a man to his chambers from his own. A firearm was quickly produced from the stables and handed over. He could not explain it but even as he told himself it could not be true, he knew his cousin would find no one in the gardens.

Darcy waited only for Richard to return from his mission to ascertain that there had not been some sort of mistake and Elizabeth and his daughter were not walking innocently along the side of the house gathering flowers to show him when he rejoined them. He need only see the look on his cousin's face as he raced back around the house to know they were not where they ought to be and kicked his horse into motion, tearing down the road after the dust trail in the distance.

All manner of thoughts ricocheted around in his head. Why had she taken his daughter? Who was the man Mrs. Lawson had seen rushing her along? Where were they going? Had she been lying to him all this time? Using her fine eyes and sparkling wit to lure him in and deceive him? Was there a woman anywhere in this godforsaken kingdom who was as she appeared to be? How could she do this to him?

He found no answers as Cerberus gained on the carriage. He could hear Richard and the footmen they had brought keeping pace just behind him and knew they would easily catch their quarry, but it eased the gut-wrenching fear in his chest not at all. If anything, anything at all, happened to his daughter, he would not be able to vouch for his highly reputed self-control. He doubted even Richard's ability to prevent him killing anyone who laid a finger on Amelia. He had promised Anne he would protect their daughter—in that he could not fail.

As Cerberus charged down the road, Darcy vaguely registered something lying beside the hedgerows in a heap of black fabric that looked suspiciously like a body, but it was far too large to be his daughter and so paid it no mind; nothing mattered but Amelia. Behind him, Richard shouted to one of the men to investigate, but the rest ploughed on.

As he came level with the fleeing coach, he pulled the pistol he had taken from the groom from his waistband. Speeding past to where the driver sat, he pointed the gun at the man on the bench only to recognise his aunt's long-time coachman at the reins.

"Stop now!" he thundered, shoving his surprise away to deal with later. "I *will* kill you, Abbott!"

"Mis'er Darcy!" the man shouted at the sight of his mistress's nephew.

The Colonel came up beside his cousin, pointing his own pistol, and the driver's eyes bugged from his head. He pulled hard on the leads, bringing the carriage to a screeching halt. A shot rang out and, for a moment, Darcy's world ground to a halt. Bringing Cerberus round to the side of the carriage, dreading what he would find when the door opened, he leapt from the saddle. A man shouted from inside the coach and he heard Elizabeth's voice cry out, but he heard nothing that sounded like Amelia and his fear multiplied. Pistols drawn, the two cousins approached the door cautiously. Darcy stood to the side as Richard reached forward and pulled on the latch.

The sight which greeted him nearly made Darcy sick. There, within the carriage, draped across the lap of the man he despised more than any other living creature, was the woman he had nearly proposed marriage to. George Wickham looked from Darcy to Elizabeth and back, grinning his hatefully smug smile.

"Fancy meeting you here, Darcy," Wickham drawled as if he had not a care in the world. His bravado fell, however, when Richard stepped forward into view. It had been only Darcy's staying hand, after all, which had prevented his cousin from gutting the reprobate when they had last met.

Ignoring his childhood friend, Darcy reached in and took Elizabeth by the wrist, pulling her unceremoniously from the carriage, only half aware of his cousin removing Wickham immediately after. Gripping her about the shoulders, he pressed her roughly against the side of carriage and looked down upon the woman he had not an hour ago believed he would spend the rest of his life with. Her eyes were glassy and her face was pale but for a dark bruise covering much of the left side of her face. Still, she was the most beautiful woman he had ever seen and he hated that. He hated that, even now, after all she had done to him, his heart ached with the knowledge that she was not what he had thought. But he could not think of that; Amelia was all that mattered.

"Where is she? Where is Amelia?" he demanded shaking Elizabeth slightly.

Confusion blanketed Elizabeth's features. "A-Amelia?" she said weakly but Darcy was tiring of her theatrics and shook her again.

"Where is my daughter?"

"Sh-she ran. In the...in the woods." She was speaking so softly now, Darcy had to lean in to hear her. But he would not allow her fear and feigned remorse affect him. She ought to be afraid!

He pulled her close and glared into those eyes which had charmed him so thoroughly. "If you have harmed one single hair on her head, I will ensure that you regret it for the rest of your days."

"Wha—no! No, I—"

"Mr. Darcy, sir!" a voice called out behind him and Darcy was grateful for he wanted to hear none of her lies. He needed to forget her, as soon as possible. It was bad enough that his heart was still calling to her, desperately trying to excuse her actions; to find any legitimate excuse for why she was in this carriage with the man he hated like no other. He shoved her away from him, back against the carriage. She stumbled and slid down the hard wood but he forced himself to turn away.

~~~*✱*~~~

Chapter Eighteen

✱

It was frightening in the woods, and Amelia did not want to leave Lizzy with that man, but her friend told her to run to Papa. So, run she did. She tried to keep to the path like Lizzy had instructed her but the path was hard to see. When she heard a cry from behind her, she stopped and spun around. That scary man was not coming, but neither was Lizzy. She needed Papa; Papa would help Lizzy.

Looking around for the path, everything looked the same. There were so many trees and the bushes were tall and thick. She turned and turned, but could not see which way to go. These were not like the woods at Pemmerley, where her papa took her walking and told her stories about grandmama and grandpapa and they would look for fairy rings. Pemmerley woods were filled with pretty birds and flowers. There was a stream where Papa would take her and let her take off her shoes and stockings. Then they would walk in the water together, laughing as the cold water rushed over their feet. She was never frightened there. But she always had Papa or Aunt Georgie by her side. There were never any bad men who tried to take her from Papa.

A rustling in the brush not far away made her jump, and she looked around, afraid that terrible man would burst through the trees and try to take her away again. But the sound moved away from her, growing softer and softer until she could not hear it anymore.

Alone and terrified, tears began to fall down her cheeks. She wanted Papa. She wanted Lizzy. But Lizzy needed help! Which meant Lizzy needed Papa.

Wiping her tears on her sleeves, Amelia looked around again. To one side of her, the trees did not look so dark and frightening and she could see a little bit of the blue sky through the leaves. She liked the blue sky, so she began to walk towards it.

Thundering hoofbeats just out of sight drew Amelia's attention. She knew that Papa and Mr. Bingey's pretty horses lived in the stable and the stable was near the house. Papa had taken her there many times to feed apples to the animals and to feel their soft noses.

Certain that was where Papa would be, because Papa loved his horses, Amelia began running towards the sound. Pleased that the trees seemed to be thinning, she ran faster. Catching a glimpse of the big house where she and Papa were staying with Mr. Bingey, the little girl nearly squealed with relief. She was almost to Papa and then they could help Lizzy.

Her foot caught on a fallen branch at the edge of the tree line and Amelia toppled forward, tumbling out of the woods and onto the small lawn that ran the length of the drive. Pushing herself to her knees, she brushed her scraped hands on her gown and looked about her. Her heart leapt when she saw, barreling down the drive, Papa astride Cerbus followed by Uncle Richard on his great big, brown horse—but they were riding away from her very quickly! She jumped to her feet and ran as fast as her little legs would carry her to catch them up.

"Papa! Papa!" she screamed but they two men turned their horses into the lane and out of sight. "Papa!"

"Miss Darcy?!" someone shouted behind her, but she paid them no heed. She needed to get to Papa before that awful man hurt Lizzy! Before she could run many more steps, however, she felt herself scooped up and enfolded in a crushing embrace. "Oh! Miss Darcy, you are safe!"

Amelia looked up into the face of Mrs. Lawson and knew everything would be well. Mrs. Lawson took care of her when Papa could not and the very nice nurse would be able to help.

"The man taked Lizzy!" she cried. But Mrs. Lawson seemed not to hear her. She placed Amelia on the ground and began feeling her arms and face. Several groomsmen and footmen gathered around, all worried for the child's well-being.

"Are you hurt, Miss Darcy? Did Miss Elizabeth hurt you?"

"Lizzy not hurt me!" she insisted, jamming her little fists against her hips. "Lizzy hit the bad man and told me to wun. But Lizzy need help! The man taked her!"

"Oh, dear." Mrs. Lawson's eyes widened as the little girl's meaning dawned on her. "Miss Elizabeth helped you?"

"Of course, Lizzy help me! Lizzy lufs me!" Amelia said as though any other notion was too absurd even to entertain.

Mrs. Lawson looked down the drive where Mr. Darcy and the Colonel, accompanied by several footmen, had disappeared in pursuit of the kidnappers. Unsure what was to be done, she turned to the gathered servants until Jasper, one of Papa's men, nodded. "I' be on it, ma'am," he said as he turned and ran towards the stables.

"Come, Miss Darcy. Let us get you inside and have some tea. Are you hurt, dear?"

"My hands hurt," —she held out her scraped and bloodied palms— "but Lizzy!"

"Your papa will help Miss Elizabeth, dear," Mrs. Lawson soothed, but Amelia saw the nurse frown and look worriedly down the drive again. "All will be well."

Unable to do anything more, Amelia allowed the kind nurse to pick her up and carry her back into the house. As Mrs. Lawson climbed the front steps, Amelia watched Jasper race down the drive after her papa. The nurse was right; Papa would help Lizzy and everything would be well.

In the nursery, Mrs. Lawson changed Amelia out of her torn and soiled gown. The little girl was bathed and the scrapes on her hands and knees washed and covered with a salve and bandages. Tea was brought in with a plate of her favourite biscuits and tarts. When she had eaten her fill, and perhaps a little more as Mrs. Lawson seemed disinclined to tell her 'no,' Amelia pulled Lizzy Doll from her bed and held her tight.

Darcy raced back to Netherfield, pushing aside every thought but for that of seeing his daughter. As soon as Jasper had informed him that Amelia had been found on the grounds of the estate, everything else faded into oblivion. He was filled with both relief and fear. Until he saw his daughter for himself, could be assured that she was unharmed, he would not be satisfied.

He leapt from Cerberus even before the horse had come to a stop in front of the house, throwing the reins at the groom without even giving orders for the beast's care. Taking the steps two at a time, he charged up the stairs and into the house. Bingley was in the entry, pacing the length of the hall. When he saw his friend, Bingley advanced, looking rather angry.

"Darcy! What is the meaning of this?! A groom came in saying the most ridiculous things.

That Miss Elizabeth had scarpered off with Amelia and some blackguard! Jane is beside herself with worry for her sister! Where is Miss Elizabeth? What has happened?"

"Miss Elizabeth attempted to kidnap my daughter!"

Bingley voiced angry objections, asserting the lady could never do such a thing, but Darcy had no patience for his friend's naïve sensibilities. With single-minded determination, he blew past his friend, sprinting up the stairs and leaving a thoroughly confused and displeased Bingley behind him.

He did not slow his pace until he had reached the nursery door and threw it open. Relief flooded his entire being when his eyes landed on the most beautiful sight he had ever seen. His daughter was there, whole and seemingly unharmed, safely seated upon her bed, the doll Elizabeth had given her held tightly in her arms.

"Amelia!" he cried, crossing the room in only a few quick strides. Tossing the doll aside, he took his precious child into his arms and crushed her to his chest, caring not one jot for the relieved tears that fell down his cheeks.

"Papa!"

"My dear, darling girl! You are safe!"

"Sir," said Mrs. Lawson.

"Prepare Miss Darcy's things. We are leaving immediately."

"But, sir—"

"Not now," Darcy barked, knowing he would regret his harsh tone later, but being unable to bring himself to care at that moment.

The father held his child as though his life depended upon it. He seemed unable to convince himself that all was well, that this horrific nightmare was over. Letting her go felt akin to putting her in harm's way once again. She would stay by his side always, sleep in his bed and accompany him everywhere he went. It was impractical, he knew, and could not possibly work, but to let her out of his sight seemed impossible to him at this moment.

When, at last, he managed to convince himself that she would not vanish the moment he released her, Darcy carried the little girl to his chambers and placed her upon his bed. He took her tiny, bandaged hands in his own and felt a white-hot rage course through him. Tempering his anger so as not to frighten his daughter, he took her beloved face in his hands.

"Amelia, dearest, are you well? Are you hurt?" he asked in a near frenzy, feeling her arms, legs, and head for injury as Mrs. Lawson had done. He breathed easy only when he was assured that there was no grave injury to his girl.

"Where Lizzy? Is her safe?" Amelia asked, tears beginning to well up in her large eyes.

"I do not know, my love. But it does not matter. We are going home. Would you like that? Would you like to return to London and see Aunt Georgie? Then we can go to Pemberley for Christmas."

"I miss Aunt Georgie," she whimpered, chin quivering. "But I want Lizzy,"

"I am sorry, dearest. We cannot see Miss Elizabeth again."

"Lizzy mad at me?" she cried as tears began to pour down her sweet, cherubic cheeks. "I wunned! I wunned to Papa!"

"No! No, my love. You did nothing wrong. But we must go."

"Who dat man, Papa?"

Darcy clenched his jaw, fighting for composure. This was the second time Wickham had attempted to take away someone dear to him. "He is a very bad man, sweetling. But he will not hurt you. I promise."

"I know, Papa. Lizzy not let him."

Darcy swallowed hard. He envied his daughter her sweet innocence. Amelia simply could not comprehend any scenario where the woman she had come to trust, to look upon as the mother she had never had, would ever hurt her. Darcy wished he could be so lucky.

"Stay here, dearest," Darcy commanded gently. "I must arrange for our departure."

"But, Papa—"

"Adams!" Darcy bellowed towards the dressing room as he stood but made no move to step away from his daughter.

"Papa?"

The faithful servant appeared instantly with a swift bow. "Yes, sir?"

"Papa?"

"We are leaving Hertfordshire immediately. I wish to be gone within the half hour. Send a man down now to have the carriage prepared. I will not stay any longer than absolutely necessary."

"*Papa!*"

Darcy spun around, terror spilling through his veins at Amelia's shout. When he laid relieved eyes on her, certain she was not once again in the hands of a ruthless criminal but standing on the bed, her tiny fists clenched against her hips, lips pouting in frustration and anger, and eyes narrowed at him. She looked so much like Anne on the rare occasion his late wife had found reason to scold him, he might have found the sight diverting were he not filled with so many terrible emotions. His daughter pointed one admonishing finger at him.

"You stop and listen to me. Wight. Now!" On the last word, Amelia stomped her little foot on the counterpane. "Lizzy need help!"

"Sir," Mrs. Lawson implored from the doorway between his chambers and Amelia's nursery. "I beg your pardon, Mr. Darcy, but it seems I was mistaken in my impressions. Miss Darcy said that a man approached them in the gardens and demanded Miss Elizabeth give over the child but the young lady refused. I am so sorry, sir."

Darcy felt as though the very earth had fallen out from under him as Elizabeth's demeanor by the carriage, her confusion at his angry questions took on a whole new meaning. She had told him Amelia ran away; he had taken that to be a confession of her guilt, an admission that their scheme had been unsuccessful. Yet, now it was so

316

horrifyingly clear; Amelia had not gotten away, Elizabeth had facilitated her escape, had put herself in harm's way to protect his child. An icy chill spread throughout his chest as his breath seemed trapped within his lungs.

"Lizzy hitted the man," Amelia declared proudly, "and told me to wun. She told me to wun and find Papa so I wunned away!" Her grin faded and she reached for her father's hand. "Papa, where Lizzy? Is Lizzy safe? Did the bad man hurt her?"

A vision of Elizabeth's bruised cheek and pale features burst upon his mind's eye. As if he had known it was there all along but had refused to acknowledge it, he looked down at the dried blood on his hands. The signs he had so resolutely disregarded struck him with the force of a bolt of lightning. The tremor in her voice, her uncharacteristic weakness, her typically bright, sparkling eyes, unfocused and glazed over. The gunshot that sounded as the carriage came to a stop. Elizabeth *was* hurt. The woman he loved had been injured and he had done nothing. No, he had done worse than nothing. He had left her.

"Mrs. Lawson," he addressed the nurse gravely, "do not leave Amelia. You are not to let her out of your sight until I return. Do you understand me?"

Once assured of her acquiescence, he turned and hurried from the room, back down the stairs and out the front door. He was halfway to the stables to order his horse once more when the sound of hoofbeats caught his attention. Turning, he recognised Richard barreling up the drive.

The Colonel leapt from his horse and addressed the groom that had come to meet Darcy. It did not escape Darcy's notice that his cousin did not meet his eye. "Is there a surgeon in Meryton?"

"No, sir. But there be one in Timmor, the next town over."

"Send for him immediately. And the local apothecary in the meantime."

"Aye, sir."

"Richard?"

"She was shot, Darcy," was the blunt reply. The fear he had been so desperately trying to keep at bay coursed through him and he only vaguely registered his cousin's next words. "There's more. Lady Catherine is dead."

"Where is Elizabeth?" asked Darcy. He would not rejoice in the death of his irascible aunt, but neither could he muster much of any other emotion.

As if to answer his question, the de Bourgh carriage pulled onto Netherfield's drive. As soon as it reached the two gentlemen, Darcy ripped open the carriage door and jumped inside. There, lying unconscious across the bench, was his Elizabeth, paler than ever and her breaths coming in shallow, raspy gasps. He took her into his arms and brushed a loose curl away from her blanched brow.

"I am sorry, Elizabeth," he gasped. "Dear God, I am so sorry!"

~~~*✳*~~~
Chapter Nineteen
₊

"Answer me, maggot," Richard demanded as he kicked Wickham hard in the ribs. For two days, the criminal had been locked in Bingley's cellar seeing no one but the footman who brought him bread and water and the maid who emptied his chamber pot. Richard had wanted him to stew in his predicament. Both men knew that it had been only Darcy's concerns for his sister's reputation which had prevented the Colonel from killing their childhood friend this past summer when he had attempted to make off with their young ward to Scotland.

The prisoner coughed then looked towards the other two men in the cellar, seeking some ally. Bingley was horribly pale and looked as if he might cast up his accounts at any moment but Mr. Bennet's face was as hard as stone. There would be no help from either of these men. Bingley would be too afraid to gainsay the Colonel, and he had kidnapped and shot, albeit accidentally, the other man's daughter.

"I can do this all day, Wickham. In fact, I have been looking forward to meeting you again for some time. So, by all means, hold your tongue." He stepped back, preparing to inflict another blow.

"I had no intentions to harm either girl," he cried, his arms held up defensively. Even still, as if he simply could not help it, a smirk traced across his lips. "I was only sent to retrieve Darcy's daughter. The other morsel was simply too good an opportunity to pass up." Mr. Bennet growled at this and Wickham flinched.

"So, my aunt hired you to kidnap Darcy's daughter," Richard inferred. "And what was my aunt's plan with the girl?"

Wickham flashed a rather self-satisfied grin up at his gaoler but feigned innocence nonetheless.

"How could I be expected to know what that old crone intended?"

"You know, you are awfully smug for a man who has just murdered the sister of an earl." Still, Wickham said nothing, only inspected his filthy fingernails as if he were not entirely at the mercy of the very angry man standing above him. "Very well, you need not tell me. Let us see if I can guess. My aunt was not a terribly imaginative woman.

"Lady Catherine believed that if she had my goddaughter, Darcy would be at her mercy and agree to marry the lady of her choosing. How have I done?" Wickham snarled but said nothing. "Good Lord." Richard shook his head. "You would risk so much for a scheme which had no hope of succeeding?"

A look of pure hatred fell over Wickham's once handsome face. "I told Darcy when he denied me what was rightfully mine, I would have my revenge and I mean to take it."

"What was rightfully yours? You mean what my uncle suggested be given you under conditions which you failed to meet yet Darcy paid you for anyway? Was it not enough what you did to Georgiana? No, you would also seek to harm his daughter?" A blank look overtook the Colonel's features as a thought had just occurred to him.

"Georgiana. Lady Catherine was behind your attempt to make off with my young cousin last summer? Ha! Oh, I am loath to speak ill of the dead but my aunt was not as clever as she ever imagined herself to be. So, you were to deliver Georgiana to Rosings for, what? A few hundred pounds, I would wager?" Richard confirmed his guess by Wickham's curled lip and twitching nose. The man had the most obvious tells. It was why he never had much luck at the card tables. "But Georgiana's thirty-thousand-pound dowry was far more attractive and so you convinced her to elope with you. Did her ladyship know you meant to betray her? I can imagine not. When Darcy spoilt your plans, you would be in no rush to cut off the possibility of further funds. And, sure enough, Lady Catherine did seek out your services once again.

"But there you were also foiled. You did not count on Miss Elizabeth's impressive courage. And when she gave herself as sacrifice to help little Miss Darcy escape, you made another attempt at your old tricks. You would demand ransom for Darcy's lady, and hang the old bat. I think you ought to reconsider your chosen career, Wickham. You seem to have little talent in the field of abduction. I mean, you will not have any time to act upon any great epiphanies, but still."

"While I do enjoy taking Darcy's money, it matters not to me that I was not successful. I have still won. Even if the lady lives, I have ensured Darcy will never look at the strumpet again."

Mr. Bennet made to lunge at the criminal at his feet but the Colonel held him back while Wickham laughed. "If you ever speak of my daughter in such a way again it will be the very last thing you do, sir."

"Explain yourself, Wickham," Richard demanded.

The captive sat up straighter and pulled at his coat sleeves as though he were preparing for a night out amongst the ton. "If I am not mistaken, and I do not believe I am, my old friend has grown quite fond of the delectable Miss. Elizabeth. Bennet. I have seen them together myself and cannot say I have ever seen the fastidious Mr. Fitzwilliam Darcy of Pemberley so utterly besotted. In fact, rumour has reached my ears that the entire neighbourhood has been on pins and needles awaiting the announcement of their engagement. An announcement which I should very much doubt will ever be made. I heard him myself. He believes his dear Miss Eliza was in collusion with me to take his daughter. He never wants to see her again.

"Now, if it were only a matter of her broken heart and dashed hopes, 'twould hardly be worth all the fuss. But you and I both know, Colonel," – Wickham raised his hand to his brow in mock salute— "that Darcy would never give his heart away lightly. He loves the chit, does he not? The pathetic, spoilt bastard must be in pure agony knowing the woman he had finally deemed worthy to bestow his exalted name upon never loved him at all. Only used him to help me seek my sweet revenge."

"You are a liar!" Mr. Bennet growled. "Elizabeth loves him!"

Wickham laughed again. "Oh, I am sure she does. But this is not about her. 'Tis about him. 'Tis about the pain and agony he is now suffering believing himself to have been used so ill by the woman he loves."

"Wickham, you are a fool," Richard scoffed. "Once I inform him that Miss Elizabeth had nothing to do with your attempt to take Amelia, all will be well. You will have gained nothing."

"Will it? Will *all* be well? Will the excessively proud, arrogant prig come crawling back on his hands and knees to beg his love's forgiveness? You know as well as I, *Fitzy*, Darcy will never admit he was wrong. It has ever been his greatest failing. He is doomed to a life of misery and loneliness, pining for a woman he will never allow himself to have. And the best part is," –Wickham sat up straighter, looking very much like an excited child who had been informed that Christmas had come early— "none of this need have come to pass if he had not denied me that which ought to have been mine. I am simply returning the favour and I have never been more delighted."

"I only hope your delight will last, Wickham," a calm, deep voice sounded from the doorway, "for it shall be your last at my expense."

"Darcy?!" Wickham scrambled to press himself against the wall, all his previous bravado fleeing. "Wha-what are you doing here?"

"What am I doing at my good friend's estate where I have been in residence for near two months? I had at one time believed you to be clever, Wickham."

"You left. Fitzwilliam told me you had scampered back to London with your brat." His wide eyes flickered between the two men.

"Did I say that?" Richard scratched his head in mock confusion. "Oh, yes. I recall now. I lied. My apologies."

Darcy peered down into the face of the man who had been, at one time, his dearest friend. The son of his father's most trusted steward, they had played together as children, fished in Pemberley's streams, swam in the lake, and learnt to ride side by side. For many years, Darcy had looked upon George Wickham as something very near a brother, even wished it to be true at one time. Gazing now upon the man he barely recognised, Darcy thought back to when everything had begun to change.

Having ever been fond of the charming young boy, Darcy's father had seen fit to bestow up his godson a gelding from among Pemberley's stables for his tenth birthday. It was a handsome grey, one that George Darcy had ridden for several years. Though aged, he was spirited, strong, and reliable. Wickham had been enamoured of the beast. He visited the stables every day, even if he had not the time to ride, just to gaze upon his horse. No boy could be better pleased with his animal.

Until a few months on, when Darcy had turned twelve and been similarly gifted with a young, sleek black stallion and a shiny new saddle. From that day, Wickham was changed. Though careful to guard his behaviour around their fathers and the senior staff, he began enacting small indiscretions; breaking trinkets in the house, stealing biscuits from Pemberley's kitchens, or tearing up flowers in Lady Anne's gardens. Darcy was a frequent target; pushing the young heir into the lake wearing his new coat, splattering his fine, white breeches with mud just before company was expected, or kicking Darcy's favourite puppy when no one was about.

As the infractions became more grievous in nature, it became clear to those willing to see that the young Wickham was being poisoned by jealousy. Every instance which served to highlight the difference in station between the future master of Pemberley and the steward's son deepened his resentment. Frequently, he would lash out at his friend, taunting Darcy with cruel words against his reserved nature and insecurities. Wickham's favourite ploy was claiming the greater share of the elder Darcy's affections.

Though Darcy loathed to admit as much, it had been an effective weapon. Rather than destroy him, however, it had pressed the young gentleman to work hard to prove himself worthy of his father's name and, one day, his place as master. As he grew older, Darcy came to see the truth of the matter. Wickham's words were empty. His father was never as gregarious or demonstrative in his affections with Darcy as he was with his godson, but the late Mr. Darcy had expressed his love for his son by giving him the necessary lessons and tools to become the best master and best man he could be. The attentions to Wickham were not but an old man's delight in an entertaining youth. What he bestowed upon his son was respect and pride in the man he was becoming. To Darcy, it was worth everything.

Darcy knew his father had believed himself to be doing the boy a favour; but in truth, it had been inadvertently cruel. With every taste of the life to which he did not belong, Wickham grew to expect ever greater advantages until he was deluded enough to believe himself entitled to that which he had no claim over and even less inclination to work for. The result was the man before him who was but a shell enclosed around a blackened heart.

Darcy stepped forward and crouched down before his nemesis, elbows resting on his knees, taking a wicked sense of satisfaction as Wickham recoiled further away.

"There is one thing which you have ever failed to comprehend, George. Happiness does not come from wealth or possessions."

"Says the man," Wickham spat bitterly, "with an endless supply of both."

With a shake of his head, Darcy sighed. "And neither have ever brought me any form of joy. Satisfaction and pride in my accomplishments and family name, indeed. But not happiness. No, true, lasting happiness comes from within. From loving and being loved."

A moment of silence followed this statement wherein four of the gentlemen exchanged fond looks and knowing nods. It was shattered when Wickham broke into maniacal, raucous laughter.

"What a load of mawkish bollocks!" he cried before turning his amused smile into an angry sneer. "Happiness is money, power, and respect. All of which you have ever denied me! But I have had my revenge. The chit you rejected? You cannot possibly have her now after what you have accused her of. Even if I believed that the high and mighty Darcy I know would ever lower himself so much as to crawl back to her and beg her forgiveness, it would matter not. Why would she forgive you after the way you treated her? I win, Darcy!"

Standing so he was towering over the prisoner, several emotions danced across Darcy's face. Anger, sadness, guilt, and despair battled for greater prominence until he breathed deeply, squared his shoulders and a look of determined longanimity settled on his features.

"You are correct, Wickham," he conceded with a resigned nod. "The Darcy you knew was far too proud ever to admit fault. My resentment was implacable. But thankfully, I am no longer that man. You see, a miraculous thing occurs when a man becomes a father. He learns patience, compassion, and just how very much he does not know." Darcy and Mr. Bennet exchanged knowing looks. "To my shame, I have wronged Elizabeth. But I *will* throw myself at her feet and beg her mercy. She has forgiven me my arrogance once before, I can only hope she will do so again. If by chance she does not, I give you leave to triumph as much as you choose for as long as you have left on this earth, Wickham. It will have no effect on me."

With a nod of grave finality, Darcy turned to leave.

"Darcy!" Wickham shouted, his voice heavy with panic. "Wait, Darcy! 'As long as I have left?' What do you mean? Darcy?! You cannot mean to let me hang! Think of your father, Darcy! He would not want me to die! You would dare dishonour his memory in such a manner? You coward!"

At the door, Darcy stopped and turned back to look on his childhood friend one last time. "I once believed as you do. That to expose the reprehensible character of a man my father so highly valued would be a stain on his good name. I have come to see, at last, that it is not my actions which dishonour his memory, Wickham, but yours. Both our fathers would be utterly ashamed of the man you have become. Goodbye, George."

Impervious to Wickham's shouts, Darcy left the cellar. When the echo of his footsteps on the stairs had faded away, Wickham turned wide, terrified eyes on his remaining gaolers. "Fitzwilliam, you must reason with him."

"Ha!" Richard barked. "The only reason you are alive today after your actions this past summer is because of Darcy's clemency. Had I my way, you would have been stuck through at dawn months ago."

"You cannot do this! The girl is fine!" Richard said nothing; only folded his arms menacingly across his chest. "I will leave the country! If Darcy will give me ten thousand pounds, I will sail to America and you and Darcy will never see me again! He owes me at least that much."

"Owes you? For what? Paying your debts these last ten years, breaking his sister's heart, or for trying to kidnap his daughter and lady? Let us not forget the small matter of murdering a lady of the peer!"

Seeing the Colonel would have no sympathy for him, Wickham changed tactics. He narrowed his eyes and raised his chin in defiance, though it could not disguise the fear in his eyes. "He will never do it. Darcy has never been able to raise a fist against me. He has ever been soft and obliging, paying off my creditors and cleaning up my messes. He will do so again. He would not lift a finger to punish me after I nearly made off with dear Georgiana. He hated Lady Catherine. I have done the man a favour! Mark my words." The reprobate clasped his hands together behind his head and leaned back triumphantly against the wall. "In a day or two, Darcy will cave and I will walk free as a bird."

A muscle worked in Richard's jaw and a self-satisfied grin stretched across Wickham's face once more. Truth be told, this was a genuine concern of Richard's. After Wickham had convinced Darcy's sister to elope last summer and very nearly succeeded in his plans to obtain her dowry, Richard was ready to kill the bastard. He had been furious with his cousin's misguided sense of honour towards Uncle Darcy's misplaced fondness for his godson. There lived the smallest shadow of worry that Darcy would, with time to consider, once again send Wickham off with naught but a harsh threat. He would be damned if he would admit as much to Wickham, however. Instead, Richard aimed a lightning quick kick to his nemesis's ribcage, smiling at the satisfying crunch and pained groans that followed.

"Gentlemen." Richard turned back to his companions. "I think we are through here. Unless either of you have any further questions?"

An ashen Bingley shook his head quickly, looking vastly relieved that the interview was over. Mr. Bennet continued to glare at Wickham. "No, Colonel. I will only say that this worthless piece of flesh is fortunate my Lizzy lives. Had she not, he would not now be alive to fret over the noose." Without another word, the angry father turned and left the cellar.

Richard slapped Bingley on the back and steered him from the room. "Come, Bingley. I shall impose on you for a short time further, if I may. I think a few more days in the dark to give our friend time to think about what he has done are in order. Nighty-night, Wicky," he threw over his shoulder just before he kicked over the single candle which had been provided for Wickham's light and stomped out its flame.

"Now, Bingley. Are you well? Darcy had some rather complimentary things to say about your coming into your own and such. Yet you look as though you did not enjoy that?"

"I daresay, Colonel, standing up to my sister, or even Darcy, is a far cry from beating a criminal confession out of a man."

The Colonel's laugh echoed through room as the door was slammed shut and bolted.

~~~***~~~

Chapter Twenty

***

Voices—some Elizabeth recognised, some she did not—drifted in and out of her consciousness. She tried to open her eyes but they felt weighed down as if by boulders. She knew not where she was nor for how long she had been there. The extent of her injuries was a mystery; though, that they existed was a certainty. She hurt all over. From her throbbing ankle to the sharp, stabbing pain in her shoulder. Her head ached constantly. But the greatest pain was the gaping hole in her chest where her heart had once resided.

Sleep. Sleep was her greatest ally. Whether her mind sought to protect her or her body was simply too exhausted from all she had been through, her sleep was mercifully dreamless and she did not relive those terrible events over and over as she did when she hovered nearer wakefulness. She did not feel the sharp stab of the pistol pressed into her side or the stinging pain of the back of that vicious man's hand across her face when she slept. The terror she felt when he had made to chase Amelia faded into oblivion. The cold, dead eyes of the woman who had sent him to steal the precious girl away did not stare at her in the darkness.

Most comforting of all, Mr. Darcy's painful accusations did not echo about in her head, his eyes, filled with hatred, boring into her soul.

Unfortunately, that blissful state could not continue on in perpetuity. She began to wake more fully and caught snippets of the whispered conversations around her. She was at Netherfield, she gathered, and Jane and Papa were with her. Once, she heard Mama wailing of her daughter's impending doom.

At some point, she felt pressure and movement about her shoulder and heard a man's voice speaking of her injuries, though she could not focus on his words long enough to determine the extent. More than once, she thought she heard a deep, familiar voice but it must have been her delusional mind playing cruel tricks. Darcy would certainly not be here, not after what he had accused her of.

She felt, rather than heard, a groan slip through her lips.

"Lizzy?" Jane's worried voice sounded far away.

"Ja-Jane?" Her thoughts raced as she tried to make sense of what had happened. Opening her eyes proved to be a more arduous task than she had ever recalled and she fought to lift them even a crack. When she at last managed the feat, blinding light forced them shut again.

"Close the drapes," she heard Jane order.

It helped a little and she was at last able to open her eyes and look about her. Looking past her pale, worried looking sister who was perched at the edge of her bed, she noted the presence of others. Her father sat in a chair beside the bed, his eyes bloodshot and looking older than she had ever seen him, while Bingley hung back in the doorway, watching anxiously.

A jumble of question burst upon her mind and the confusion very nearly pushed her back into sleep. Reaching out with her tongue, she licked her parched lips, only to realise her mouth was too dry to have any effect. As if reading her thoughts, Jane reached over to a side table and poured a glass of water from the pitcher sat thereupon. Carefully, she held the cup to her sister's lips and Elizabeth sipped gratefully.

"Amelia...safe?" Elizabeth asked when her thirst had abated.

"Yes. Miss Darcy is well," answered Jane and Elizabeth sighed her relief. "But you, dearest, were shot. And in the confusion, you were not attended to as...as quickly as you ought to have been. You lost a good deal of blood and with your other injuries, you have been unconscious for nearly three days."

Looking down carefully, she saw that her right arm was resting in a sling across her middle, inhibiting her ability to move it. From her shoulder emanated a dull, throbbing ache.

"Other...injuries?" she asked, but speaking was proving to be excessively tiring. Thankfully, Jane possessed an endless supply of patience.

"Yes, dear. There is a terrible bruise on the left side of your face but the doctor says there is no damage to your eye."

"Hit...hit me."

"He hit you?" Jane asked, a trembling hand held to her lips. Elizabeth could only nod once, which was painful enough. She heard a sound resembling a growl to her left and shifted her gaze to see her father looking as severe as she had ever seen him. His teeth were gritted in an angry grimace and his fists clenched on the arms of the chair. She slowly reached out her unimpeded hand to him. He took it in his own, bending down to place a kiss on her knuckles.

"What else? My...my ankle...hurts."

"Yes. It is broken, dearest. Mr. Graham has set the bone but you will have to curtail those walks you love so dearly for a time," Jane answered with a feeble attempt at levity.

Elizabeth attempted to smile but she could not know how successful she was. Fatigue was quickly claiming her once again. Mr. Graham was not a name familiar to her; or was it and she was simply too tired to recall?

When next she woke, it was necessary for her family to explain her injuries once again and reassure her of Amelia's wellbeing. She did not ask after Mr. Darcy and seemed to be overcome by a fit of coughs whenever anyone mentioned him.

Unwilling to do anything to hamper her recovery, none of her family pressed the issue.

Unable to remain entirely ignorant, Elizabeth asked after the identity of her would-be abductor. Though her father did not know the whole of the history, he had learnt enough from Darcy and Colonel Fitzwilliam to satisfy her. George Wickham, she was told, had been raised at Pemberley, the son of the late master's steward. The senior Mr. Darcy had held the elder Mr. Wickham in high esteem and had taken particular notice of the son. This, it seemed, was enough to fill the young man with thoughts of grandiose entitlement.

Wickham leant heavily on the Darcy name to garner lines of credit with merchants all across the country from Derbyshire to Kent. He used his good looks and charming manners to court favour with the higher classes and woo young ladies of all stations; often to their ruin.

When the elder Mr. Darcy died, he had suggested in his will that a valuable living within his gift be offered to his godson should he choose to take orders. Apparently having expected a vast deal more, Wickham refused and demanded a substantial remuneration instead. Only two years later, when the incumbent of the living died and Wickham's funds dried up, he returned to

Pemberley to claim the living but was denied. Filled with a burning hatred fueled by soul-withering envy, he vowed to seek revenge on Darcy for a lifetime of imagined slights.

When Mr. Bennet had finished telling all he knew, Elizabeth nodded her satisfaction and looked away. She did not know what to make of all that had occurred. She had read novels where damsels were kidnapped by ruthless criminals and debauched uncles; never had she imagined any such thing would happen in sleepy old Meryton, and certainly never to herself. Unable to find the words to match her feelings, she expressed a desire to sleep and allowed Jane to tuck her tightly into the bedclothes.

"We are so pleased you are well, Lizzy. I do not know what I would have done if..." Jane bit her lips together and wiped a tear from her cheek. "Well, there is no use canvassing that. You *are* well, and that is all that matters."

"Thank you, Jane," Elizabeth whispered. "You always take such good care of me."

"'Tis the least I can do after the care you took of me when I was ill. And for being the very best sister anyone could ask for."

"I love you, Jane."

"I love you, Lizzy." Jane pressed a soft kiss to her sister's brow and quietly slipped from the room.

Her gaze drifted to the open window as she processed all her father had said. Everything that had happened to her roiled around inside Elizabeth's brain until her fear and grief gave way to anger. Anger at Wickham and Lady Catherine for daring to put Amelia in harm's way. For the fear and anguish they had caused her family to suffer.

She was angry with herself, as well. If she had not suggested taking Amelia into the garden without the gentlemen, if she had only been a little patient and joined the gentlemen in returning to the house, Wickham could not have taken them. But Elizabeth had selfishly relished the idea of spending that time with the precious little girl she had hoped to call her daughter and it had very nearly cost too great a price.

And she was angry at Darcy. While she could accept the blame that was her due, she was not guilty of the crimes of which he had accused her. It had been his very own aunt who had sent a deranged criminal to steal away his daughter, yet Darcy had accused Elizabeth; without question, without hesitation. Without even affording her the opportunity to defend herself.

After all the time spent in one another's company, had she not demonstrated how dearly she cared for both father and daughter? That he could believe, even for a moment, that she would harm even one hair upon that dear child's head was like a dagger to her heart. Every time she remembered the look on his face as he held her against the carriage and demanded his daughter from her, when she heard the hateful words he had flung at her in his fury echo in her mind, the blade twisted deeper.

Then, he left. Left her with that man, bleeding in the road, as if she had never meant anything to him at all. She wondered now if she ever had. Not long ago she had felt certain that he loved her, but could he? Could he truly love her and yet think her capable of such heinous actions? She could certainly not imagine accusing someone she loved of such vile acts.

"Ahem." Looking towards the sound, Elizabeth's eyes landed upon her father, standing at the corner of the bed, arms crossed, studying her with a curious expression.

"Papa? I thought everyone had gone."

"Oh, yes. You do need your rest," he said but made no move to leave the room. Elizabeth knew her father well enough to be able to see there was something he wished to say, but it would likely be unpleasant.

"What is it, Papa?"

Mr. Bennet hesitated only a moment before he said, "Mr. Darcy is here and very desirous of speaking with you. Would you like to see him?"

Hurt warred with her heart. Yes, she wanted to see him, to see him looking upon her with those loving eyes. She wanted the reassurance of his nearness, to smell him and hear him promise he would never leave her again.

But the things he had accused her of would not quiet in her head. The look in his eyes when he had gripped her firmly by the arms and demanded she tell him where his daughter was, the threats he had spat at her she feared would forever be branded on her heart.

"No. No, I do not wish to see him, Papa."

Mr. Bennet sighed and she knew he was disappointed with her answer, but it was the only one she could give. "You ought to hear him out, my dear, before you cast him off." He held up a staying hand when she opened her mouth to argue. "I am not saying that you must forgive him. That is entirely up to you. But he does owe you an apology and a great deal of thanks. Both, I know, he is eager to deliver. But, more than that, Elizabeth, he is a good man."

"How can you defend him, Papa? After what he accused me of?!" Her throat was beginning to tighten and burn with building emotion. "It is the worst sort of insult!"

Mr. Bennet chuckled and his daughter turned an icy glare on him. "I seem to recall hearing some tale of your having insulted not only Mr. Darcy but young Miss Darcy, as well, once upon a time."

"Papa! It is hardly the same thing!"

"It is true that Darcy's recent mistakes are orders of magnitude greater, but you must consider that so were the risks. In a state of heightened emotion, you insulted a man and his daughter whom you had never met. The worst which could have come of that evening was that you learnt to despise one another and suffered through a good deal of discomfort and mortification until he left the neighbourhood. In contrast, under the influence of fear of the most acute kind, Mr. Darcy was faced with the prospect of losing his only daughter at the hand of a man who holds a history of abusing his name and using those in whom Darcy had placed his trust to enact terrible threats against him. I can defend him, my love, because I know the love of a father. I, too, very nearly lost a most beloved daughter to that man that day. Tell me, my dear girl, were Amelia your daughter, what might you have done? Think on it, my dear."

Mr. Bennet then left the room but she heard the murmur of his voice through the closed door, though she could not make out the words, and the deep voice which responded. She could not be certain as the solid oak obscured much of the sound, but she imagined his voice to hold a deep disappointment and sorrow. It touched her heart and she very nearly called out for him to enter. The words were on the tip of her tongue before she stopped herself. She could not so easily set aside what he had done, not matter how dearly she wished to.

Taking her father's advice, Elizabeth thought on little else but Darcy, the accusations he had lain at her feet, and the words her father had spoken for the next several days. Her feelings vacillated wildly from one moment to the next. When she thought of the days they had spent together, walking in the gardens at either Longbourn or Netherfield, swinging a giggling Amelia between them, sitting in the parlour like a perfect little family, reading to the sweet little girl when Elizabeth had cared for Jane, or the kiss he had given her behind the roses, her heart nearly overflowed with love and compassion for Darcy. In those moments, she felt there was nothing she could not forgive.

But when she remembered what she had been through and how he had so callously thrown her aside, thinking she could ever do anything to bring any harm upon his daughter whom she loved so very dearly, her heart broke anew. Beyond her anger, she was deeply saddened that she had bestowed her heart upon one who could think her capable of heinous actions. Then she would be angered again when she realised how dearly she loved him still. She wished she could cast him away as easily as he had her.

She tried not to give too much credence to her father's wisdom, yet her rationality could not but acknowledge that he was correct. Elizabeth had not a parent's heart. As dearly as she loved Amelia, she could not know what Darcy had felt upon being told his daughter had been taken. Had she a child, would she have behaved just as he had if told Darcy had been the cause? She still could not think so, but she also could not say for certain. Until she knew the love of a parent, she would likely never know the answer.

Her mind drifted back to the night she had first met Darcy, to the tale Mr. Bingley had shared with her and Jane. A gasp escaped her lips as she thought on all Darcy had lost and the realisation that much of it had been at the hands of, or at the very least in connection with, either this George Wickham or his mother's sister, Lady Catherine de Bourgh. Her heart softened slightly to think of how he must have felt to learn that these two people who had already wreaked so much havoc in his life had sought to do so again; and had involved the woman he had given his heart to.

By no means prepared to absolve the gentleman—but neither set against it—Elizabeth at least felt equal to speaking with him. Thus resolved, she reached for the bell kept by her bed and rang for the maid three days after the discussion with her father. The wait, short though it was, felt interminable. Her hands trembled, her heart raced, and her stomach roiled in such a way, it felt as though her breakfast might very well escape her. She was not confident she would not simply fall into his arms the moment Mr. Darcy entered the room. Her love for the man battled greatly with her anger at him. Truly, she did not think she would know what she would do until she laid eyes on him.

At long last, the maid who had been attending Elizabeth entered with a curtsey. "Can I help ye, Miss?"

Forcing a calm into her voice she did not feel, Elizabeth made her request. "Yes, Molly.

Would you ask Mr. Darcy if I might have a word, please?"

"Mr. Darcy, Miss?" The young maid's eyebrows furled and she looked as though Elizabeth had spoken in an heretofore untranslated language.

"Yes. It is quite alright, Molly. You will remain in the room while we speak."

"Oh, no, Miss." The maid shifted uneasily on her feet. "'Tis no' tha'. 'Tis on'y tha', well, Mr. Darcy is no longer in residence."

Elizabeth looked up sharply from where she had been nervously twisting the bedclothes in her hands. "What?"

"Aye. He an' the little Miss Darcy lef' fer London some three days ago."

Elizabeth could not quite account for the sinking feeling in her chest. Moments ago, she was not even certain she wished to see him; now that she could not, she felt the loss acutely. *What else did you expect?* she chastised herself. *Why would he remain when you made it clear you did not welcome him?*

"Please, um…" What did she want? She scarcely knew. Fighting back tears, Elizabeth requested her father be summoned. He, at least, would come. Both Mr. Bennet and Jane had taken rooms at Netherfield to be near Elizabeth as she recovered.

But Mr. Bennet had little else to add to what the maid had already told her. Mr. Darcy left Netherfield the very day she had refused to see him and had taken Amelia with him, which was not surprising; only crushingly disappointing. Her father at least gave her some little hope.

"There is a good deal to be done in regards his estate in Kent now that his aunt has died." The explosive sound of gunfire echoed in Elizabeth's head at these words and the vision of the dead woman burst upon her memory. She squeezed her eyes shut as her breaths came in shallow gasps. Mr. Bennet, gazing absentmindedly around the room as he spoke, was ignorant of his daughter's discomfort, for which she was glad. She had not yet been made to give a full recounting of all that had occurred and was given to understand she would not be required to give testimony to the magistrate as the perpetrator had confessed all.

"But," Mr. Bennet continued on, a merry twinkle in his eye, "I have every confidence he will return in due time. If I have taken the man's measure accurately, and I think I have, he shall not give up on you so easily, my dear."

~~~*✲*~~~

<u>Chapter Twenty-One</u>
✳*✳

Darcy's mind wandered back to the last time he had travelled this road. Though it felt a lifetime ago, it had only been a few short weeks and the carriage had been carrying him the other direction. Reluctant to leave London at the time, he had felt as though he were abandoning his dear sister in her darkest hour. He had believed then that leaving Georgiana, heartbroken and vulnerable, was the most difficult task he would ever undertake.

Oh, how unbelievably naïve he had been!

Georgiana was young girl of sixteen in the throes of her first heartache; likely there would be more. In London, she had their kindly, beloved aunt to confide in and lean upon. She was humiliated and mistrustful of her own judgement, but she was whole and healthy. Above all, she did not hate him.

Darcy had not blamed *her* for the situation she had found herself in. In fact, Darcy had taken great strides to assure his sister that she was not to be held responsible for having been taken in by a depraved scoundrel; though, by all accounts she was far more culpable than he was willing to admit aloud for having thrown out all she knew about proper behaviour and decency. Given an excellent education and sound principles, Georgiana knew very well that to elope was wrong. She had allowed herself to become caught up in the flattering attentions of a charming snake and led by the misplaced encouragement of the corrupt companion who had been hired to guide her. Still, Georgiana had known her actions were foolish. She had demonstrated as much when she instantly confessed the whole of the plan to her brother when Darcy had joined her unexpectedly in Ramsgate.

What he had felt then paled in comparison to his current condition; he could not recall ever feeling as miserable as he did at this moment, returning to London. If he could go back to that last journey when his greatest worry was his young sister's first clash with disappointed hopes, he might happily give up his entire fortune.

The woman he loved despised him, and quite rightly so. She had very nearly given her life to protect his child, a victim of the very same people who had preyed upon Georgiana, and he had lain the blame at her feet. Were this the worst of his crimes, still he would feel the vilest blackguard imaginable. But, no. He had left her laying in the road, injured and bleeding after callously throwing his accusations in her face, refusing to hear her defense. Were he even of a mind to seek it, he could not find the slightest shred of justification to condemn her for not being willing to hear him out. He had not afforded her the same courtesy, after all.

Mr. Bennet's advice before Darcy had left Netherfield drifted across his mind. His beloved's father had encouraged him to leave, quite certain Elizabeth needed only time. If he remained, she would feel pressured and put upon, and there was no surer way to strengthen his most stubborn daughter's obstinacy, Mr. Bennet had assured him. But if he were to leave and she could be made to feel his absence, she would certainly come round soon. Darcy wished he could find it within himself to be so optimistic.

Regardless, he left. There was much to see to in the wake of all that had happened. Wickham was turned over to the magistrate to be sent to Newgate prison to await his fate and Richard had taken on the task of seeing Lady Catherine's body delivered to his father in London for burial. The lady had desecrated Rosings enough; Darcy would not see her buried there. Perhaps it was juvenile, but he felt as though this could be an act of retribution for all the vile woman had put her family through.

But he would need to see to the estate itself. Had he done so long ago, he castigated himself, none of this might have happened. Had he only stood up to Lady Catherine when he married Anne and removed her mother from Rosings as he had desired, she would have known he was not a man to be trifled with. But Anne had feared what her mother might do if removed from her home. Would she come to Pemberley and continue to reign over her daughter with tyranny and force? Though Darcy would never have allowed any such thing, Anne would not rest easy until she had his word that he would leave Lady Catherine be. At Rosings, his late wife had contended, her ladyship was occupied with her own importance and would leave them to live their lives at Pemberley. Darcy could not agree, but had relented.

After the death of his wife, Darcy had been much occupied with the raising of his infant daughter, young sister, and the running Pemberley. Before he was even aware of it, several years had passed and he had still taken no steps towards dealing with his heinous aunt. A steward had been hired to manage Rosings, a man in whom Darcy believed, until recently, he could trust. It was exceedingly uncharacteristic of him to give in to such indolence; he had never avoided onerous tasks before.

To Rosings, he would now go. He would see to it that every token of Lady Catherine's mark upon the place was removed, the house restaffed and redecorated, and Mr. Malvern released from his position. A new steward would be found and the estate let or sold, he cared not.

Looking around the carriage at his companions, a variance of emotions warred for dominance in his heart. Beside him sat Amelia, quiet and subdued. She had been thus since he had told her that Elizabeth had been hurt and they must leave to give her time to recover. He could not bring himself to confess to his darling child that they might never again see the woman they both loved so dearly because of his foolish mistakes. The sight of his daughter invoked both extreme relief and the deepest despair. She was safe and unharmed, but he could not forget at what cost.

On Amelia's other side was her nurse, Mrs. Lawson. Towards that woman he fought valiantly not to harbour any ill will. She could not be blamed, not truly. She had only acted upon that which she believed she had seen and in the best interest of her charge. In fact, had she not witnessed the scene outside her window, there was no telling how much time might have been lost. Wickham might very well have succeeded in his scheme. Such reasoning did not stop Darcy from wishing she had exercised perhaps a little more prudence. No, he could not blame her in the least. Had he not also failed to implement sound judicial reasoning and leapt straight to believing the very worst of the woman he professed to love?

Mrs. Lawson had apologised profusely and even offered to tender her resignation in light of events, which Darcy had immediately refused; though it garnered a certain amount of pain to look upon the nurse and recall how her frantic alarm had sent him charging blindly after Amelia. Elizabeth, he knew, had exonerated the woman entirely and he must, as well.

It was towards the final member of the party which Darcy experienced the most unexpected sentiment. In all the years that he had been friends with Charles Bingley, never had he ever fostered any form of jealousy towards the man. He had, on occasion, vaguely wished he possessed his friend's easy manners and ability to charm those around him, but he had never held such against him. It had been the younger man who had always looked upon the elder with something akin to awe. Bingley had always followed Darcy's every lead, taken his advice as near gospel, and ever placed the man upon a pedestal.

Yet, now, as they rambled towards Town, Bingley gazed absentmindedly out the window with a euphoric grin—of which he was likely unaware—plastered on his face. He was going to London to speak to his solicitor regarding his marriage articles. Never in his life had Darcy wished more that he could change places with a man. Bingley had not offended the object of his affections. Bingley was secure in his lady's adoration and good opinion. In a few months, Bingley would be married to the woman he loved with nary an impediment.

"Are you well, Darcy?" Bingley asked warily. Darcy started and realised he had been staring—or more likely, glaring—at his friend for an indeterminate length of time.

"Ah, uhm." Darcy shook his head to clear his thoughts. Bingley was his dearest friend and he would not begrudge him his happiness. "Yes, I am...I am well," he finished somewhat dejectedly. Truthfully, he was far from well. Were it not for his daughter's comforting presence beside him, he might very well be downright dismal.

"Listen, Darcy. I am sure Miss Eliz—"

"Stop, Bingley," Darcy interrupted his friend. Softening his features and voice, he looked Bingley in the eye. "I appreciate your sympathy, truly, I do. But I have no wish to canvass it at the moment."

The sigh Bingley let loose told plainly that he had no wish to relinquish the topic, but did not push it any further. "As you wish, my friend. Will you go straight to Kent?"

"No. I will stop first at Matlock House to leave Amelia with my aunt and Georgiana. When do you expect to return to Hertfordshire?"

"As soon as I possibly can! I have no wish to be apart from Jane any longer than needs be!" Bingley laughed but quickly sobered. "I mean, that is. I, uh..."

Darcy shook his head again. Would it forever be like this? His acquaintances tiptoeing around him as if he were a dandelion gone to seed? Fearful that if they upset his sensibilities, he would fall apart and scatter on the wind? This he could not abide.

"I would not expect anything less. I am happy for you, Bingley. Truly."

The conversation turned to rather mundane topics; acquaintances they might see whilst in Town, Darcy's sister, Bingley's sisters, whether or not Bingley would take a house in London. Miss Bingley had long been pressuring her brother to do so but he had always been happy enough in his rented rooms at a respectable boarding house—or imposing on Hurst or Darcy's hospitality when the fancy struck him. They spent some time debating whether the new Miss Bingley would still harbour such desires. She had been much more pleasant of late and it was really anyone's guess where her true wishes lie.

At last, the carriage pulled up before the Hurst's Townhouse at Portman Square where Bingley would stay for the short time he was here. They parted congenially; Bingley made a silly face at Amelia and pulled the first laugh from her Darcy had heard since his troubles had begun. Darcy offered one of his carriages for Bingley's return to Netherfield should he wish for a slower return journey than horseback would afford. The offer was laughingly refused and soon the Darcys were making their way towards Grosvenor Square where his uncle, the earl, lived.

Lord Matlock's anger over the actions of his sister was righteous, if nongermane. What purpose could there be in raising one's ire against the actions of a dead woman? Some time was spent half-heartedly discussing what ought to have been done, when it ought to have been done, and who ought to have done it; but, in the end, such arguments were meaningless. What was done was done. Amelia was safe, Wickham in prison, and Lady Catherine dead. None of her relations would express aloud the relief they felt knowing they would never again be made to contend with her ladyship's unreasonable nature, relentless demands, or irascible temper; none, perhaps, except Richard.

"Shall we raise a glass to Aunt Catherine?" he suggested, holding up his own brandy in his father's study. Lord Matlock and Darcy shared a dubious look before slowly raising their own drinks. "To Lady Catherine. May she be reaping her just deserts in hell!"

"Richard!" his father chided while Darcy could only chuckle as he sipped the fine brandy.

"Tell me you do not agree the old bat got just what she deserved after all the trouble she caused this family over the years?"

"Of course, I do!" Lord Matlock confessed as he pulled at his cravat. "Still, 'tis damned indecent to speak so." Richard merely shrugged and took another pull from his drink. Shaking his head, the earl turned his attention to his nephew. "What will you do now, Darcy?"

"I must go to Kent. With any luck, Lady Catherine has not run the entire place into the ground and I shall not have too much difficulty selling it."

"Sell Rosings?!" Richard cried as his lordship coughed and sputtered over inhaled brandy.

Darcy reached over and slapped his uncle on the back a few times. "Indeed," he confirmed calmly when the earl was able to breathe easier, as if they were speaking of nothing more than selling off a few horses or an old carriage. "Why should I keep the place? Anne hated it there."

"But what of Amelia's inheritance?" asked Lord Matlock.

A bark of humourless laughter met this inquiry. "Come now, Uncle. There is no cause for concern in that quarter. She has already an exceedingly handsome dowry and, in the likelihood that I father no more children, Amelia will have Pemberley. I have never particularly liked the idea of my daughter settling so far away, in any case."

"I grant you that, Nephew, but why should you have no more children? You are young yet and there is not a single lady in the country who would not have you."

"You would be surprised, Uncle," murmured Darcy, draining the last of his brandy. "I have married once for duty. I shall only marry again for affection. As the woman I love currently despises me, I shall not venture to foster much hope in that corner."

A pregnant silence fell following this proclamation as Darcy stared into his empty glass, his thoughts some thirty miles away with a bright-eyed woman with a sparkling wit; the other gentlemen exchanged anxious glances. Several times they opened their mouths to speak words of encouragement or comfort, yet neither could seem to find their voices.

"Have you spoken with Lord Dorchester to clear up any misunderstandings which may have arisen from Lady Catherine's interference?" Darcy asked his uncle at last.

"I have." Lord Matlock shook his head before taking a deep pull of his brandy. "And it only serves to highlight just how grand were my sister's delusions. Apparently, Cathy paid the duke a visit telling—yes, telling—his grace that she had a husband for his daughter. Lord and Lady Dorchester agreed that it would be a fine match, but that they had no intentions of promoting a marriage for Lady Prudence at this time, the young lady being, after all, only just seventeen. She has made her come out but they wish for her to have at least one season before even considering any suitors. It seems, as was always her way, that Cathy chose not to hear any of this, acknowledging only their agreement to the suitability of the union."

"Bloody hell," Richard cursed.

"Indeed."

Another silence descended on the trio as they all contemplated the seemingly endless supply of arrogance her ladyship possessed. To think she could dictate to a duke to whom he ought to marry his daughter was outside of absurd.

"I wonder," Darcy broke the silence again, turning to his cousin. "Might you be available to accompany me to Kent, Richard?"

"Oh, ah. Yes. I think I might be able to do that."

"Thank you. I shall leave first thing in the morning. Might I impose on you and my aunt to watch over Amelia whilst I am away, Uncle?"

"Of course, Darcy. You know we love to have her. Your aunt especially." Darcy nodded and nervously twisted his glass in his hands. Understanding his nephew's concern, Lord Matlock placed a fatherly hand on his nephew's shoulder. "She will be well protected, Darcy. You have my word."

Swallowing down the lump of fear in his throat, Darcy could only nod.

"Mr. Darcy!" someone called out as he stepped out of his carriage before Rosings' front door and Darcy groaned. Turning, he saw a tall, paunchy man in unkempt parson's garb scuttling up the drive towards him. Stopping a few feet from where Darcy stood, Mr. Collins dropped a deep bow; or rather, he doubled over, clutching his side and breathing heavily. After a few minutes to catch his breath, the ridiculous man righted, but remained hunched in a most subservient manner. "Oh, Mr. Darcy! How relieved I am to finally see a member of my most esteemed patroness's family! I have been at a complete loss! When last I heard from her ladyship, she bade me to remain and await her instruction but I have had no word from her in,"—he paused and looked skyward, his lips silently counting— "eight days! It was fortunate she had already approved my sermon for Sunday last or I know not what I might have read to the congregation! But now it is Friday and Lady Catherine has given me no instruction for this Sunday's sermon! What is more, I have received the strangest letter from my bishop and I know not what to make of it! I know it must be some gross mistake for there can be no cause for such action! But this all pales in light of the worry I harbour! When her ladyship left for Town, she was so very distressed and I fear for her most dreadfully! She was for Hertfordshire to collect her granddaughter away from the dangerous influence of my vile relations and I fear they may have brought harm upon your most excellent, venerated, noble mother!"

As the parson droned on, Richard stepped down from the carriage and stared in amazement. He looked to his cousin but Darcy could only shake his head. After only a moment in the man's presence, a headache was already beginning to form.

"Do you know this man, Cousin?" asked Richard when the toadying parson had, at last, ceased speaking.

"Unfortunately, I do." Mr. Collins looked bewildered at these words but Darcy continued on before he could launch into another agonizing monologue. "This is the rector to whom our aunt awarded the Hunsford living without my say."

"Ah, I see." Knowing very well the kind of people his late aunt preferred to gather around her, no further explanation was necessary. "This ought to be a treat."

Shaking off this exchange he would no doubt find a way to explain away as some form of noble condescension, Mr. Collins took several shuffling steps nearer Darcy, who quickly backed away. "My patroness? Pray, tell me your most benevolent, respected mother is well!"

"If you mean Lady Catherine, my *aunt* is dead."

The shriek which emanated from the parson's throat was a sound which neither cousin had ever heard from any man's throat. Both gentlemen took a step back and stared at the pitiful vicar in disgust. Mr. Collins fell to his knees and crawled across the gravel to Darcy and grasped at the hem of his coat.

"No! No, no, no, no! This cannot be! It cannot be! There has been some terrible mistake! Her ladyship was the only one who can speak for me! She must write to my bishop and vouch for my loyalty and service! I cannot be defrocked! Oh, my wicked cousin and his horrid, grasping, sinful jezebels! They have done this! I will swear to it! Fear not Mr. Darcy! My evil relations will not escape justice for the crime which had been committed against your—"

"Enough!" bellowed Darcy, pulling out of the man's sweaty clutches.

"What is this lunatic on about, Darce? What have his relations to do with anything?"

"He is Mr. Bennet's cousin and, until recently, the heir to Longbourn."

"Dear me, Cousin. Should you succeed in winning fair Miss Elizabeth's forgiveness, you shall certainly be gaining a deplorable relation. At least your most shameful relation is now dead."

"No! You cannot possibly think to marry any of my devilish cousins, sir! I can see you have been beguiled by their sinful beauty! I, myself, was very nearly caught up in their loathsome trap! But you must marry the lady chosen by your most excellent mother! You must! You must! You cannot ally yourself with the very people who have slain the brightest light in the—"

"Mr. Collins! I said that is enough! I was not beholden to Lady Catherine's desires while she lived, and I am even less so now! The Bennets had nothing at all to do with my aunt's demise. She conspired to kidnap my daughter and was murderer by the man she hired to do the job."

A horrified silence followed this statement until Mr. Collins started as though he had stumbled upon some marvelous idea. "Was it Mr. Bennet?"

"Good God, man!" The Colonel cried. "I know her ladyship enjoys surrounding herself with witless idiots, but you, sir, surpass them all!"

"Wait," Darcy said as Mr. Collins' earlier words burst upon his mind. "Did you say you have been defrocked?"

The man began wringing his hands together and shifting his eyes in every direction, refusing to meet the eyes of either gentleman. "A-a-a-a ma-mistake, I am sure. Quite sure. There can be no question that my service to her ladyship, the noble and honourable Lady Catherine de Bourgh, has been everything faithful and exact! Of course, it will be more difficult for her ladyship to dictate the letter informing my bishop so if she is...now that she is...dead. Oh!" The bumbling fool turned to Darcy with a look that might very well have been mistaken for having very instantly fallen in love. "*You*, Mr. Darcy, are the master of Rosings! *You* may write to my bishop and set matters to right! I have no doubt Lady Catherine has informed her most beloved son of my excellent service and value in the parish. Oh, you are too good, sir! Too good!"

"First of all, Mr. Collins, and I shall not repeat myself, Lady Catherine was not my mother, but my mother's sister. For a brief period of time, I had the greatest misfortune of being required to claim her as my mother-in-law. Secondly, it was I who wrote to your bishop regarding your reprehensible behaviour towards the Bennets."

"My behaviour? *My* behaviour?! 'Twas my deceitful, ungrateful, artful cousins who disregarded the well-intended olive branch I so graciously extended at the excellent advice of your most noble moth—ah! Aunt!" Mr. Collins corrected himself, cringing at the sight of the dangerous look on Darcy's face. "Had they not been so intent on reaching far above their own station and corrupting honourable, noble gentlemen such as yourselves with their wicked arts, proving themselves to be nothing more than common trollops, Cousin Elizabeth, perhaps most of all, they—"

In an instant, Darcy had the parson by the collar and slammed him against the side of the carriage, toes barely scraping the ground. With his nose mere inches from Mr. Collins face, Darcy's voice was low and dangerous. "If I ever hear you speak a single disparaging remark against the Bennets again, especially Miss Elizabeth, I promise you, sir, it will be the very last thing you ever do." He released the man and Mr. Collins slumped to the ground. "Now, you will remove yourself from Hunsford parsonage and never show your face near Rosings again. Am I rightly understood?"

The trembling Mr. Collins gave a tremulous nod and a pitiful squeak. More than ready to be done with the odious man, Darcy and the Colonel turned away and walked towards Rosings' front door. Alas, Mr. Collins found his voice and called out.

"Wh-where am I to go? I do not—"

"I care not, Collins. I am done with you. Be gone."

The remainder of their stay at Rosings passed much less eventfully. The cousins wandered through the house, taking note of missing paintings and valuable artifacts; no doubt sold to bribe the steward to ignore Darcy's instructions in favour of Lady Catherine's. Mrs. Bithers, Rosings longtime housekeeper, followed the young gentlemen through the bedchambers and primary rooms, accepting orders for the changes Darcy wished to be made.

Mr. Malvern was summoned and released from Darcy's employ. The steward was wise enough to voice no protests. He made no excuses for his conduct and offered a sincere apology for his lapse in judgement before quietly accepting his last month's wages and leaving the estate.

Darcy's last bit of pertinent business was to write to Anne's uncle, Jeremiah de Bourgh, to offer him first rights of refusal to purchase Rosings. The de Bourgh family had never gotten on with Lady Catherine and were excessively displeased that such a woman would be mistress of their family seat. It gave Darcy immense satisfaction to think of his belligerent aunt's reaction if she could know he would be handing her home back to the family she had so long despised, but of whom his late wife had retained many fond memories from visits in her childhood.

He had just sealed the letter and was standing from the desk to seek out the butler to have his letter readied for the post in the morning when the man entered the room with a bow and a letter on a silver salver.

"I beg your pardon, sir. This express has just arrived for you."

"Thank you, Harper." Darcy took the missive and handed over his own. "Please see this letter delivered in tomorrow's post."

Refusing the offered drink from his cousin, Darcy took a seat in an armchair before the fire staring at the letter postmarked from Hertfordshire. With trembling fingers, he opened the note. His eyes scanned the page, his heart quickening with every word. When he had read it twice over, he sprang from his chair and yelled out to no one in particular to have his horse made ready.

~~~*✱*~~~
Chapter Twenty-Two
✱

Darcy knew he ought to be grateful for his cousin's eminently wise insistence that he not set out on his journey to Hertfordshire the moment he had received Mr. Bennet's note. Indeed, had their roles been reversed, Darcy would have suggested just the same. Riding out after dark at break-neck speed was foolhardy in the extreme. It was quite difficult to care about that when he had a letter in his hand stating that Elizabeth had asked to speak with him.

"You cannot mean to go now?" Richard had looked pointedly out the darkening window when Darcy made to push past his cousin, determined to get to Elizabeth as quickly as possible.

"I can and I do."

"Darcy, just stop and think. If you were in my shoes and it was I rushing off into the dead of night in agitated spirits, what would you tell me?"

A growl slipped out his throat as he begrudgingly acknowledged that Richard was correct. "I would advise you to wait for morning," he admitted through gritted teeth, his fists clenched tightly at his sides.

"It will do neither you nor Miss Elizabeth any good should you come to harm in your haste to accept your lashings," Richard had teasingly argued. He was, of course, correct, but that did not mean that Darcy had to like it any better.

So, he had set out at first light this morning trying to feel some form of gratitude for his cousin's sage advice. As he barreled down the road to London on his stallion at the break of dawn, he fought down annoyance at the hours lost which might have been spent grovelling at Elizabeth's feet.

His journey was further hindered by his decision to trade his mount for the slower carriage for the remaining distance to Hertfordshire; though this was a necessity he would not forgo. He would not leave Amelia behind. Already he had been parted from his daughter for longer than he liked after coming so close to losing her. Even if such were not the case, he wanted Amelia to go to Netherfield. She wished to see Elizabeth and he felt certain Elizabeth would feel the same. It may be that she could never forgive him, but she loved his daughter and he would not keep them apart.

Amelia jabbered the entire way to Meryton, happily anticipating seeing her friend again and holding tight to the doll Elizabeth had given her. Darcy envied his daughter as her tiny slippered feet swung back and forth where they hung off the carriage bench; she had no qualms about her reception by that lady. It was not Amelia who had laid horrendous accusations at the feet of the woman he claimed to love after that very woman had nearly given her life to defend his child. Then, against his better judgement, he had left. He had not offered his apologies nor even thanked her for the selfless service she had proffered him. He had just left.

For one weak moment, he considered not returning at all. Already Elizabeth had refused once to see him; what hope had he that she could ever forgive his insufferable behaviour? Like as not, she wished only to scold him as she had the night they met, and she would be wholly justified now just as she had been then. After all she had been through, he had no desire to further her discomfort. Would it not be kinder to simply refrain from inflicting his company upon her?

But he could not refrain. It was, perhaps, selfish of him, yet he could not bring himself to give up hope that she might yet love him enough to forgive him. The long ride to Meryton was passed by playing all of their interactions in his head. He remembered her every look, touch, and scent. The teasing way she spoke to him, the kiss she had granted him in the garden; the waltz they had shared at Netherfield; the hopeful, tender look she had bestowed upon him when he had asked her to join him for breakfast that final morning before all had gone so terribly wrong. No, he could no more leave her behind than he could remove his own bleeding heart from his chest.

At long last, yet, somehow before he was prepared, the carriage turned up the lane that would take them to Netherfield. Whether he was more anxious or nervous, Darcy could not say. Amelia was a tiny ball of energy, climbing up onto his lap to eagerly look out the window wondering out loud if she might see Elizabeth out walking. Though he knew it was impossible that her injuries would allow her to venture out, Darcy could scarcely prevent his own eyes from scanning the gardens and lawns for that light and pleasing form that he loved so dearly.

Amid fervent protest, Amelia was taken directly to the nursery. Her father gave his every promise that she would see Elizabeth after he had spoken with the lady and been assured that she was well enough for visitors. The little girl pouted but relented.

Now, he stood outside her chamber door, the very same one she had occupied not so many weeks ago. It was oddly reminiscent of the times he had walked her to her chambers and then simply stood here after she had gone inside, wishing he could think of some reason to knock and bring her back out again. Only now, he lacked not a cause, but the courage. A brief meeting with Mr. Bennet revealed that which Darcy had feared. His leaving Netherfield had not softened her heart as her father had believed it would; upon learning that he had departed Netherfield without so much as a word, Elizabeth now felt he had abandoned her a second time.

She was being ridiculous and she very well knew it. Why she should be disappointed that Darcy had honoured her wishes, Elizabeth could not say. She had told her father she did not want to see the gentleman and he had left the very same day. She ought to be relieved; yet she was not. Inexplicably, she was even angrier than she had been before.

What did he mean by leaving? Was she not worth fighting for? She who had very nearly given her life to protect his child? Though, she could not deny that she would do so again and again for Amelia, even given beforehand knowledge of what the consequences would be.

Her father had said that Darcy wished not only to thank her, but apologise. Was she not owed that? Why then, did he leave? He had been prepared to ask her to be his wife, she was quite certain; did he no longer wish to marry her? Did she still wish to marry him? Should not he have remained, refusing to depart until she agreed to hear him out? What sort of poor lover was he to quit the field after the first sign of trouble. Albeit, this was certainly not an average quarrel...

Yes, she was being excessively silly. Of course, she still wished, more than anything, to be Darcy's wife but her anger was warring heavily with her heart. Yet, now it was likely purposeless to worry over the situation. Darcy was gone; he had wished to speak with her and she had refused even to see him. What man would remain after such a rejection?

Her confusion was helped not at all by her growing frustration at being confined to this confounded bed. An active young lady, Elizabeth had long been accustomed to walking out her problems in Longbourn's woods or upon Oakham Mount's gentle slopes. The sunshine on her face and fresh breeze in her hair had never failed to bring clarity to her mind; even if the solution she came to was nothing more profound than that there was little to be done for whatever conundrum she pondered but to release it and move on.

But with a broken ankle, Elizabeth could not even walk about the room! She struggled just to sit up without aid with her arm trapped in this blasted sling as it was. The tedium was rapidly wearing on her good humour. Papa brought her books from his library, commenting regularly on the despicable state of his future son-in-law's collection. But Elizabeth had, for once, little patience for reading. Jane sat with her for hours every day, often accompanied by Caroline and Louisa. Elizabeth put forth a great effort to appreciate their kindness, but it was difficult. Her sister's suffering aside, Jane was incandescently happy and it showed upon her face, even if she took great trouble not to speak of it.

Louisa, as well, said little of her own joy but her hand nearly always rested tenderly upon her middle when it was not busy knitting tiny stockings or hats. Even Caroline, who might have the greatest cause to commiserate with Elizabeth, was buoyed by her newfound resolve to get out of her own way and seek happiness. These ladies who had every reason to rejoice and be congratulated on their good fortune walked on eggshells around her and she felt a crushing sense of guilt over it.

Determined that she would no longer be a wet blanket to her friends' enjoyment, she was on the verge of asking Jane about the overly extravagant plans Mama was making for her wedding or inquiring after Louisa's health when a firm yet gentle knock sounded at the door. Instinctively, Elizabeth knew it was Darcy. Only he could convey both such tenderness and strength in a simple rap on the door. Before she could form any reasonable excuse to prevent it, Jane had crossed the room and opened the door. Her soft gasp informed Elizabeth that she had been correct.

Looking up, all breath fled Elizabeth's lungs. Though she had not forgotten how handsome he was, it was still something of a shock to be reminded of his overwhelming manliness. His tall, broad-shouldered form was framed in the doorway, making the portal seem almost too small. Even though his words were directed at Jane, his dark, brooding eyes never left Elizabeth's across the room where she was propped up against the pillows on the bed.

"Good afternoon, Miss Bennet." His deep timbre washed over her and chipped away at the feeble anger she still harboured against him. "I hoped I might have a word with Miss Elizabeth, if she will allow it?"

"Oh, yes. Of course, er...I mean, ah...Lizzy?" Jane looked to her sister with wide eyes. She was of such an agreeable nature, she obviously wished to grant Darcy his wish immediately, yet was painfully aware of Elizabeth's conflicting feelings on the matter.

Unwilling to see her sister discomfited, who had been so patient and kind during these difficult days, Elizabeth gave a short nod to signal her acquiescence. A flurry of activity followed that action. Jane stepped back to allow Darcy entrance while Caroline and Louisa rose from their seats with looks of encouragement towards Elizabeth. She nearly laughed when Caroline fixed Darcy with a stern look of warning before she exited the room. Though she could not be certain, she thought she heard her new friend hiss something along the lines of "What did I tell you?" as she poked him in the chest.

Jane was the last to leave, exchanging one last look with her sister. "I will leave the door open?"

"Of course," Darcy agreed, though his eyes never strayed from Elizabeth. For her part, she could suddenly not bring herself to look upon him and so fixed her gaze on a spot on the counterpane upon her lap. After a few moments of awkward silence, she nodded towards the chair beside the bed in invitation. Darcy wasted no time in crossing the room and taking the seat, as if he were eager to show that he would eagerly obey any and all commands she might give.

After several awkward moments, Darcy at last spoke. "Your father tells me that you are mending well. Are you? Well, that is?"

"As well as I imagine I can be. My shoulder aches and my ankle will not be healed for several more weeks. More than anything, I tire of being confined to this infernal bed."

"I know this must be especially difficult for you."

"You do? You suppose you know me so well, do you?"

"Elizabeth—"

All the anger and hurt burst from her of its own volition. She had truly meant to hear him, to allow him to speak his piece. But her anger would not have it. The subject which bubbled just under the surface like molten lava between them erupted forth from her lips.

"I fear you do not know me at all! You accused me of kidnapping your daughter! You condemned me and left me to die!" she cried, shaking in anger as tears of fury fell down her face. Unwilling to show him her weakness, Elizabeth turned away from him and clenched her eyes shut.

For several moments, there was silence, broken only by her shuttering breaths. She thought, perhaps, that Darcy had left the room and, inexplicably, her heart broke even further. Then he made a noise that sounded somewhere between a throat clearing and choking.

"I did," he said, his voice thick with emotion. "Should I live a thousand years, I shall never forgive myself."

She hated that she could hear the sincerity in his voice for it went a very long way in dispelling her anger towards him. Yet, she could not absolve him just yet. "How? How could you think, even for a moment, that I would ever wish to harm you or Amelia?"

"I have no excuse, Elizabeth. Only to say that when Mrs. Lawson burst in shouting that you had taken my child, a fear I have never known before took over my mind and all rational thought fled. I had already failed to save Anne. I could not fail in my promise to protect her daughter. The moment Amelia told me what you had done, how you had put yourself in danger that she might escape, I knew I had made a terrible mistake. I knew—I *know* you would never put my daughter in harm's way. I owe you everything, Elizabeth. You have my eternal gratitude for protecting Amelia when I could not. I understand if you wish never to see me again, for what I accused you of is unforgivable. But please, please allow me to say how very sorry I am for thinking, even for a one foolish moment, that you could ever betray me in such a manner.

"I will importune you no further. Perhaps I ought not to have come at all." Darcy hesitantly reached over and gently pressed her hand as a teardrop fell down her cheek onto the bedclothes. His voice was thick and cracked with emotion as he spoke. "But I would have you know, though you may no longer desire it, my heart is yours, Elizabeth. Forever it will remain so, for I will love you for as long as I live."

With a final squeeze of her fingers, Darcy started to rise and panic rose in Elizabeth's chest. Before he could step away, she tightened her grip on his hand, holding him in place beside her. What remained of her anger melted away at the look of hope and longing shining from his beautiful eyes. She knew, deep within her soul, that if she allowed him to walk away now, she would regret it for the rest of her life. Her words came out in a hoarse whisper, but they contained every ounce of love she felt for this man.

"I do desire it, Mr. Darcy. I very much desire your heart. It seems only fair, as you have mine."

"Elizabeth?" Darcy fell to his knees at her bedside and pressed her hand to his lips. "You are too generous to trifle with me. Does this mean, my dearest, loveliest Elizabeth, that I am forgiven?"

"Well, I am still displeased with you."

"I should be exceedingly surprised if you were not."

"Very well, Mr. Darcy. I forgive you. I think that in such cases as these, implacable resentment is unpardonable. Besides," said Elizabeth with a spark of her customary playfulness lighting up her bright eyes, so tired was she of holding on to anger and bitterness, "I do so miss Amelia and cannot very well maintain the acquaintance if you and I are at odds."

"Oh, I see how it is!" The relief he felt was blatantly apparent in the wide smile he wore. "'Tis not I with whom you wish to associate but my daughter! I ought to be offended, madam!"

"I shall neither confirm nor deny your supposition, sir." With a look of contrived hauteur, Elizabeth turned away and made to cross her arms over her chest, forgetting in her levity her injury. She cried out when she attempted to move her aggrieved shoulder and Darcy leapt to his feet, taking a step back clearly fearing he had somehow caused her harm.

"My love, what is the matter? Did I hurt you?"

"No, Mr. Darcy," she laughed, though it was painful. "'Tis only this bothersome shoulder. I simply forgot in my happiness that I cannot move it."

"Oh, Elizabeth. Forgive me! Here I am, revelling in your delightful company when I ought to go and allow you to rest." He bent over her good hand once again and pressed a kiss to her knuckles. "Thank you, my darling Elizabeth, for being far more understanding than I have any right to deserve."

"Excuse me, Mr. Darcy," said Elizabeth when he straightened and made to leave. "Are you not forgetting something?"

Darcy looked about him as though he might spot a dropped handkerchief or a book he had not realised he had brought with him. "I, ah…I do not believe so?"

Pressing her lips together, Elizabeth steeled her courage for the bold move she was about to make. It was, perhaps, precipitous; he would likely proceed on his own as soon as she was recovered. But she found she had no desire to wait weeks for what could be done now. She needed no great romantic gesture nor the perfect setting. All Elizabeth need was Darcy. And Amelia.

"If you do not ask me to be your wife before you quit this room, I shall be very vexed with you, sir."

"Are you certain, my dear? Would you not wish—"

"Ask me, Mr. Darcy."

For a moment, the gentleman only stood and stared at her in disbelief. Elizabeth feared she may have pressed her luck a mite too far. Then a devastating grin stretched across his face and butterflies erupted in her stomach.

"As you wish," said he, sitting on the edge of the bed and taking up her uninjured hand in his. With his other, he reached over and cupped the side of her face, gently stroking her cheek with his thumb. "My darling Elizabeth, you must know how ardently I admire and love you. You are far and away my superior. My daughter loves you and I could not imagine spending this life with anyone but you. I would consider myself the most fortunate man in all the world if you would grant me the great honour of agreeing to be my wife and Amelia's mother. Dearest Elizabeth, will you marry me?"

"Oh, Mr. Darcy!" she cried in feigned surprise. "This is so very sudden! I hardly know what to say."

"Say yes, you minx."

"Very well, Mr. Darcy. Yes, I will marry you." Sobering, she looked deeply into his eyes. "There is nothing I wish for more than be your wife."

Darcy leaned down, stopping mere inches from her face. "Then I should very much like it if you would call me Fitzwilliam."

"Fitzwilliam," she complied in a breathy whisper.

She had only a moment to appreciate the exultant look in his eyes before he pressed his lips to hers and she was lost in a euphoria of her own. In that kiss, the painful past was forgot and only the memories which could be recalled with pleasure would be allowed. There was far too much joy to be anticipated to spend even one minute regretting anything that had gone on before. They were, both of them, committed to being the happiest couple in all the world, setting forth to demonstrate to one and all the true meaning of connubial felicity.

Whistling a jaunty tune, Colonel Fitzwilliam followed the limping guardsman down the dank halls of Newgate prison, endeavouring to ignore the foul odours which assaulted his senses and the pathetic cries for clemency from the cells he passed. His surroundings certainly did not inspire cheerfulness but Richard simply could not suppress his good humour. This was a visit he had been looking forward to ever since he left Hertfordshire. He was exceedingly glad his cousin did not waste any time obtaining his lady love's forgiveness. Even with the weight of an earl's influence, a hanging can only be put off so long.

The turnkey stopped at the end of the long hallway and banged a fist against the bars of the cell. "Ye've go' a visita'." He nodded towards the pile of filth in the corner and limped off.

Richard looked into the cell and was inordinately pleased when he hardly recognised his old chum. Wickham had ever been excessively proud of his good looks and ability to charm many a lady out of that which she ought to keep most sacred. Now, with his long hair hanging in greasy sheets about his face, a great bloody black eye, and being covered in grime, Richard doubted the bounder could inspire even the loneliest of widows to so much as flutter her fan in his direction.

"Ah ha," Wickham barked out a laugh. Richard nearly laughed himself at the sight of several teeth missing from the reprobate's mouth. He had clearly been up to his old tricks during his residence in this hell-hole yet had met with far less than his usual success. "I knew Darcy could not stomach sending me to die. It would not please his dear old papa to allow any harm to come to the godson whom he favoured over his own heir."

"I do say, Wickham," Richard replied lazily as he leant a shoulder against the bars and crossed his arms, "if I did not know you to be such a coward, I might have spoken for you myself. His majesty could certainly use more men with your bravado on the frontlines against Old Boney."

The smile on the prisoner's face slipped a fraction. "If Darcy was going to allow me to hang, I would be dead already."

"What you seem to forget, Wickham, as a deplorable lack of vision has ever been one of your greatest failings, is that I am the son of a powerful and influential earl. The very earl whose sister you murdered, as it were. Had he so wished it, I am quite certain Lord Matlock might have had you to stay at the palace whilst you awaited your fate. Now, we would never have countenanced such a thing, but you do see my point, do you not? You are alive, you useless ratbag, at my pleasure."

Wickham eyed his visitor warily for several moments before a hesitant grin crossed his features. "You are bluffing. Why else would you be here if not to secure my release at Darcy's command? You always were his faithful little lap dog."

Richard reached into his inner jacket pocket and pulled out a folded piece of newsprint. "If I were bluffing, you would never know. You always have been lousy at cards. I have come to give you this. Darcy may not care what you think of him, but I simply could not allow you to go to your death thinking for even an instant that you had bested my most excellent cousin in any way. He is far and away a better man than either of us and I wanted to make sure you knew that before your appointment with the hangman's noose."

Wickham cautiously approached and took the paper the Colonel slipped through the bars. A wicked, self-satisfied grin spread across Richard's features as he watched the blood rush from his companion's face. In his mind, he pictured the words Wickham was now reading.

Lord Andrew Fitzwilliam, third earl of Matlock,
is pleased to announce the engagement of his nephew
FITZWILLIAM GEORGE ALEXANDER RYAN DARCY
to
ELIZABETH MARIANNE BENNET

"You see, Wickham? You lose. You took nothing from Darcy. His lady has forgiven him and they will wed and live happily ever after. And you will die. Tomorrow, by the way. Ah, but the cream is this: had you but shown even the slightest inclination to live an honest, respectable existence? There is nothing Darcy would not have done to assist you. You have spent your entire life despising and envying the man who might have been your greatest ally had you not been such an utter waste of human flesh."

Seething with anger and hatred, Wickham charged the bars of his cell, reaching out to grab at the Colonel but Richard stepped deftly away, chuckling. The guard hobbled over, yelling for Wickham to come to order. Smiling to himself, Richard turned away.

"Goodnight, Wicky. I shall see you bright and early in the morning. I would not miss it for the world." He left, his childhood friend screaming invectives and obscenities after him, feeling an immense sense of satisfaction.

Finis

~~~*✳*~~~

Epilogue
Pemberley, Derbyshire
June, 1815
✳*✳

Sitting in the warm sunshine on the veranda off her favourite parlour, Elizabeth Darcy gazed contentedly over the beautiful grounds she had come to love so dearly since her marriage nearly three years ago. From her first glimpse of Pemberley, it had felt like home. Indeed, before even she had come to Derbyshire, she had felt a strong affinity for her husband's estate. Darcy had spoken so fondly of his home during their too-long engagement, she had determined to love it, if only for his sake.

Thankfully, Pemberley was as near perfect a place as Elizabeth could possibly imagine. Situated in a low valley among the foothills of the Peaks, there were beauties everywhere she looked. To her vast delight, the grounds had been left much as nature had intended them, with only a few cultivated lawns and formal gardens kept near the house. The woods and paths provide as much entertainment and opportunity for exploration as any lover of nature, such as herself, could ever wish for. The lake served as a wonderful backdrop for picnics and cooling one's feet on hot summer days. Her husband would often say fondly that she seemed designed for Pemberley, to which she would tease that she rather thought it was the other way around.

Running a hand over her very swollen abdomen, Elizabeth released a sigh of contentment. Though the last three years had been exceedingly happy, they had not been without trial. Having loved being raised with so many sisters, she was eager to provide Amelia with siblings and Darcy, his heir. Alas, despite applying an abundance of enthusiasm to the task, Elizabeth remained nulligravida for more than a year. Darcy assured his beloved that it made no difference to him if they had ten children or none. He was perfectly content with a wife and daughter he adored already. Indeed, they were an enormously happy family; still, there was a certain longing within Elizabeth's heart which she struggled to suppress.

As they neared two years of marriage, Elizabeth began to suspect she was, at last, increasing. She had missed her courses for two months together, suffered acute illness in the morning, and had developed a staggering aversion to eggs and her previously favoured kippers in the mornings. An encouraging letter from her dear aunt, an experienced mother five times over, gave wings to her hopes.

In the spring of the year '13, however, just when she had expected to feel the quickening, Elizabeth was taken to bed with horrid pains in her abdomen. Her husband, with whom she had not yet shared her suspicions for fear of raising false hopes, was beside himself with terror for his wife. Darcy sent for the local apothecary and surgeon as well as his physician from Town. After two agonizing days of torturous pains, a blistering fever, and a good deal of bleeding, the child within Elizabeth's womb was lost.

For weeks, Elizabeth was nearly consumed by her grief. Most days she remained abed. When she did venture to rise, she did not leave her chambers. Dark thoughts filled her mind; jealousies towards her sisters Jane, who had just the week prior to Elizabeth's convalescence written to announce her anticipation of a second child, and Mary, married not a year ago to the rector at Kympton and recently delivered of her first babe. She raged at God for her pain and, at her weakest, most shameful moment, threw blame at her husband. His own mother, after all, had lost many children.

It was another letter from her wonderful aunt that finally roused her. Aunt Madeleine reminded her niece that she still had much for which to be grateful; most of all a beautiful young daughter. an adoring husband, and a whole life ahead of her. Not a creature made for melancholy, Elizabeth took her aunt's words to heart, tucking her grief into the recesses of her heart and attacked life with renewed vigour.

Her husband was another matter altogether. His wife's difficulty had brought to mind with excruciating clarity the loss of his first wife all those years ago. Still struggling under the guilt that it had been his actions which had taken the life of his cousin, Darcy stubbornly abstained from his wife's bed for several months. The sorrow he felt at Anne's death, a woman he had taken to wife with nothing more than familial affection, had been terrible; the very thought of losing Elizabeth, the woman for whom his heart beat, was nearly enough to tear him apart.

It was not until his wife demanded he attend her in her chambers and explained, with loving patience, that many women suffered such losses, that his fear began to subside. She told her husband that, after having known intimacy with him, she refused to continue on in a celibate marriage. While he was by no means instantly convinced, Darcy quickly—and with great relief—came around to his wife's way of thinking and, very soon, Elizabeth believed she again had reason to be hopeful.

Cautiously optimistic, she shared her suspicions with Darcy as she had promised she would not withhold such suspicions again. They cherished their hopes quietly until Elizabeth had felt the quickening for a solid month; at which point, Amelia was the very first to learn of their joyful news.

Now, in the eighth month of her increase, Elizabeth was lost in musings on the future. Would her confinement go well? Would her child be healthy? Would it be a boy or a girl? Jane, who now lived at Rose Hill Hall with Bingley only 20 miles distant from Pemberley, had accurately predicted the sex of both her daughter and son. She had told her sister early in her first pregnancy that she simply knew and that Elizabeth would, as well. Smiling at Jane's misplaced confidence in her abilities, Elizabeth had no such notion of her child's sex, even now. Mama wrote often with her own absurd advice on what tells to look for to inform her of such things—from specific food preferences or aversions to which side she favoured when she slept to the shape of her ever-increasing waistline; but Mama was hardly an authority. She had sworn throughout each of her five increases that she was carrying her husband's heir. Truly, Elizabeth did not care if she was delivered of a son or daughter, so long as the child was healthy. Darcy repeatedly made similar sentiments known, only varying to include the health of his wife, as well.

"Ma'am!" a maid stepped onto the veranda and punctured Elizabeth's amusing ruminations. "I beg your pardon, Mrs. Darcy only...um. It's Miss Darcy."

Elizabeth slowly sat up. "Oh? What about her?"

"Um, well, it's just that...we can't find her," the maid admitted nervously.

"What? Oh!" Standing as quickly as her rotund figure would allow, a wave of dizziness washed over Elizabeth. Her mind flashed to a pair of wild eyes that still haunted her dreams on occasion and the feel of a pistol pressed into her side. She trembled all over and her breaths came in shallow gasps.

"Mrs. Darcy, are you well?"

"I...I am." *Pull yourself together, Lizzy!* she admonished herself. Forcing herself to take several slow, deep breaths, the dizziness passed and the world came back into focus. Nodding to herself, she looked on the maid. "Has Mr. Darcy been told?"

"Not yet, ma'am. He's still out riding the estate with Mr. Chavers."

"Send for him at once. Tell him he is needed at the house immediately, but nothing more." She would not have her husband unduly concerned. Amelia had a tendency to hide when upset and it was likely such was the case now and she had simply found a better hiding place than usual.

Dropping a quick curtsey, the maid turned and rushed off to carry out her orders, Elizabeth shuffling along behind her as quickly as she could manage. Her mind raced, thinking of all the usual places her daughter liked to hide, dismissing the most obvious as likely having already been searched by Mrs. Lawson and Miss Drake, Amelia's governess. Mr. Jeffries, Pemberley's longstanding butler, met her in the vestibule and Elizabeth ordered every available footman set to searching every inch of the large house.

For a moment, Elizabeth stood alone in the grand hall and thought over the last several days, looking for any clues as to where Amelia might hide. The six-year-old little girl had been rather sullen of late, and seemed often on the verge of tears. Though she was as affectionate and engaging as ever with her father, she seemed to shy away from Elizabeth and had even begun calling her Mrs. Darcy instead of Mama.

"Mrs. Darcy?"

Elizabeth turned and saw Miss Drake standing nearby. "Yes? Have you found her?"

"No, ma'am, but I thought maybe it would help if you knew what Miss Darcy spoke to me about this morning."

"Go on."

"It seems Miss Darcy has some concerns over the arrival of your baby. She seems to think there will be no place for her once you have a child of your own. Of course, I assured her that was not true but she said that she wished she could have her own mama."

"Thank you, Miss Drake. Keep looking and send for me the moment she is found." Elizabeth watched the governess hurry away, contemplating her words. A memory from just shortly after Darcy had proposed to her surfaced. The newly betrothed couple had taken tea with the little girl in Elizabeth's room at Netherfield to inform her of their marriage.

"What mean 'marry?'" Amelia asked.

Darcy turned such a tender look on Elizabeth, she felt her insides melt a little. "Well, sweetling, Elizabeth has agreed to be my wife. Which means that she is going to come to Pemberley to live with us." He then looked to his daughter. "Would you like Elizabeth to be your mother, my love?"

"Lizzy be my mama?"

"Yes," answered Elizabeth, gently taking Amelia's small hand in her own. "If you would allow me to be."

Amelia's angelic little face scrunched up adorably as she considered Elizabeth's words. She looked to her papa then down at her hands fidgeting with the hem of her gown. "But, what about my mama? In heaven? She not watch me anymore?"

"Oh, my darling girl." Darcy pulled his daughter onto his lap, wrapping her in a tight

embrace. *"Your mama will always watch over you. She loved you so very much but she knew that she could not be here to with you. So, do you know what she did?"*

"What?" Amelia asked in wide-eyed wonder.

"Just before she went to heaven, your mama asked me to find a wonderful lady who will love you and care for you just as much as she wanted to do. I think that Elizabeth is that lady, do you not agree, my dear?"

"Yes," the child replied after a moment of very serious thinking in which she stared at Elizabeth with those dark, soul-searching eyes she had inherited from Darcy. *"Lizzy be my mama."*

With a sudden clarity, Elizabeth knew where she could find her daughter. Looking around, she spotted Pemberley's faithful butler and beckoned him to her.

"Mr. Jeffries, when Mr. Darcy arrives, please tell him that I require his presence in the Rose Room."

"Of course, Mrs. Darcy. Forgive me, but has the young Miss Darcy been found?" the obviously worried man asked. Elizabeth was filled with gratitude for the wonderful staff at Pemberley who loved her family as dearly as she did. Indeed, many of those who served this wonderful house had begun to feel very nearly as family to her.

"Not as yet, but I believe I know where she is." She squeezed the dear servant's arm as she turned to waddle her way up the grand staircase to the second floor where a sitting room the late Mrs. Darcy had favoured was located.

Uninterested in erasing the previous mistress's presence from the house and knowing Amelia might like to have some of her mother's things readily at hand, Elizabeth had requested that all of Darcy's first wife's belongings be moved to that room when she came to Pemberley and took her place in the mistress's suite. From time to time, Amelia came to the room to look through her mother's belongings or admire with the jewelry the lady had brought with her from Rosings. Instinctively, Elizabeth knew this was where Amelia was hiding now.

She approached the door and knocked softly before letting herself in. It took only a brief glance to discover her daughter, curled up as she was on the soft pink floral brocade sofa wrapped up in the heavy Indian shawl that had been her mother's. Slowly, Elizabeth crossed the room and sat on the far end of the sofa, carefully giving the aggrieved girl space.

"Amelia, darling. What is the matter?"

"Go away!" a muffled voice demanded from beneath the heavy fabric.

"I shall, if that is what you wish. But I should like to know what has caused you so much trouble of late. I am worried for you, my dear."

"I am not your dear! I am not even your daughter!"

This pronouncement stung bitterly but Elizabeth knew the girl spoke from a place of anger and hurt and so checked her own emotions in favour of comforting her child. Gently she asked, "Have I not treated you as my daughter since even before I came to Pemberley?"

There was a light pause wherein the shawl shifted slightly. "You have," was the quiet response.

"Are you certain? If I have been at all remiss, I beg you would tell me so that I may correct the error. I should be terribly ashamed if I learnt you have felt yourself at all neglected."

The shawl moved again and a mass of silky, dark blonde curls and one dark brown eye that matched her father's peeked out. "I have not been unhappy." The next few words tumbled out of the girl's mouth almost as if she had not meant to speak them at all. "But that will all end when the baby comes and you have a child of your own. Then you will have no need for me and will send me away!" The one visible eye widened in alarm before the shawl was pulled hastily back over her head.

Movement from the other side of the room caused Elizabeth to turn and she was met by the sight of her husband standing in the doorway, looking both concerned for his daughter and offended for his wife's sake. With a shake of her head, Elizabeth warned off the rebuke she knew was poised on the tip of his tongue. Divided as he was between devoted father and doting husband, she was sure he would fumble his words and only confuse the situation. With a look, she implored that he allow her to handle the distraught little girl. She received his acquiescing nod with relief.

"Amelia, dear. Where on earth did you get that idea?" she asked.

After a brief hesitation, Amelia responded, though there was uncertainty in her voice. "Lottie Dobbs said that when you have your own baby, you will have no need of me anymore."

"And what, pray tell, does Lottie Dobbs know of the matter?" asked Elizabeth, though she very well knew the answer.

"Lottie told me that when new mamas give papas babies, the old children are sent away for they are no longer wanted. And she knows!"

At this explanation, Elizabeth sighed. Lottie Dobbs, three years Amelia's senior, had come to live at the parsonage at Lampton some months ago after the brother of the vicar's wife had remarried. When the new Mrs. Dobbs had delivered the heir to her husband's very modest estate, poor Lottie had been sent away by her step-mother. Mrs. Carver, Lottie's aunt, had expressed her extreme disappointment in her brother's poor choice of wife in an unguarded moment to Pemberley's mistress. Though she was excessively vexed that the girl would cause her daughter such distress and fear, and there would be a conversation had with the residents at the vicarage, Elizabeth could understand young Miss Dobbs bitterness and pain. She felt great pity for the poor child.

"My dear, I shall not dissemble and say that such things do not happen, for poor Lottie is proof that they do. But I will tell you, with every assurance which I can give, that no such thing shall happen to you. First of all, your papa would certainly never countenance such a thing! And, secondly, I love you too dearly to ever let you go." The shawl lowered a fraction, enough to peek over the edge. "Besides, I shall sorely need your help when this baby arrives."

Amelia's head emerged from under the thick wrap and she sat up. "You shall?"

"Of course! I am but a poor country squire's daughter. I shall need your help to know best how I am to raise a child of the master of Pemberley."

"I can do that," Amelia eagerly volunteered then threw herself into Elizabeth's arms, toppling her back into the cushions with an "oof!" "Oh, forgive me, Mama! It was silly of me to think you would not want me any longer."

"It was, darling. But we are all entitled to be silly from time to time. Someday, I shall tell you all about the time I broke my arm because John Lucas said I could not climb higher than he in the old oak at Meryton."

"Truly?!"

"Truly."

"I love you, Mama."

"I love you, my precious child. Now, why do you not run along and find Miss Drake to let her know you have been found."

Amelia pulled away from Elizabeth's embrace and cried out. "Oh, dear! Miss Drake must be terribly worried!"

"That she is, dearest. Go and relieve her."

Scampering away, pausing only to throw a quick hug around her father's middle, Amelia hurried to ease her sweet governess's concern. Shaking his head, Darcy advanced into the room as Elizabeth struggled to free herself from the deep sofa. The man ought to have been commended for checking his amusement at the absurd grunts and groans his wife made as she shimmied and shifted and, at last, gained her feet just as he came to stop before her.

"My dear, what are you doing. You ought to be resting."

"Well, I was before you daughter engaged the household in an impromptu game of sardines!"

"Come, you must sit and I have the perfect seat for you."

"But I—"

Before she could point out that she had only just stood and that it had been enough of an undertaking for one day, Darcy had sat himself upon the sofa and gently pulled her down onto his lap.

"Fitzwilliam!" she laughed even as she tried to scold him. Deciding that it was, indeed, a rather comfortable perch, she gave in and wrapped her arms around his neck. "I shall crush you, I have grown so large!"

"Nonsense. You are lovelier than ever." Gazing adorningly into her eyes, Darcy released a contented sigh. "Have I told you recently, my beautiful wife, how very dearly I love you?"

Enjoying the delicious tingles which being the object of this man's admiration still inspired, Elizabeth beamed at him. "In fact, you have, my wonderful husband. But it does not follow that I would object if you were to tell me again, for I cannot imagine I shall ever tire of hearing it."

"Then allow me to tell you, Elizabeth Darcy, how ardently I admire and love you."

The kiss which followed this pronouncement had the power to steal her breath and curl her toes. Unwilling to cease what he had started, Darcy stood, scooping his wife up into his arms and carried her away to their chambers where they remained for several hours. When they were well and truly spent, they lay entangled in one another's arms and little else. Elizabeth's fingers twirled and teased the dark hairs on her husband's chest while his traced delicate paths up and down her arm. Both might have been quite contented to remain thus forever were there not a daughter to raise and an estate to run.

"I do not know what we would have done without you, dearest Elizabeth," Darcy whispered, breaking the silence.

"You were doing perfectly well before I came along and disrupted your very ordered life, my dear. I am sure you and Amelia would have managed perfectly well without my wild ways."

"Not at all! I was blundering along, trying desperately not to muck everything up too terribly. We were a father and daughter, carrying one another along. But you, my wonderful, darling wife, you have made us a family."

Darcy pulled her more tightly against him, pressing a kiss into her silken curls and silently giving thanks for the abundance of love and joy in his life, all of which he owed to an impertinent young lady from Hertfordshire with exquisite eyes and a saucy smile.

I want to thank my amazing husband and my wonderful children for their encouragement, enthusiasm, and patience for all the hours I was locked away in a dark room obsessing over this book! I am even grateful to them for the ridiculous suggestions they offered when I hit brick walls and asked their advice. Though I did not include any of the alien abductions, monster attacks, or Cthulhu raids that were suggested, they kept a smile on my face through this whole process.

Thank you to Bridget, Carolyn, and my mom, Ann, for reading my book, even when I only gave you half and left you hanging for months! Thank you for your suggestions, edits, encouragement, and patience.

And thank you to all the JAFF writers who entertained me and inspired me to take a shot at something I never I'd ever do but discovered a deep passion for.

About the Author

Melissa first discovered Pride & Prejudice at the age of eleven when visiting family while her aunt was recording the BBC miniseries from TV to VHS and instantly fell in love. A voracious reader, this led her to the novel which, in turn, led to the discovery of Jane Austen's other excellent works, Persuasion being her favorite. She stumbled upon the genre of JAFF in 2019 and was hooked, having read over 500 titles since that time. After reading so many variations and imaging storylines of her own, she began writing them down and, for the first time, discovered her passion in life.

Melissa lives in Alaska with her husband of fifteen years, a delightful combination of Mr. Darcy, Mr. Knightley, and Mr. Tilney, their five children, and their behemoth of dog, Knightley. When not reading or writing, which is not often, Melissa enjoys camping in the wide Alaskan frontier, hiking, traveling and watching all the adaptations of Jane Austen's works on DVD. And sleeping. Sleeping is the best.

Printed in Great Britain
by Amazon

68745599R00241